A RUNAWAY WIFE

A Runaway Wife

❦

Sayidet Al Hijaz

iUniverse, Inc.
New York Lincoln Shanghai

A Runaway Wife

All Rights Reserved © 2004 by Sayidet Al Hijaz

No part of this book may be reproduced or transmitted in any form or by any means, graphic, electronic, or mechanical, including photocopying, recording, taping, or by any information storage retrieval system, without the written permission of the publisher.

iUniverse, Inc.

For information address:
iUniverse, Inc.
2021 Pine Lake Road, Suite 100
Lincoln, NE 68512
www.iuniverse.com

ISBN: 0-595-30120-7

Printed in the United States of America

houbby

Contents

❊

The Bridge 1
Jaddah 43
Mama 74
Mary 104
A Taste of Freedom 146
About the Author *179*

The Bridge

There have been cold and dark days, but this night, on that plane, beats them all. It is the second time I board a BA777. Carrying my laptop on one shoulder, the carry on bag on the other and a back pac on my back I walk down the aisle looking for my seat. I look at my boarding card: *21D* and walk till I find it. I place all my luggage in the overhead compartment and remove the seat belt then sit and buckle up. The seat is comfortably wide and I have everything at my reach. There's also a TV screen with a remote control and on that same remote control I see a telephone. Oh! How I wish I can just lift it up and call my children, but I don't dare. I think of how I left them, *all in tears.*

That last time I walked down the stairs, I remember my household help waiting to bid me goodbye. I had been up and down those oak-colored swirled stairs so many times, but they had never been that long, seemed like eternity this time. I take a step down with one foot but the other does not want to follow. Yet, I know that I have to; I have no choice. I go to, each and every room in the house. Here is where I usually sit to have lunch. That is his seat; I remember and see everyone sitting down having lunch. My six children each have their own seat and no one ever dares sit in the other's place.

"Deema can you pass me the rice?" Sam, my eldest son, with his greenish-hazel eyes, begs politely. He knows that in order to get anything from his sister he has to be extremely nice. Deema, a beautiful girl is as stubborn as her mother, unwillingly, passes the rice:

"Is it too far for you"? She tells Sam.

"Oh, com'on Deema," I add, "he *is* being nice, right?"

My other two daughters, Dalia and Rana are twins and always share everything, even their steak; Dalia is five minutes older and assures Rana of that difference all the time, teasing and reminding her that she is the older sister.

"Mama, I'm as old as Dalia, right?" Rana asks me, always seeking maternal reassurance.

"Yes *habeeby* (my love), you're twins," I answer smiling.

I know that my kids, all six of them love teasing one another. They get that habit from me I guess. As a little girl I was horrible; I would tease anyone and anything and wouldn't even spare a stray animal on the street. So God never forgot that and He gave me six kids, who drove me crazy, yet I didn't mind it and as a matter of fact, I loved it.

I then look at Amr, who is only four, the baby boy of the family sitting next to his brother Kareem his strongest defender. Kareem, my second son, knows how the three girls always fight with Amr for no reason whatsoever, so he is always siding with him. Sam, who is fifteen, is also another staunch protector of Amr. Everyone is at peace eating, teasing, playing and communicating in one way or another when suddenly we hear an explosion: a bomb!

"What's this Fairooz?" he screams, "there's no salt in the beans!" I jump off my seat as Ali shouts my name out. He grabs the bowl of beans and throws it over the plate of rice. Down come the bowl, the beans, the sauce and the lamb traveling all the way up in the air almost hitting the ceiling; crashing and breaking all its surroundings. It all hits the plate of rice, and there goes the rice jumping away, making room for this strange aggressor that suddenly hits its territory. I can feel the rice saying:

"*Hey, what the hell's happenin' around here?*"

"*Sorry,*" replies each bean, cut of meat and even the paste and tomato, each grain or piece defending itself, "*sorry I had no choice I suddenly found myself up in the sky and down targeting you, really no choice whatsoever.*"

Although it was years ago, I can still feel how that food felt; all tormented by such an experience, the attacker and the attacked. Glass is all over the table, tiny bits of finely crushed glass covers the floor, too. The beans like fish dying in the wide Red Sea. Yes, red because the sauce is red, made of tomato paste and freshly squeezed tomatoes. Or are those beans birds, innocent loving birds flying in a red sky, a sky full of rage and hate.

"How many times have I said that your cooking sucks? This is the last time I'll sit at the table with you," Ali yells and storms out of the house.

Over the years I've been totally shocked and scared by this strange man in front of me. Now, sitting on the plane, I clearly remember how I felt: utter paralysis! For about three seconds, not a word said; my brain stopped working and my senses went numb. All I could say then was:

"Dada (the nanny), come here please and clean this mess."

I stood up and tried to clear some of it myself as I stare at the children to see their expressions: utter shock and fear. They all run to their rooms. Of course, no one finished the meal, full of shattered glass. How can he do this to my family? To his own money? I still can't believe he broke my favorite *Limoge* set!

Till this day I've never understood why he has done that. I was too naïve to suspect anything. Ever since that incident, whenever I sit at the table, or even pass by the dining room, I always remember that wild man, all red with anger; how I spent a whole day in the kitchen, trying to fix a meal and how he just came and spoiled it, over a pinch of salt! I used to do the cooking myself, then; I had help with the preparation of the meals, but I always did the cooking. That incident was what stopped me from cooking and since that day I had taught my Philippino help how to cook. Ali never liked having someone else do the cooking, but he left me no choice. I was not prepared to spend hours in the kitchen only to have such a horrible act performed at the dining table. Since then, I didn't do anything around the house except supervision.

I remember the last day at home as I walk down the stairs saying good bye to every piece of furniture in it. I look at the cabinet in that dining room, which has some precious pieces of souvenirs and antiques. I check the bathroom there and say to myself, *well, dear toilet I'll miss you, though you aren't what I wanted. I wanted you in a different color and different tiles all over you, but of course I had no choice in choosing you! You know, Ali chose everything!* I remember what he had to say when I wanted to chose what I like:

"Fairooz we can't have what you want, this paint and those tiles are cheaper," he told me.

Nothing in that house is according to what I had dreamt of having, yet I loved it.

"Ladies and gentlemen, this is your captain speaking. Welcome aboard BA777. Thank you for flying with us. Please don't hesitate to ask for any help. We would like to apologize for the delay and the inconvenience. We're flying at an altitude of thirty-seven thousand feet. The outside air temperature is -59°C and our approximate speed is nine hundred and fifty kilometers per hour."

I feel relieved to be pulled out of my past memories and back to the present. Looking out of the window I can see everything floating beneath. My life passes by, as these clouds, each in separate pieces and now and only now I feel I can put them together. It is like an enormous puzzle, which I can at last assemble. I feel like a god, sitting on top and looking at everything beneath me. It is an amazing feeling I just cannot believe it. Free at last, just like those clouds, roaming not knowing where they are heading. At last I'm free yet a bit lost and afraid of the unknown, not knowing what life is holding for me or what is going to happen. A new place a new life is awaiting me. However, in a weird sense I know exactly what I want. I want to get away. Away from that miserable life, I was leading. It took me such a long time to decide on what I wanted. For years, I was going around singing: *I'm leaving on a jet plane. I don't know when I'll be back again.* I knew that I was leaving but didn't figure out when; and now at last I made up my mind. Well, what will one expect of a Libra but indecisiveness; yet once I make a decision, it usually is the right one.

Suddenly my mind switches back to the day I was leaving home. I just cannot leave behind all those memories without at least reminiscing over them. Weighing every step and move I ever made. Why? Why did I take all this? That is what is so puzzling to me and that is why I have to go all over it again and deeply think, as to why I acquiesced?

I remember passing by the guest-room, that gorgeous part of my house: every painting hanging, every piece of art work on its walls, on the tables or on the floor; every piece of antique, lying on its floor, every tile, every spot of paint on its walls, every plant, everything in that room cries deeply: *"please don't leave!"* And the plants look so sad and lonely as they say: *"who is going to caress us, talk to us, play us some music, water us and open the windows for us?"*

This is the saddest moment in my trip around the house because everything in that room is related to me in some way or another. The porcelain flowers I made in the art class I took a couple of years ago: black and yellow flowers representing my favorite football team *Itty* back home. The wooden mirror I engraved, with beautiful Japanese print, which I colored too. The glass mirror I painted with tiny brushes, which were my first introduction to this kind of art; before this mirror I had never done any art work, painting or anything, but as soon as I touched those brushes I knew that I had a hidden passion, one I had never thought existed within me.

Oh, my mom's old sewing machine! The oak old machine she had had for more than forty years. How did they ever work with those machines? Use a handle? It is torture to use the modern machines nowadays, but now one can imagine the patience and endurance women had then.

I then pick up my grandfather's glass, the one he used to take his tea in. A glass that resembles a mug yet, it can't be a mug, as it is two inches long. I touch it, rub it close to my cheeks, smell it and kiss it. I even put it close to my ears hoping to hear his voice. Oh how I loved and feared that man. That is strange! How can love and fear mix in one heart? Yet I can see his scary eyes staring at me through his glasses, eyes that are as green as jade.

My knees suddenly bend down quickly, yet gently and with both arms I stretch out and pick up my grandmother's scarf; tears run down my eyes. I have no control what so ever over them. It's a yellow scarf, printed with tiny colorful flowers with an embroidered yellowish (not as dark a yellow as the scarf itself, a bit lighter) lace all around it. My gorgeous grandmother always had that scarf on. Tears always linger in my eyes whenever I think of her, but now tears literally shower and wet my cheeks. I hold the scarf tenderly and really hug and squeeze it close to my heart. I can actually feel my grandma now, that loving tender-hearted woman.

Sitting by the window on the plane I think again of the house I left behind. There, under the stairs is another old oak sewing machine: it's my aunt's, Noura, but it is different to my mom's. My mom's has to be set on a table and this one is an oak treadle machine, a *Singer*, of course. My aunt, a professional tailor, buys nothing but *Singer*. The machine itself falls into the top to form a flat surface, which can itself be used as a table. It has a treadle and an electric foot pedal so one can use it either way. On the top of it again, rests this beautiful gramophone, another piece of antique that's so dear to my heart.

I remember now my aunt, Noura, who is the most beautiful woman I had ever seen and who looks so much like Elizabeth Taylor. Her dark brown eyes take up half of her face, with eyelashes almost touching her well-built cheekbones. Her lips on the other hand, are thick and full leaving no room for her chin. Her rounded face is a piece of art with the most beautiful complexion and her black soft-curled hair adorns her gorgeous face. When I remember my aunt I cannot stop thinking how beautiful she is, yet at the same time I cannot believe that my own aunt, my mom's sister, is the one person in the world who had harmed me most; *she is my mother-in-law too,* I think trying to remind myself of that fact.

Yes, my mother-in-law is my aunt too, I tell myself again because back where I come from people marry their cousins. And believe it or not, she was the cause of all the quarrels and the problems that I had with Ali. So Ali is my first cousin too and being related to my husband was not such a wonderful thing; I could never express my true feelings towards my mother-in-law; never could tell her how horrible she was to me. She was after all my mom's sister and if I upset her, my mom got upset too; it was so hard on me to just hide those feelings. I try hard to put all those sad memories out of my mind, but no they would not let me alone.

Walking back in that guest-room, I look at my six beautifully engraved samovars: the first one I bought in 1980 in the States from an antique shop. It is a brass seventeenth-century Russian samovar. The other two are silver-colored, they were my mom's; she used them, when she first got married about fifty-five years ago. The fourth and fifth are brass too, which I bought at an auction in Jeddah (my hometown) around 1989. The last and one of my favorites belonged to Mohammed's mother. He was a dear friend who died so young. I could never forget his black round eyes looking at me. His humor filled my ears whenever I looked at that samovar and his laughter, oh his laughter, that loud happy giggle so full of life and joy.

I remember the three antique chest boxes, which I bought at the same auction, where I got the two samovars. The first one is Indian and mahogany, so old.

"It's a fifteenth-century piece," the salesman at the auction informs me.

"Does it have a certificate to prove that?" I ask.

"No, sorry it has none."

I loved it so much I just believed him and bought it. It is printed with all sorts of horses and warriors that resemble the Arabian Night legend; such paintings cover the top and all four sides of it. The cover itself is stunning! I love just looking at it. It is divided into two halves. Its back is glued to the rest of the body and doesn't open while the front part slightly slopes to the marbled floor it is standing on. A warrior on a horse seems to be falling off of that top and that is why I keep that front end open all the time to save the two of them from hitting the ground. Amazing craftsmanship! Everything is hand-made. Of course it belongs to an age when man was still needed and machines had not invaded his world yet.

The second one is a bit larger and it is oak and engraved again with Indian architectural designs, but it is quite different to the first one. It portrays lovers in different positions: standing facing one another, holding hands, lovers sitting down and caressing one another and the last portrayal is of lovers intensely kissing with eyes shut. The top on this one opens all the way up.

The third chest is the largest and the most beautiful. It is mahogany and hand engraved with delicate Arabesque designs. It opens from the front and is very roomy inside. The drawings on it are absolutely fabulous, as they represent a Harem. Small squares, of a mosaic, each portraying a picture and each has the same sheikh, surrounded by over twenty women and every woman is catering to please him. One square has a woman who is massaging his right foot with some paste out of a bowl, while another has his left foot in a bowl of liquid probably salt and water, massaging it. One of his Harem's members is again giving his right hand a manicure, while another is working on his left hand.

Another portrait shows the same man surrounded by a group of women again and while one is fixing his hair the other is putting his left sock and shoe on and the third is fiddling with his right sock and shoe. Other squares have him sitting in the middle with another group of gorgeously dressed women dancing all around him; and another square has him sitting with more women smiling and flirting with him and with each other.

His Harem has all these lovely young slim women with long black or brown hair down to their knees, large round beautiful eyes either black or brown painted with lots of *kohl* to give them that exotic shape. They are all dressed in colorful belly dancing outfits: beaded tops and shear beaded skirts and each outfit has a different color and a slightly different design.

What a life? By the way, a lot of men envy this kind of life and mind you, a lot of men convert to Islam to have more than one wife and their own harem; that is because they can always divorce one of the four wives and marry a new one, as they believe that it is possible to do so as long as they just keep four at a time. However, having four wives at a time is a misconception that men enjoy practicing, a whole notion of an enjoyable convenient game which they play and invent their own rules as they go along.

What is so sad about all these chests is that they are all full of precious antique: old pots, glasses, sugar bowls, plates, trays, silverware and more; everything I collected through the years from almost every member of the family and some were even given to me by my friends, who knew of my great passion for antiques. One of my dreams was to have a room especially for those precious antiques; but do dreams ever come true? Tears are lost in my eyes as I think how all these things are going to be ignored and neglected.

I reminisce passing by my children's bedrooms. First the boys', where I have their pictures hung all over the walls. Sam is such a handsome boy with big heavy-lidded greenish long-lashed eyes and a nicely formed nose with an upper thin-lipped mouth and a slightly thicker lower one. He had blonde hair as a child, till the age of twelve, it then turned to brown. Kareem, on the other hand, always had black silky hair. It reminds me of a horse's tail so beautiful and so black. His bulging-shape eyes are round and his thick black long lashes cover their hazel color and make them look black. You have to stare at them to know their true color. His lips are even thinner than Sam's and his nose is tinier.

I remember where I used to lay in bed with Sam and Kareem to tell them bedtime stories. Oh, how I miss each piece of furniture that reminds me of them. Their cologne hits every hair in my nostrils, as they shower with it, not just spray it on, just like their dad.

I also remember how I repeatedly relate the story of the black duckling to Amr, my baby. His big round hazel eyes always show his dislike to Dada because she is Eritrean, so all I did then was relate the black duckling's story and how this black duckling, which nobody loves is so loving, brave and honest; how she sacrifices her own life to save her brothers and sisters from drowning; and now at last he loves Dada, yet he has to tease her and play Tae Kwon Do with her all the time, that poor nanny. I realize how hard it is trying to implant the tiniest values into my children's heads.

Then I look at the walls again and there is Amr's picture. Amr has blonde shaggy hair. I used to give my kids and every kid in the family a hair cut then. I love cutting hair as I am a licensed beautician. Oh how Amr hated the color of his hair and wished it were black. I remember how each day he used to stand before the mirror and ask me:

"Mama isn't my hair black?"

"I think it's blonde, but if you think it's black, then it is black!" I comfort him.

His eyes are again adorned with long thick lashes. His nose nicely fits his face and his lips are so similar to mine, as a matter of fact everyone thinks that he looks a lot like me. Maybe that is why he is my baby.

I smile as I remember how everyone who has ever been to my house asks the same question:

"Fairooz do you have an interior designer to decorate your house?"

But no I don't. I decorated and designed every corner of that house: it's my baby too and I was very cautious, as to how it looked, was adorned and taken care of.

I then walk to the girls' room. Messy as ever; I will certainly miss every bit of that mess! I will miss the scent of perfume of each of those three beautiful girls. I look up at the ceiling and think how I hung each one of those stuffed animals up there. "Dada, give me the ladder, please," and up I'd go hanging them. I did the same to the boys' ceiling. Deema, my third child, is eight in that picture on the wall: a gorgeous girl. She and one of the twins, Dalia have heavy-lidded eyes; hers are beautiful brown while Dalia's are similar to Sam's: leaning on the greenish side and Rana the other twin has the same the same eye color, but her eyes are bulging big eyes as Kareem's and all three girls have brown long curly hair. The pictures on the wall again capture my eyes and emotions. How can I just leave those beautiful girls alone without a mother to befriend them? How can I ever forgive myself for doing that to them? How can I live with my conscience? But then I remember I had no choice, he left me none whatsoever.

Walking down the corridor I pass by the small kitchenette on my way to the living room; that room where I spent most of the days, all alone; I always felt that I was a prisoner in it. The TV set is right in the center of the room. The video and Satellite receivers are in the same cabinet where the TV is. It is a huge living room with sofas all around. Again I never chose those sofas they were brought back by Ali from one of his trips to Korea. The walls have paintings and all the children's pictures; *I remember this one painting,* I think as I stare at the wall and recall how everyone used to sarcastically ask me:

"Fairooz, what's this painting suppose to mean? Tape stuck all over it?"

I used to get really upset at the beginning, but then, I ignored any such humiliating comments. I chose to leave all this history behind for a new life when Ali at last signs the form for me to fly away.

"We'll be crossing the Red Sea from Jeddah to Luxor and Asyout. We'll then continue north to the west of Alexandria. Crossing the Mediterranean we'll come to the Southern air space of Greece over to the West of Rome on to the North of Italy. From there we'll pass over Geneva, Switzerland, then to France and then to our destination: Heathrow Airport in London. Once again, I hope you enjoy your flight with BA."

I thought that the captain's announcements were over, yet I was thrilled that he once again ripped me out of such sorrowful memories and a five minute break were a relief, before my thoughts suddenly rush back to that day I was leaving home: such a gloomy evening that seventh of March, 1998. It was only yesterday yet it seemed like it was a long time ago. Such a warm day: evening or not the weather during summer is awfully hot in Jeddah, yet right now I'm chilled to the bone.

We all get in the car, a brand new blue Expedition, Ford. Ali always thinks that material things will please me and make me accept any harm he inflicts upon me, but he was wrong because money is the last thing I ever care for. I'd rather have him the broke student I married years ago, than that rich stranger I don't know any more. He gets into the front seat next to Ridah, the Indonesian driver; Amr, Rana and Dada are in the back seat and Dalia, Deema and me in the middle seat. It's strange but he cannot even look at me, not even sit next to me.

The cars are fast as usual, as if racing. People seem like zombies to me. Drivers are driving like they have black shields over their eyes. All the faces are sad and you rarely see a couple or a family laughing or talking in their cars, so depressing; it is such an unhealthy environment to raise a family. I feel so hurt and know exactly how my children feel, so I keep trying to comfort them as much as I can, as I say: "you all know how much I love you, don't you?" I tell them on the way to the airport. "Remember that I never would have left you, but I can't take it any more."

I look at each one of my four children and their nanny. Not a word! They are all sobbing, tears running down their cheeks and not a word said. I have to do all the talking trying to console them and to convince them and myself that I have to leave and go on: "don't cry please, don't cry. We'll always be together. Nothing can keep us apart." Again not a word just tears and sobs.

I look at the front seat at him. Twenty-eight years of marriage and now I am leaving for good and not a tear shed! I don't want your sympathy, tears or love all I want is to get away from you, from your tyranny. Then, I look back at my lovely kids, who are sobbing so hard, I feel they will lose their breath. I turn to one of the twins:

"Hey, Dalia come on we'll always be together. Please stop crying," I grab her closer to me and squeeze her. Then I pull her away and try to wipe the rushing tears off her greenish eyes. Her long wet eyelashes are dripping too and her thin-lipped mouth is shivering even more. "Hey come on. Please stop you can't do that to me. Don't you love me?"

Dalia vigorously nods and her brown silky short hair moves back and forth covering her oval face then I hear more sobbing. I take a peek in the back and find that Rana, Amr and Dada are crying out loud now. Deema next to me again can't stop. What can I do? I hug Deema. "Come on Deema you're my big baby. You can't do this. Just think that we'll be together real soon and no one can ever keep us apart O.K.?"

These words seem to have comforted everyone in the car except for Amr, who is looking out of the window and is just sobbing. He knows that now that I am going away, he has no one to talk to. His dad is always out and busy, his sisters are together and if he ever tries to get closer to them they just fight him. I turn around and sit on my knees: "Amr," I put my arms out for him, "come here. Come closer. Amr you know that this isn't easy for me, to leave you and go, but all this crying makes it even harder. You're breaking my heart. Listen, don't you love me?"

"M...a...m...a," he nods and stutters as he calls my name and his warm tears wet my T-shirt.

"So please all of you just stop!" Tears never leave my eyes either. I'm fighting them back, but how can I? I look at Dada. "Come on Dada. Not you too? You know that if you weren't with those kids I'd never leave? You know that I trust you with them more than I do myself? I know that you'll take care of them better than I will, so please don't you do that to me. Please stop." I even stretch my arms further trying to reach her and touch her shoulders to comfort her. Dada touches my hands and tries to kiss them but I pull them away quickly.

"Amaaty (Madame) you know that I love you and this family more than any one else. I had been with you for twenty-two years. Your kids aren't yours alone they're mine too and I'll never leave them. I'll take care of them more than if you were around," Dada sobs clearing the tears off of her dark black eyes. Her dark Eritrean complexion glitters as the tears rush down her cheeks and her thin lips shiver as she speaks.

"I know and that's why I trust you so much with my life and theirs." These words comforted Dada so much, that she turns toward Rana and Amr and touches them; she tries to comfort them and tries even harder to stop crying. They both get closer to her feeling her warmth as they too fight those tears.

The road to the airport is gloomy and the sky is dim and starless: not a star. Is the sky sad to see me go? The trees aren't even moving. Not even the faintest breeze in the air. Everyone and everything is sad except him; after all those years?

I remember how weeks before this trip, when I decided on leaving I told him:

"I'm going; I can't take this any more."

"How can you go? What will you do?" He adds in a sarcastic tone.

I didn't realize that sarcastic tone then, but now that I'm looking at the clouds on the plane I think that he probably believed that I was bluffing and that I would actually come back. Now that I remember that look on his face, he was probably thinking to himself, *she'll just go meet her supervisor as usual and come back. I know her too well she just can't live without me.*

Well he is absolutely wrong. This time I'm not bluffing I really have it in mind to go and never come back but his arrogance blinds him from seeing the true feelings behind my words.

As the car stops in front of the terminal I sadly ask myself: *we're already here?* It usually takes twenty-five minutes to get to the airport but this time it's such a fast drive. Seconds, it seemed to me! We all get out, as the car stops in front of the terminal. Tears and sobs, though everyone is trying to stop, no one can. I hug each one at a time, although it is not usual to hug and kiss so much in public, but I don't care and my husband leaves us to get my passport checked and get the boarding card. He is so cold I cannot believe it; how can a human being be that emotionless?

"Now I have to go. You must remember how much I love you and how hard this is going to be on us all but you know I have to do it," I say and again, not a word. The sobs are louder and the tears are racing down. Everyone at the airport is staring at this woman in tears extensively hugging and kissing four children and their nanny, all hysterically in tears. I cannot let go and even if I can I will not. I just will not, but now I have to. I try hugging them all at the same time, but that is impossible. "Remember that I love you more than anything in this world," I go on, "I never ever thought this would happen. You all know that I'm leaving you because I started thinking of harming myself and that it is better for me to leave than have people tell you later on in life that your mom was crazy and had killed herself. Please remember, that I would never leave you, if I hadn't thought of that."

I can see their eyes saying, "*we know Mama and can understand. We don't expect you to have done anything but that. Remember we love you too and we'll always love you. We know that you had never left us before and that this time you have to. It's horrible but we do really feel with you. We're always on your side and some day you'll be proud to have all six of us.*"

Their eyes spoke together in one unified voice. Dada can't believe this is happening.

"Please Madame don't go we all need you," she says hugging me and squeezing me to death.

There he comes. Smiling to himself still thinking, *it's a bluff, I know.*

He then signs the papers to let me get on the plane. See in my country we have some strange laws, one of them is that you cannot leave the country without a man's consent. Not even run away. You cannot even run away if your husband doesn't sign your papers. No woman, no matter how old she gets can leave the country without the consent of her guardian: her father, husband, uncle or even a younger brother. Is that slavery or what? Fredrick Douglass, the Dixie-line, Maryland and Georgia all rush to my mind.

"You take care of yourself now," he says on my way into customs. *I know she'll be back within a week,* he thinks as he grins.

He gets closer to kiss me but I just give him my cheek I do not even want to kiss him. How can he dare act like he loves me? He is quite an actor. Wants me to give him a kiss? Not even on the cheek, I will not even do that. I am after all leaving my kids, parents, family and loving country because of him. I'm going to a strange land and going to start all over again, and why? Because my presumably devoted husband after twenty-eight years of marriage got him another wife! A young Moroccan as old as his eldest son half his age; and he expects me to accept this awkward new situation? He knows better. He knew that once I found out about this secretive marriage I'd be leaving him but he never thought I would leave everything behind, even my kids. Well he was wrong.

Why all this memory right now on the plane? Why? When I am all alone on that dark cold lonely plane? The lights are off and I look around for a familiar face but see none. The woman in the seat across the aisle is pulling a blanket over her thirteen year-old boy; fixing the pillow for her fifteen year-old girl. *My heart's bleeding, where are my own? I wish it's them I'm covering right now*, I think almost weeping, *my lost motherhood*, still looking at her and now that she is sure that her son and daughter are comfortable she puts her head back and tries to get some sleep. The man in the back seat is probably reading. He has his light on. No one to talk to; I who can never stay quiet, with my mouth shut for one second. I look at the young man in the seat next to me fiddling with his briefcase and just turn my head back and keep my eyes fixed at the back of the seat in front of me, to avoid looking into his briefcase. I never like looking into other peoples' affairs. Flash backs of my last trip to London hit me hard. *No not now! I can do without you. Please don't come now*, I keep thinking and try to keep those horrible memories away.

"*No way, we're coming like it or not?*" those terrifying memories yell back, "*you have to get all of this out of your system and this is the only way you can do it.*"

Having no choice I submit and talk back to those memories: "*maybe you're right. I have to leave the past behind and live hoping for a brighter future.*"

So here I am back in December 1997, just three months ago, I am back in my burgundy-color wall living room and remember telling Ali:

"Ali I need to go to London to check my school papers."

"When?"

"Any time, whenever you can: when you're free."

"Me? What do I have to do with your trip?"

"I want you to come with me."

"You know I can't leave the children alone, either one of us has to be with them."

"Oh come on. Just for a few days. We haven't traveled alone since we had Sam. It's been twenty-four years."

"No I can't leave my work."

"Ali you can if you want to."

"Let me think about it."

Next morning at ten I get a call from the office:

"Good morning Madame."

"Good morning."

"Mr. Ali wants me to ask you if leaving on the fifteenth of December and coming back on the nineteenth is O.K.," asks his secretary Abdou; I can see his frail body and black eyes as he speaks to me over the phone.

"Ya, that's fine Abdou."

"O.K. Madame I'll have to get his passport and if you can send me yours."

His passport? Then he's going with me, I think and wonder why has he changed his mind? "Wait, Abdou please reserve the return seats for the twenty-second instead of the nineteenth," I tell him. *We need more time together and we'll have a better chance of settling our problems, maybe another honeymoon? I doubt it but I'm willing to give it another try. I can't believe it, he doesn't even tell me he's going with me and lets his secretary do so, that is how close we are,* I'm thinking while Abdou is writing down the new dates. So we get all ready to leave within a week. I'm worried about the kids and think that they'll be upset.

"We'll only be away for a week," I tell them.

"Mama, you can stay longer if you like," Deema answers with a devilish smile, "it's O.K. and don't worry about us. We'll be fine."

Each and Every one of the six children has inherited something of my naughty self. They had to, where else would it go? What I still have within is enough to last me a lifetime!

"You just take your time and have fun," adds Dalia the older twin.

"Yes, yes, yes, have a good time there," replies Rana the other twin who is such a devil just like me.

"Mama I'll miss you but you can stay longer if you like," Amr lovingly says.

I know that he'll really miss us. The girls want some freedom without me on their back all the time. I know that as girls they feel choked, but what can I do? I have to act protective in such a place. Go with the tide. When I was their age in Egypt, I had all the freedom I needed, but look at them now! It breaks my heart to think that I had more freedom at their age.

It's a chilly Friday night when we get to the airport. The children are there with their nanny. "Take good care of yourselves and God bless you," I tell them as I walk into customs.

"Mama don't you worry we'll be all right," Deema answers, wanting to push us into the plane.

I remember it is a BA777 also. We sit next to each other and I try to get close as he pushes me away; six long hours to get to Heathrow and not a word said. As soon as the plane takes off he falls asleep. Is he pretending? Or does he force himself to sleep to avoid me? I can just tell how the trip is going to be like: *a second honeymoon, sure?* I smile and disappointedly ask myself.

After six long boring hours the plane lands at Heathrow. I know my way pretty well. I have already been here several times and for the last two years I have come all alone to meet Jane my professor, but I still have to act like I don't know anything and follow him. It is a cold day and I put on my black suede gloves, a black and white hat and cover my neck with a matching scarf, *all that extra clothing and I'm still freezing,* I say to myself.

"Where to Sir?" The taxi driver asks.

"Intercontinental Park Lane, please."

"Park Lane?"

"Yes London Intercontinental."

"Yes sir."

It is four in the morning and the streets are quite busy. Once again I feel like I'm out of place in the cab, as it drives on the wrong side of the road; such a long, tiring and boring flight; and all I've done is read and watch the movie but I haven't even concentrated on anything, just thinking how this trip is going to be like? How can this gap between Ali and I disappear?

"Oh Ali look at that bus!"

He uninterestingly gives it a glimpse and that alone tells me how excited he is. I reach out and try to hold his hand but he pulls it away and reminds me that we're in a cab. *In a cab? So what? I'm not trying to seduce or rape you, all I want is to touch you,* I angrily think. I try so hard to be nice and close for forty-five minutes and I do all the talking for about ten minutes, then I just resign. It is the worst thing that can happen to me: being forced to keep quiet; but living with him through the years, I learned how to restrain my poor tongue, keep my lips zipped and suppress my most intimate thoughts and feelings. It is amazing how a human being can adapt to its surroundings.

At last, the cab stops in front of the Intercontinental. The lobby is huge and exquisitely furnished. The concierge is to the left hand side as we walk in and the reception is facing the main door. We walk down straight to the reception.

"Good morning Sir, Madam."

"Good morning. I have reservations."

"And your name is? Please."

"Mr. Al-Arab."

"Mr. Al-Arab? One second, please," the receptionist checks the computer.

"Yes Sir. It's room 708 on the seventh floor. This is your key and the porter will have your luggage up in a minute."

"Thank you."

"Thank you Sir. Have a nice stay."

The people at the hotel know me and the concierge smiles at me walking back to his desk:

"Good morning Madam."

I stayed at this same hotel on my previous trips to meet Jane and I actually feel at home. We walk straight, pass the reception and turn left toward the lifts, where a gigantic mirror is on the facing wall and walk immediately into the lift, not a word said and not a word mentioned about me or to me. He doesn't consider me there at all. Am I really there? I now start doubting my own being. He doesn't even look at me and once again I try to hold his hand and again he pushes it off; so mad now, I just keep away.

Where's the room? 701, 703, he talks to himself and doesn't even try to ask me or acknowledge my presence at all.

"There it is," I say. He stares at me and looks extremely upset as he doesn't want me to act smart at all. It's so hard for me to act stupid but that is what is expected of women in my country. So many times I would come up with ideas and make them look like they are his, to give him all the credit and after a while, he actually comes to believe that he is the one, who has come up with them. I can never show that I'm smarter or know more. He opens the door and goes in and I walk in behind him.

"Oh! What's this, a baby crib?" I feel faint asking.

"Oh I don't know what this is doing here? Salih reserved the room. It's probably a mistake."

Salih is Ali's close friend, living in London. I know that Salih probably thinks that it is Ali's second wife and the baby that are accompanying him and not me. By this time Ali has a new wife and a new baby boy too.

"Salih, who does he think is with you?" I ask teasingly, trying to be nice and stupid. No one can see my anger and my mixed emotions. Still, I cannot make a fuss out of it and I just let it go and pretend to believe him.

"I swear I don't know what this crib is doing here," he irritably says.

"Oh, it's O.K. don't you worry."

"I'll call house keeping and have it taken away," he adds abruptly.

That was the first stab: a crib in my hotel room! It hurts so much. How can I try to be nice any more? But coming from such an oppressive society I force myself to learn how to change and acquiesce. I have no right to express any rage and simply accept whatever my husband does. Although a rebel in nature, I got used to being lead into this way of living, as society forces me to abide by its cruel rules to endure.

"Fairooz, I'll go in and have a bath."

"Go right ahead! I'll just lie in bed while you finish," I smile and silently think, *I wish you'd slip in that bathtub.* Now I try to cool down and only now do I notice the room. I notice this computerized system; they probably installed it after my last visit. The TV's on with a message: *Welcome Mr. and Mrs. Al-Arab.* The room is nicely furnished with a king size bed, a small mini bar and a desk quite nice and simple. I look out of the window. Seven stories high, what a view? Hyde Park is right down there. I wish we could walk down there some time, though it is freezing; but I know he would not, so I save my dignity and don't even ask. *Walk in a park? You must be crazy. Do you think we're lovers or what?* I think of what his answer would be. It's like when I had asked him, so many times, back home, if we could walk or sit by the sea.

"Why should we? We have a house and we can certainly sit in it," he would always say.

Ali suddenly comes out of the bathroom. He disturbs my thoughts as he appears with the towel wrapped around his waist. Shocked, I jump like I had seen a ghost. "Done with the bath?" I ask him pretending to be calm.

"Yes, that feels so good. Are you going in?"

I nod and obediently go in. I turn on the water. Ah, that's nice and warm. I can never take a cold shower like Ali, even if the weather is hot. I then wet the loofah and scrub my body real good. Since he had re-married, I scrubbed myself so hard. Maybe I don't like him sleeping with me any more? Or maybe I want to clean my skin of his touches, smell and breath? I don't know what it is I try to do in the bath, but I almost bleed scrubbing myself, then I start singing, *I feel good.* Singing in the bathroom, is a relief; I brush my teeth and wash my face. Then I start rubbing my body with my favorite lotion: *Dolce Vita.* I put on a long T-shirt and go out. All nice and fresh! He is in bed waiting. How could he think that after that crib and after ignoring me throughout the trip I'll just jump into bed with him? I do get into bed but with different intentions: I want to nap.

"Why don't you get close Fairooz?"

"I just want to take a nap."

"A nap? Come on not now."

Men are so strange, if they want to make love they think that they cannot be rejected. It is a switch with them: on and off. They forget that a woman has feelings and sometimes has no desire what so ever. If a woman on the other hand, is dying to have sex, a man can just shun her. Just like that. Switch her off! So his hands move under the blanket and touch me. *Oh no don't*, I want to scream. But who is to listen? He gets closer pulls me to him and starts caressing me. He reaches out and puts the lights off and two hours later he fiddles around and I wake up.

"Fairooz, I have to meet Sheikh Mohammed. He is staying here at the hotel."

"You have to what?"

"It will just take an hour."

"I thought that this is a vacation for the two of us, only. Now you have to do some business?"

"Oh come on, don't start. It'll just be an hour or so."

"O.K.," what else can I say? Do I have a choice?

"I have some papers I need him to sign. When I get back we can go out."

He then gets a file out of his bag and leaves. Once again I'm all alone. A prisoner held at my own consent and all I can see now are the four walls of the tiny suffocating room. The crib is gone! I start fiddling with the remote control. There is a film on BBC 1. I watch it but I'm not really there. My thoughts and mind are somewhere else. What is happening to me? How long can I take all this? I cannot believe it all. Is this really a test set by the Almighty, but why me? I've always loved Him so much.

"Excuse me Miss, do you mind? I would like to pass," asks the man next to me on the plane.

Thank God, he saved me from that horrid past; but twenty-eight years of my life cannot just dissipate: memories and more memories. It is like running your computer and going over all the files you have stored. Or running a movie and watching every incident carefully. I'm once again on that same trip to London, in 1997; on the third day we are in a cab, going to Heathrow to pick Sam up—he is passing by London for a few hours on his way back home for Xmas—and before we get to Heathrow I turn to Ali and say:

"You know Ali, Sam doesn't know about you remarrying, I didn't tell him."

"Really," he is so pleased, "he doesn't know?"

"No, I never told him. I don't want to upset him when he's all-alone over there. You can tell him if you want," I knew he wouldn't dare. It's a pity when a man gets vulnerable as he makes a mistake and feels so ashamed in front of everyone, especially his own children. An hour later the cab stops in front of terminal three and we walk straight to Saudi Arabian Airlines to meet Sam.

"Mama you look so good! It's so good to see the two of you all alone on a trip."

I keep thinking, *he doesn't really know how good the trip is!* And as soon as we get back to our room Sam throws himself on the bed, almost asleep. Ali and I are sitting on the sofa.

"Sam you look so tired why don't you nap a little?"

"No I feel fine Mama. I want to stay with you."

"So how's school?" His dad asks.

"I'm getting better now, Baba (that's what we call a dad nowadays). I'm taking thirteen hours. I only have a year and a half to go."

"At last you'll graduate?" His dad sarcastically asks.

"Yes I am working hard now."

"I'll have to wait and see to believe you," he says this with a smirk.

He is always harsh on his children. So harsh! Just like a soldier. *I'm so glad you're not my father,* I look at him and think. "When you go home Sam you can spend all the time acting as head of the family until we're back," I say jokingly trying to break the ice.

"Mama I haven't slept for two nights, I'm so excited about this whole thing and so happy that you called and told me that I can come home this Christmas, it was a lovely surprise," he looks at his father saying that and then goes on, "and look at you and Mama, you are so happy having a second honey moon, huh?"

He knows how we usually are at home: strangers. So now he thinks we're happy. He doesn't know the act we're both putting on, I say to myself and wish I can say it out loud, but just can't.

"Yes we are," Ali answers immediately pretending it is true.

How long will this pretence last? I cannot handle it any more, I think of the past two days, when he had to meet Sheikh Mohammed every night. I then look back at Sam, who's out and already snoring; he is dead tired, all the way from Melbourne, Florida, when suddenly Ali says:

"Fairooz I just have to meet Salih for fifteen minutes."

I wonder if there really is a Salih, I wonder. I've never seen this Salih. Maybe he is an imaginary friend? He leaves me all alone except for Sam, who is fast asleep and an hour later he is back.

"He's still sleeping? Wake him up," Ali says as he walks into the room and sees Sam on the bed.

I look at him and think, *why do I always have to do the annoying dirty work? Why don't you wake him up? You can never talk to your children. If you don't like anything, you ask me to speak to them. Why do you always have to look like an angel and make me look like the devil? I keep giving orders and pushing them around just as you want,* and again I do as told: "Sam baby, wake up; Sam come on," I tickle him and he starts giggling, "do you want a massage?"

"Aha."

I then massage his back legs and arms and again tickle him, "come on; you've had enough spoiling."

"What? Is it time to go?"

"Yes, come on. Wake up. It is time to go," answers his dad.

It seems like he just wants him gone before he finds out the truth about his marriage. It is hard to let him go although I know that I'll see him in four days. We take him back to Heathrow and when we get to the gate I hug and kiss him: "now call us as soon as you get there."

"Sure Mama. You have fun with Baba," he says teasingly.

I feel so cold on that plane. I have goose bumps all over my arms. Is it because I'm cold? Or is it because such memories are so horrifying, like horror movies, where one's hair sticks out? I call the stewardess and ask for a blanket, and while she's getting me one, I try to free myself from those depressing memories and press the button for the TV screen in front of me, as it pops up I check the outside view. I'm willing to do anything to get my mind off of that trip! I start reading the screen:

Head Wind	6 mph
True Airspeed	552 mph
Time since Departure	1:37

The screen switches every minute, each time it reads different information:

Head Wind	12 km/h
True Airspeed	892 km/h
Time since Departure	1:37

And before my eyes read any more, my memory slips back to that same trip, in December. On our flight back home Ali acts completely different. He is not the same person who flew with me a week ago. First, he covers me with a blanket and hugs me to make sure that I'm warm enough. Then he gets on his knees takes my shoes off, rubs my feet and puts on the socks we get on the plane, to make sure I'm completely comfortable. He pampers me and treats me so nice all the way till we land in Jeddah.

A handsome Sudanese man is sitting next to us and doesn't stop staring and smiling at this loving man, who cannot keep still, trying to please this woman next to him. It's funny how appearances deceive people, but there is a reason for everything. I didn't tell Sam about his dad's marriage, yet his dad doesn't appreciate that, so as soon as we get to our room, after dropping Sam off at the airport, he turns to me and says:

"Fairooz, today I have to go out and have dinner with Salih and two more friends," and leaves immediately.

Again? Why is he so secretive? Why didn't he tell me that when he came back earlier from his meeting? Has he been scared that I'd tell Sam then? I'm fuming on the inside now; and this time he doesn't take any papers with him, he just takes off. He leaves me all alone in a strange place and goes to meet his friends. *Why am I taking all this shit? Why? I don't have to stay any longer with this asshole. I will not. I don't care what happens. I don't care what anyone thinks. I will not stay with him any longer. We're supposed to mend our life, not add breakage to it and look at what he's doing? Hurt and more hurt! No consideration for anything that I've been trying to do. Everyday he has a business meeting, comes back and takes me out and then makes love to me. This is not the kind of life I want. Not any more!* I angrily think; and suddenly I get back to my stubborn old self. Everyone in my family knows how stubborn and hard-headed I am. I am after all, knick named as: *the hard-headed girl.* "So, do you always have to go out and leave me all alone?" I ask, before he shuts the door, full of rage.

"You know I have to get my work done."

"No I don't, know. So when is she coming home?" No more fooling around I want straightforward answers.

"Who?" He asks nervously.

"You know who," I add insistently.

"Oh, I don't know," he says.

Then he sees the look in my eyes and immediately answers:

"Maybe she'll be back by January."

"You have to make up your mind. I can't live in the same city with her. It's either me or her."

"Oh I don't know."

"I'm telling you if she comes I leave."

"Listen I can't promise you that she won't come. I can't keep her away if she wants to come back to her home, but I'll try."

"You keep lying to me all the time and I pretend to be a fool and to believe you but not any more. You can go home and leave me here."

"What? Are you crazy?"

He knows I mean what I'm saying and waits for my answer: "no, I'm crazy if I go back."

"What about Sam? He's coming back to see you. What will he say if you just don't go back?"

"Don't worry about him. I'll tell him why I'm not going back."

"Fairooz please don't. How can I leave you here? You don't know where to go. Come home and then if you insist on leaving, I'll arrange things for you," he begs.

I cannot believe my eyes looking at him crying, I ask myself: *who's this man? Where's the man I married? Oh, how I respected him so, he had been a second god to me, and his words had been divine, right down from the sky; and now look at him. What's happened?* Then I say out loud: "don't you worry about me I can manage. I'll go to Newcastle stay at the hotel and look for a place at the dorm. You know I can."

"But what would everybody say? I can't just leave you. Come back, please and I'll try to work things out."

I don't answer. Not a word. I go into the bathroom and lock myself in. Fifteen minutes later he knocks at the door:

"Fairooz, what's wrong? Open the door." No answer!

He goes back to the sofa. Thirty minutes later he is back and he can hear me crying:

"Fairooz, what's the matter? Open the door. I need the toilet."

I know he's lying, but I open it.

"Fairooz, why are you sleeping on the floor?" He can see two towels, one spread on the floor and the other wrinkled on top.

"Leave me alone, please."

"What's wrong? Come on. Why in the toilet?"

Not a word out of my mouth or even a faint expression to satisfy him.

"Oh what's wrong? Why here?"

"I'm just like shit and I belong here, because I'm taking all this; that's where I really belong."

"Fairooz, please come."

But I refuse to go to the room and leave the freezing toilet floor and lie on the carpeted floor of the room by the door. I again, get two large towels. Fold one underneath my head and cover myself with the other. *It's so cold,* I think to myself, *but I'll sleep here,* and I don't even move. After a while he comes to me, I cannot tell how long I've been lying on that cold floor as I don't have my watch on and all I know is: I'm freezing;

"Come on please Fairooz let's talk."

Now he wants to talk? I ask myself only I don't even want to talk to him but the cold floor makes me get up and lie on the bed while he is sitting at the desk next to the bed.

"Please, Fairooz. Try to understand what I'm going through."

"Oh my God I can't believe that after al these years? How can you? I've been such a faithful wife, right?"

"You know you've been a great wife, that's not the reason."

"Then why?"

"You know that our sex life hasn't been as great as it used to be?"

"Maybe it's because you've already started whoring around? Of course a wife, who is part of your routine a piece of your furniture, seems as dull as a wall, no matter what she tries to do."

"No. That's not true."

"So hand it to me, why?"

"How many times have I asked you to stop eating onions?"

"What, I can't believe it?"

"Yes, at times I wanted you so bad, but when I got closer to you, I could smell the onions and that shunned me off."

"Oh my God, say something else, Onions?" I want to laugh but keep looking serious.

"Yes, you don't know how much that put me off."

"God! Oh my God! I can't believe that. You're so trivial! After twenty-eight years of marriage, you get yourself another wife, because of maybe, a bite of onions? You could have offered me a piece of chewing gum but no, you have it going some where else, so you just give up."

"Please, Fairooz. Don't be so mean."

"Me mean? Oh I can't believe all this. Am I dreaming? Pinch me. I can't believe I'm not sleeping. I'm not going back with you, and that's final."

"Please, just come back and I'll try to solve this problem," now he's really sobbing.

Wow! I can't believe it. The man who is so strong and with no feeling is crying, wiping his tears, begging me to go back with him, I stare at him in doubt and my mind keeps racing: "I need a logical answer to all this," I finally say.

"Come on Fairooz please."

"My God! For two years, two whole years, you know that you didn't even touch me for two whole years? Not a touch and when I asked you why? You always said that we were getting old and that you were too busy and your mind was too preoccupied with your work, that you didn't even think of sex," I can't believe how calm I am now, after finding that he never was, worth my time. *I never missed your touch I just felt sorry for you. I didn't want you to feel less of a man,* thinking and more thinking.

"Please don't bring that about."

"No, let me just remind myself of how dumb I was, so what did I do? Remember?"

"Please…"

I interrupt: "I went to my doctor and asked him for some hormones or any type of medication for you and what for? God I can't believe it."

"Please stop."

"No let me finish, this is really funny. Oh, all the guts you had? You took the medication and you even asked me to bring you some *Royal Jelly* capsules, every time I go to London to meet my professor. Remember? Not a touch, for two whole years!"

"Stop, Fairooz."

"I just can't believe it, now all the pieces of my puzzle fit together: your outrageous behavior for the last fifteen years, your continuous absence from the house and from any family gatherings and your trips to different places of the world, especially to Paris and Morocco, business trips huh?"

"Come on Fairooz, stop this. You're hurting me!"

"I'm what? Hurting whom? Tell me who's hurting whom? You call that hurt? Then what's this you've done to me, my children and family?"

"I told you I'll try to mend things up. I will try."

"Try is that all you can say?"

"What else can I say?"

"Please just stop. Don't say another word," still trying to be as calm as possible; I always try to be as cool as possible, when we discuss our problems. "You make me sick. I'm sorry but I don't believe anything you say. I just don't and while we're at it tell me, what went on between you and Sonia twenty years ago? I never forgot that." Sonia's been my friend. She had a crush on Ali then, and I always suspected an affair between the two of them; he even had her in his dreams once and called out her name while sleeping.

"I swear nothing ever happened between us, nothing," he says and thinks, *boy! She was beautiful, had a great body and such a flirt!*

God I don't believe a word he's saying, I also think to myself. "Please I want to sleep right now and I will stay here. You can go back home and tell everyone that I won't come back with you," I add trying to end this discussion.

"You can't stay and you know that I can't force you to come back with me. We're in a country that won't allow it. So please come back."

"I know and I also know that once we go back you'll never allow me to leave the country. Remember the law is always on your side? It is a man's world."

"Please just come and see Sam and if you still want to leave, I'll arrange everything for you. I promise."

Promises, promises I've had enough of those false promises, just let me sleep now and I'll think about it when I wake up, I keep thinking. I don't speak out loud still trying to salvage the breakage; our marriage is after all, falling apart, but I still want to try my best to save what's left of it.

"You don't want to go out? I have reservations at a Spanish restaurant, but I don't have to go with my friends. We can go together instead."

"Go out?" I cannot believe this! "I just want to nap. When I wake up I'll see," I then turn and give him my back. Suddenly he gets in bed and gets close, his hands moving to my breasts.

"Stop! I'd like to sleep," but he doesn't. He turns me over, gets on top of me and starts kissing me all over: my breasts, to my nipples and up towards my lips. I keep pushing him away but he pushes himself on me. I move my face from one side to the other, making sure that he cannot get a hold of my lips. He fights me and holds my hands down; kissing me so hard on the lips, even more than kissing: biting. I'm hurt and I keep trying to get away from him.

Then he pushes himself into my body. I kick him off and twist my body to get him out of me. It is the first time I ever felt like this. I despise him so much. Everything about him disgusts me, but my rejection makes him even more excited. Throughout his performance I keep pushing him off, pulling my body and lips away from his grasp. I want to scream, but I don't want a scandal. People might call security and it will be a big mess. All this doesn't stop him; he just goes all the way through, till he climaxes and relaxes! Has he really enjoyed it? He might as well have made love to a dead woman. I feel my lips with my fingers and they are literally swollen.

I go to the bathroom and scrub myself again harder than ever. *Get him off, I couldn't get him out at least I can scrub him off,* I furiously tell myself. When I come out, I go right to bed to sleep and find him on his mobile, telling his friends that he's going out with me. Then he comes to bed and gets close and holds me tightly, but I'm too exhausted to fight back again and immediately fall asleep. An hour later we wake up.

"Well, how do you feel?"

"Very sore, look at my lips!" I wish he could understand how bitter I feel.

"Are we going out?" He asks.

"O.K. if you want to," I might as well go out than sit and get raped again. This is not the way I want to be, but I'm trying to play this strange person's role, to keep the ball rolling. I do have six kids after all and I'm willing to do whatever I can to save this marriage. I'm even willing to act as a dummy and go with the tide. I get out of bed and put on a short black sexy chiffon dress and put some make up on, trying to lift my spirit up, while he gets dressed, too.

"Mick will be here in half an hour?"

"Why Mick? Can't we take a cab?" Mick is Salih's driver. I want some privacy and don't want anything to do with Salih.

"We don't know how to get there. We'll have Mick drive us there and we can take a cab back."

I know we can always ask the concierge, but I just go along. We go down to the lobby, not a word said. He tries to be nice and I pretend to be happy. We find Mick waiting in the lobby, Ali knows him, so he goes straight towards him:

"Good evening Madam, Sir. How are you this evening?"

"Fine how about yourself?" I ask.

"Just fine, are we going to the Spanish restaurant?"

"Yes please," Ali answers.

It took us fifteen minutes to get there.

"When shall I come back for you?" Mick asks as he closes the car door behind me.

"It's O.K. Mick we'll take a cab," Ali says.

"No Sir. I have nothing to do I can come back whenever you want me to."

Ali looks at me and I displeasingly nod "O.K.," I say.

"Let's say one?" Ali asks.

He again looks at me for approval. I cannot believe it, how he once again wants my consent. It has been so long since he has done that. "That's fine with me," I answer. Always pretending, not myself at all.

"See you then. Have a good time," Mick says, as he gets back in his black Mercedes.

As we walk into the restaurant the receptionist greets us as she takes our coats:

"Good evening."

The restaurant is so romantic. The lights are dim; candles and a vase with a red rose embellish each table. The walls are all decorated in a lovely Spanish style. The ceiling is engraved with drawings of dancing couples dressed in the traditional Spanish costumes.

"Good evening Sir. Your reservation is for…"

"Mr. Al-Arab."

The waitress checks her book.

"Right this way please."

We follow her to a table in the front, right by the dancing floor.

"Is that a good table?" Ali asks, awaiting my approval again.

"Yes," I respond with a false smile on my swollen lips. Once seated, the waitress comes back with the menu. We pick the menu up and start looking for what we would like to order. A few minutes later he asks me:

"What would you like?"

"I don't know. I think I'll take fettuccine," I say and think silently, *I'd rather swallow poison at this moment. I feel so embarrassed like everyone around me knows what I'm going through.*

"I think I'll take braised fish. Would you like an appetizer, a soup or a salad?"

"Yes I'll take a small salad."

"I'll take chicken corn soup. Then we can share, right?"

"O.K.," I unwillingly respond. *"Share food with you? I can't stand you. How can you ask me to share? I'd rather spit in your soup than share,"* my eyes mutely say. We wait for the waitress and a few minutes later she notices that our menus are closed and lying on the table, so she comes over and starts taking our order when Ali asks her:

"Can I have the wine list?"

"Sure," she then comes back with the wine list.

He orders the wine and starts looking around him. Looking at everyone at the restaurant and avoiding my eyes. The food comes and we start eating.

"That's real good. Would you like a bite?" He asks me offering me some of his fish.

"O.K. just a small bite," I lean forward to get a bite. *Doesn't he know that I don't like fish? What's he trying to do to me? Is he testing my patience and endurance?* I quietly ask myself.

While we're eating a dancer comes out dressed in a beautiful traditional red dress. Black frills on all its ends. Her red shoes match her red and black dress. And her black hair is decorated with a beautiful red carnation. She is thin and about five, six. I cannot concentrate on my food. I'm trying to watch every move she makes. It is a hobby of mine: to watch new moves in a dance. That's my way to learning new moves. I clap while my eyes are fixed on the dancer's feet. Ali is too busy eating; he never appreciates dancing and even when I dance he tries to discourage me, so I consequently stop and never dance before him anymore. *Wherever I go people love the way I move but not him*, I tell myself. The dancer is so serious while dancing. I've never seen anyone as serious as this woman right there on stage. She is superb and keeps on moving for about fifteen minutes. She then sits down and another thin tall, but younger dancer, dressed up in another gorgeous purple dress, comes out and starts dancing. I involuntarily start comparing the two dancers, *I think I like the first one more. She looks more like a professional and her moves are typically Spanish*. Another fifteen minutes pass and then the older dancer starts dancing again, but this time the second dancer dances with her for about five minutes and then sits down. The whole act is so good and when they finish the people clap so hard, even Ali claps! I start eating, when the dancers leave the floor.

A band comes out and starts playing slow tunes. A few minutes later everyone's dancing. *Everyone's dancing except us he won't even look at me*, not a word said.

That is so typical of him. Ignoring me is his game. It's been so for so long. I cannot wait till we finish our dessert and I immediately ask: "do you want to dance?" looking at my chocolate mousse and peeking at his chocolate cake I add: "when we finish I mean."

"No, not really," he answers.

So I sit there watching everyone having a good time. Kissing, touching and caressing. A few minutes later he says:

"Do you want to dance, now?"

Oh how I want to say no, but I just get up to dance. It is very strange but I'm trying my best to be nice, though I'm so hurt. I'm pretending to be loving, sexy and most of all happy. Am I trying to compete with the second woman, his other wife? As we're dancing I think, *what's this? What's the matter with this man? Why is he so cold? He really believes I'm part of his property? Only when he wants me, he gets close!* The song ends, but I wanted to go on dancing; I can dance all night long. I love it, although he is a bore, dances like a robot and without any feelings, I still wanted to go on dancing. He then pulls me off the dance floor:

"That's enough. I'm tired."

What happened to him? He's not acting anymore? Not trying to be real sweet and nice? He's back to his normal self. As we sit at our table, he notices that a young man is making advances at me and dancing right in front of our table, such sensual dancing, just staring at me.

"Fairooz come on, I'm really tired. Let's go."

Unwillingly I get up and we leave heading back to the hotel. Ali calls Mick and tells him that we're taking a cab back and that he doesn't need to come back for us, as it is just eleven. When we get to the room Ali notices that I'm so unhappy and he's so scared that I'll throw another tantrum so he apologetically starts telling me:

"Fairooz, you know I told you that I've made a mistake and I just can't ignore everything. I will try to mend our life, but I can't just abandon her and my son now. I will try to ignore her as much as I can, until she gets fed up and leaves back to her country."

Liar, liar, I keep thinking and then say: "you think she'll just pack and leave you. After all that you've done for her? All the jewelry you bought her? And the house she owns back in Morocco? You really think I believe you? Leaving this luxurious life you're offering her?"

"Ladies and gentlemen this is your captain speaking. We're approaching Heathrow. The temperature is 14°C, and the time is four in the morning. Thank you for flying BA. We hope you've enjoyed your flight and hope to see you again soon."

My life is saved again, thanks. It is strange how memory rolls! So many incidents; incidents that took years and months flash by in just a few hours. Twenty more minutes and we'll be there. Once again the reel rolls, I remember then how only four months ago at the beginning of November 1997 he told me that he had a business trip to Yemen. By this time I had already known that he was married; so he went all right and he called several times a day. Not only that, he even gave me his number there and that was the first time he had ever given me a phone number to his whereabouts. I thought then that this was a good sign of a better relationship. When he got back he told me all about Yemen and how the houses were built of clay and no signs of modernization at all.

Then a week later he said he had another trip to Yemen, but this time he left and never called, for ten days; he never even asked about me or the children. At this time Amr was acting strange in school and they suspended him; and his loving dad did not know anything about that. How could he when he had never called? I checked the hotel he stayed in last time in Yemen, but he was not there. I then called the Yemen airlines, on which he said he was traveling and his name was not there, either. I called his secretary Abdou, but of course his secret keeper would never betray him. When he got back Amr asked him:

"Baba how was your trip?"

"Oh very boring all I did was read this book," he holds up a book on Islam, "there's nothing to do. No TV or anything. I stayed at a camp and not at a hotel, like last time. I miss you all so much."

"Oh that's why you didn't call?" I stupidly ask.

"Yes, how can I? It's so far away from any civilized area."

There is something strange about this whole situation. I can sense it. I may be naïve but I'm getting wiser. At least I can doubt now, when I trusted so much before. He seems a bit nervous and can't look me in the eye. He is talking and his eyes are looking straight ahead, trying to focus on the TV or anywhere but my eyes; what is he hiding?

"I need to take a bath. I'm sorry but all my clothes are dirty. There was no where I could wash them there."

"Don't worry. It's O.K. You asked me for extra clothing before leaving. Was it enough?"

"Oh, yes just barely. Amr, do you want to come to pray with me?"

It is a Friday and he always takes Amr to the prayers, in the Mosque.

"Oh, Fairooz you wouldn't believe how primitive that area is? My last trip I think was odd, but this one was so different. There was nothing; I didn't even have good food to eat and all ate was bread and cheese. So how about a bath, want me to scrub your back?" He asks.

"Sounds great," I go to the bathroom with him. I know what he wants, yet I want to know what is he's hiding. *Scrub my back? There is something fishy going on here,* I warn myself. I don't want him to even touch me, not until he tells me what he's hiding. We get in the bedroom and he locks the door and starts undressing me and undresses himself and leads the way to the bathtub.

"Oh, I miss you."

"I was so worried about you and I even tried reaching you everywhere, but couldn't get a hold of you," I tell him while he starts scrubbing my back. Then he turns me around and starts caressing me.

"I miss that body," he tells me, staring at me.

"I miss you too," I say, trying to move away, "hey, we won't have time for anything and you'll miss the prayer." I then step out of the bathtub, put on my robe and start leaving.

"When I get back?"

"Yes." Then he gets out and raps his body with his towel. He pulls me back to him and starts to untie my robe and once again starts caressing me.

"That feels so good."

"Ali the prayer," I have to find out first; then he lets me go and gets dressed.

"Amr, are you ready?" He asks.

"Yes," Amr answers, dressed in his clean *Thoab* (traditional men's attire).

They kiss me good bye and leave. The girls are in the living room watching TV. I then go back to the bedroom, lock the door behind me and start emptying his suitcase. Yuck everything stinks! Nothing's clean. I remove it all and put it aside so Dada can wash everything. *"Fairooz check his handbag,"* a voice tells me. What is this strange voice, coming from within? Maybe it's my wake up voice? I never thought of going through any of his things. *Shall I, why not?* I tell myself. So I start opening his handbag, shocked I speak to myself, *God! Saudi Airlines ticket? I almost faint! I thought he said he's going on Yemen Airlines. He showed me something from the Yemen Airlines to prove that he's going there. I can't believe how naïve I am! I thought it was his ticket and didn't even take a good look at it, I truly trusted him,* I think as I remember that it was the first time he had shown me his ticket, that is strange; but come to think of it, when he showed it to me he held it in a funny way, as if he was hiding parts of it, so I wouldn't know what it really was.

There is something fishy about this whole thing. Now I'm so confused. I read the ticket I'm holding in my hand now: *Jeddah-Casablanca, Casablanca-Jeddah* and ask myself, *what, Casablanca?* I read it over and over again. Then I check the date on the ticket: *November 20th–29th*. No, it can't be true I must be wrong and I read it for the tenth time. Yes, he was there! Then I start looking for his passport. That is one thing I cannot be wrong about. I find it among his papers and run through the pages. That is to the US, an old one. So many visas and no clues yet. O.K.! That is Yemen's visa, but the date on it is that of the previous trip. Where is this last one? I flip the pages so fast. Oh my God! Two full pages of his trips to Casablanca? I go through them all. Aha, that is it: entry visa on the twentieth of November and exit on the twenty-ninth of this year. That is it! That is what is so strange about that stranger. Yes, a stranger, but at last I'm getting wiser. I pick up the phone and dial a number. *Oh please answer. I hope you're there I need you,* I think in despair. The phone keeps ringing and after five rings my voice shrieks:

"Samia?" Samia is my best friend and my secret keeper and advisor. She is a very smart well-educated woman a very good listener and an excellent counselor. Deema and her daughter Mona are best friends. I met her at one of the mother's meetings at Deema's school and we just talked and found out that our daughters are best friends. Then, we too became best friends. Samia is Syrian, with a smile that never leaves her round face and her sparkling brown eyes are always grinning. She is always nicely dressed and I always think that she is so lucky, because she is petite and looks ever so young.

"Fairooz? What's wrong? You sound strange? Is everything all right?"

"Samia I don't know what to say?" I listen to my voice: so hysterical.

"God, Fairooz? What's wrong?"

"Remember I told you that Ali didn't call all the time he was in Yemen?"

"Ya and you told me he's coming back today. Is he back?"

"Yes and I wish he never was"

"Fairooz just calm down and tell me."

"Well guess what? He wasn't there."

No, don't tell me my guess is right? Samia on the other side of town thinks. "No?" She says trying to be calm, but she is so mad, boiling and sounds hysterical, too.

"He went to Casablanca."

"Fairooz, are you sure?" She knew that he was there.

"Yes, yes I checked his handbag and found his ticket and passport," I say almost sobbing.

"Fairooz, don't worry. Just take it easy, shall I come and see you?"

"Oh he'll be back in a short while. He's at the mosque now."

"Listen Fairooz, don't be so upset, when you told me that he didn't call before, I knew he was there, but I didn't tell you."

"Oh Samia, you really thought he was in Casablanca?"
"Yes, and you know I went through all of this myself."
Samia was another victim of a viciously segregated society, where men and women each have their own lives; and her husband too was married, but she never told him that she suspected anything.
"So? What shall I do?"
"Fairooz it's so hard to tell you what to do now."
"I want to face him with it all. What do you think?"
"Maybe you should."
"I want to leave him I can't stand looking at him."
"Fairooz, you can't. Remember your children."
"My children want me to leave. They can't see me crying day and night even in my sleep."
"Listen, you have two choices either you keep quiet like I am, or confront him and see what happens."
"No, I'll leave."
"Fairooz please you're upset now. Cool down wait and see what happens."
"O.K.," I answer not really convinced.
"Fairooz will you please?"
"O.K. Yes I'll wait. You know how much I value your advice. Samia I love talking to you, you always let me cool down. I don't know how I can survive through a lot of my problems without you?"
"By the way are you still on the Prozac?"
Samia was so worried and knew about my previous breakdown cases and as a matter of fact, she was the one who advised me, to go on Prozac.
"Yes, oh yes."
"Keep taking it for about six months and it will make you feel good."
"It's working like a miracle, I really feel great using it."
"That's so nice to hear Fairooz. I love you. You are so dear to me."
"I love you, too Samia."
"You sound better now."
"I feel better, too."
"O.K. now I'll leave you and I pray that everything will be all right. Take good care of yourself Fairooz. O.K.?"
"I will. Don't you worry; I'm getting stronger each day."
We hang up and I already feel such a relief and go to the kitchenette to boil some water. I open the cabinet and bring out a sachet of chamomile. I heard that hot chamomile calms the nerves. I take my mug and go back to bed. Lying

down and sipping my drink I start wondering and cannot believe what is happening to me. Is this the same guy I married years ago? Everything happening to me now is absolutely shocking! Is it a nightmare? Or is it a bitter reality I have to cope with? Where is that other man I married? I wish he would come back. I suddenly open my eyes and find him there in front of me. He kisses me and goes out to see the girls.

"Deema, Dalia, Rana where are you? Don't you miss Baba?"

I can hear him and think, *miss whom? Where have you been for ten days? Haven't you missed them? Couldn't you have just made one call and asked how they were for ten whole days?* I'm so furious, *"but no, cool down,"* that voice tells me again.

"So what are your plans for today?" He asks the girls.

"Baba today is Friday and we're going to Sitto (grandma, my mom)," answers Deema, coming out of her room and buttoning her blouse.

"Baba, why don't you and Mama come along any more?" Innocently asks Rana. She reminds him so much of me: so out spoken.

"I'm tired right now. You just go ahead and say hello to everyone."

He knows that he cannot go there any more. Everyone is so mad at what he had done to me. So sad, he was so much loved by all and now they are all mad at him, his own cousins. Ten minutes later, I hear running down the stairs, the door slams and they are all gone.

Oh how I miss those gatherings at Mama's and his mom's, but I'm so ashamed of myself to have accepted such a situation and I never go there again. At least not when the families are gathered, how can I meet any of his family or mine? I feel that I'm a failure; and feel so embarrassed about what has happened to me. Where ever I go, even if when I go shopping, I feel that people, strangers, are staring at me and saying: *this is the woman, whose husband neglected and married another woman.* I feel that I failed myself, my kids and every woman around me. How can I face any one after what has happened to me? It is a strange feeling a woman gets, when she feels betrayed by the man in her life; how she emotionally and physically depends on him for her self-esteem and loses it all when he leaves her. I feel like I can never live any more. I'd rather die than go on living; I lost all my self-confidence, because the one person, who provided me with such assurance, let me down.

My memories are still concentrated on that horrible Friday, when I found out about Ali's trip to Morocco. I remember how Amr was grounded that Friday, but because I wanted to be alone with Ali and get the truth out of him, I called him:

"Amr." He comes running from his room, with a wide smile on his face as he knows what I'm about to say: "Amr it's O.K. you can go to Sitto, because Baba is here and he's asked me if you can go, so go get dressed." He runs to his room, so excited and quickly gets dressed in shorts and a T-shirt, puts his sneakers on and runs behind his sisters; luckily they were still waiting for the driver to get dressed.

"Fairooz, if you want to go you can. You don't have to stay because I'm not going," Ali says.

"Why don't you go?"

"You know I won't go until I solve my problems. I can't face anyone there, but why don't you go?"

What does he want? Does he want the true honest me? Does he miss that? Maybe he feels that I've been acting for too long? I haven't been myself for over two months, acting and more acting, I think "You know you're not the only one; who is ashamed of what had happened; I can't face anyone anymore: not my family nor even my friends. I haven't been to so many parties; I can't meet people anymore. I even apologized to that party at your mom's last week; and everyone was upset and the next day, I was told that everyone was really sad and that your mom cried throughout the party. They say that even the singer asked about me! I guess they have to get used to me, not being there?" I at last say out loud.

"But no. How long can you go on doing that?"

"Until you settle your problems and decide on what you're going to do." He then reaches out and touches me. His right hand reaches out to my breast and his left is already on my thigh. *God, are you nuts? Is that what you think I need right now?* Not a word said, I just stare at him and think. Now, being alone he makes advances but I just want to let him know that I have changed and that I know everything. He keeps touching and gets all excited and starts undressing me, when I reach out and pull his hands away.

"Where is Rosie?" He asks about the Phillippino help.

"She's down in her room probably."

"What do you say if we go to the bedroom?"

He pulls me up. *Let's see where all this is leading to? I'll play this game his way and see how it ends,* I think. We then walk to the bedroom his hands all over me never stopping. I cannot take it any longer. Shall I ask now? Or wait and see? He pulls me to bed and starts undressing me while kissing and caressing my body. *Now is the right time,* I smile as I pull myself away and lie with my hands and breasts on his chest. "So, how was Yemen? Did you really miss me?"

"You know I did. I missed you so much," he starts kissing me again.

"Were you really in Yemen?"

"What do you mean? Of course I was; where else?" He answers with an irritated voice.

"Tell me why didn't you call at all? Didn't you worry about me or the children?"

"You know that as long as you're with them I can never worry about them and the compound I was staying in had no telephones. I had to drive five hours to get to the nearest phone."

God, why does he have to make it sound so morbid to prove his point? I smile thinking, then say, pretending to be surprised, "five hours? That must have been an awful place?"

"Yes horrible, I didn't think that you'd be so worried or I would have driven all the way to call you."

"Oh no I would have felt terrible if you would have driven five whole hours. We were all right. I just missed you," I feel myself smiling secretly.

"Now, let's stop that talk and get some work done."

His hand is pulling my head closer to his face and before his lips touch mine I pull away again. "Ali, I know where you were."

"What do you mean?" He tries to smile.

"You know what I mean."

"No I don't. What do you really mean?"

"How was Casablanca?"

"What?" He angrily asks.

"How was Casablanca?"

"Casablanca? How should I know?"

"Ali, can't we speak like grown ups for a change and stop this acting game?"

"What are you talking about? When will you stop these hallucinations of yours?"

"You know very well that I'm not hallucinating."

He gets so furious and pushes me off of his chest and turns around giving me his back.

"So you were there?"

"No. You know very well that I was in Yemen. Didn't I show you my ticket before leaving?"

His voice is so loud and he is so mad, or pretending, at least to be furious. I can feel the heat off of his body and can see how red his face is.

"You are really crazy!" He screams at me.

Aha! At last he's back to his normal self. The raging man I was living with for over twenty-eight years. No more acting. There goes the sweet guy I briefly met, for the past two months; so sweet trying to cover up for what he did, now I feel better and again ask out loud: "Ali why don't you just admit it?"

"Admit what? Listen, you're just blabbing and I want to go to sleep."

I jump out of bed and bring a small book. "Before you go to sleep, just swear on this Koran that you weren't there."

"Why should I? Don't you believe me?"

"There's nothing to worry about if you swear, is there?"

"You can't believe me?" He is so angry now.

"Just swear. Please, just swear." He puts his right hand on the Koran and strangely looks at me and says:

"O.K., I swear that I wasn't in Casablanca. Are you happy now?" His hand is still glued flat on the holy book.

"No, swear that you weren't there this year, between the twentieth and twenty-ninth, of November."

"This is a bit too much?"

"Come on just do it."

"O.K., I swear that I wasn't in Casablanca this year, between the twentieth and twenty-ninth, of November. Are you happy now?"

"Yes." God I can't believe it. *How can I live with you? How can I trust you? I can't believe all this is happening to me,* I smile and think.

"Now can you leave me alone?"

I've never seen him this mad and I just look at him and give him my back and try to sleep. Two hours later, I wake up and find him on the floor, looking out of the window onto the swimming pool. I get down and sit next to him. He cannot look at me and sits sideways only. I stare at him and can feel how he's avoiding my eyes. I just want him to know that I know that he was there for sure, because his look, tone of voice and everything about him, makes me feel that I'm making it all up. "Can I check your passport for a second?" I ask him.

"Why? Not again?"

I don't wait for his answer and pull the passport right out of his handbag and flip the pages. "So where does it say that you were in Yemen?" I ask in a sarcastic tone.

"I don't know," he adds in such a feeble tone.

"So, did you go to Casablanca?" I'm pretending to go through all the pages. "Aha? What's this here? This is the visa to Yemen almost three weeks ago. Is this a visa to Morocco? Yes, it is. Entry visa on the twentieth and exit…"

"Did you go through my bag?" Once again he speaks in such a weak voice.

"No, but I checked the manifest for the Yemen Airlines to see if your name was on it and I checked the hotel you stayed in last time and you weren't anywhere. So were you there?"

"Yes, I had to go and make sure my son's name is officially registered. I couldn't tell you, I knew how much that would hurt you."

"Your what?" My eyes bulge as I jump off and almost strangle him, but he swiftly moves his head back to avoid my rage.

"Fairooz, I'm so sorry," tears in his eyes, he comes closer again and tries to hug me.

"Keep those dirty hands away!" I hysterically scream at him and once again he moves back. "So when was that *son* of yours born?" I furiously shout.

"On the fifth of November," now tears rush down his face.

"I will not stay! I'm leaving you with the children!" I roar weeping.

"I can't tell you not to. You have every right to, but if you do you'll leave me in such a bad situation. I won't be able to take care of my work with the responsibility of the children and the house. Please don't leave. I promise I'll work things out."

"So she's coming over here?"

"She has to so I can register the boy here, too."

"I'll give you one last chance. I'll stay, but Sam has to come home for Christmas. I miss him so much. And I'll never tell the children where you'd been and how you never lifted the phone to ask how they were."

This whole episode was before the trip to London in December and before Sam came back home for Christmas. I don't like what I'm doing. I'm in such a powerful position and look at him he's so weak, tears falling down his cheeks. Now, I have to blackmail him to bring Sam home for Christmas.

"O.K. I'll call him and get his tickets ready. When is his Christmas vacation?" He tries to speak, but chokes on his tears.

"I don't know?" No feelings what so ever. Is that really me? Where are my emotions? "I'll call him today and see." I can't believe how he has become. *I guess we're all humans we can laugh and cry, be strong or weak. It all depends on the situations we find ourselves in. It's shocking how society imposes our roles and formulates our characters and attitudes?* I can't stop thinking. Suddenly my horrid train of thoughts and memories are interrupted again:

"Excuse me Mam."

Thank God. He saved my life again, constantly thinking I look at the man next to me on the plane, coming back to his seat. He is about thirty-five. His black hair is brushed back and I can't see his eyes but now as he stares at me I can see that they are deep brown almost black. His loose fit blue jeans match his multi color T-shirt. He has a nice smile quite a friendly looking guy. His looks make me get away from that horrendous film I was viewing.

"I noticed that you were sleeping most of the time. Are you that tired?" He asks.

"Ya I guess so," I answer and more thinking, *sleeping, how I can I sleep?*

"You know, I've come from Riyadh and I can see that you have an Arabic magazine out."

With his looks, he can easily pass as an Arab but I'm not sure and I want to switch to Arabic but I ask:

"Are you Lebanese?"

"Oh no do I look it?"

"Ya you know in the Arab world we have a mixture of looks."

"No I'm American," he smiles to himself as he says that.

As he smiles I can see a nicely-formed set of teeth. I can tell that he feels good to be taken for someone from my region.

"Oh! So what were you doing in Riyadh?" I ask.

"I work at the American Embassy."

"Oh so how do you like it there?"

"It's quite different and if it wasn't for the people I work with and the activities we have I'd think I was in a desert, it's a city with no people."

"How is that?"

"You see, you don't see anyone on the streets and I really miss the family life over there."

"Really? You're kidding, right?" I ask with a funny look, like I don't know; I myself cannot stand going to that city; he is so right no people anywhere on the streets and no friendly face in shops either.

"Before I answer this question I like to ask where are you from I know you're an Arab because of that magazine. You know I don't read Arabic but I can tell if the letters are Arabic and I never would have thought you were an Arab if it wasn't for that magazine. So where are you from?"

True I have a magazine on my lap, but I didn't have the chance, to even open it, I smile and silently tell myself and at last I answer his anxious face, "well, I'm from Jeddah."

"Jeddah? No can't be?" He astoundingly asks.

"Why? Why do you have that look on your face?"

"Well, really because you never see Arabian women in Riyadh I never thought you'd be from there. Tell me, how come I can see your face? Why don't you have that black thing head to toes on?"

What kind of a guy is this? I silently ask; *is he making fun of women back home?* I feel at liberty to criticize anything concerning my country but cannot take it when other people do.

"Please forgive me if I am out of line," he adds in his American accent, as he notices my displeased look. "I don't mean to be sarcastic, but truly in Riyadh I never saw a woman, in all my two years there. All I saw was a black dress walking down the street; they call that an *Abaya*, right?"

"Yes and I guess you're right. In Riyadh they're very strict but haven't you ever been to Jeddah?"

"No. Is it any different?"

"Well, it's not as bad. We still have to put on those black tents but we don't have to cover up all over, or even put on gloves like women in Riyadh. We do have some freedom compared to the women there," I tell him and think mocking my own words, *some kind of freedom?*

"See, that's what I mean over there you never see a family together on the street. It's always someone in black accompanied by kids. You can't even tell if it's really a woman."

"I know exactly what you mean. You know sometimes men dress up in those tents and no one knows about them. Years ago, they say that men used to attend *only women* weddings," I place a lot of emphasis on my words, "disguised as women and no one knew about them, till one day a man was caught and since that incident no one with a tent on was allowed to weddings."

"So, how come you don't have this *Abaya* on?"

I hate those questions, but I'm going all the way along to see what happens, I think as I look at him and then ask: "you mean now?"

"Yes."

"You must be kidding? I can't believe I'm out of the country, so I can just take it off." I don't mean to be rude but I feel so dried up so tired and he doesn't want to leave me alone.

"So tell me what are you going to London for?" He asks.

"Actually I'm taking another flight to Newcastle," I answer and hope this is his last question.

"Newcastle? Where's that, is it in England?"

"Yes it's up North."

"You're on a business trip?"

Gosh this guy is even worse than me. "Well, kind of. I'm going to study there," I know his next question so I go on: "I'm going for my Ph.D. in American Fiction." Now I'm really tired of talking about myself so I divert the question: "how about you, why are you going to London? Is it a business trip?"

"No I'm catching a flight to Alabama, Georgia," he says and only now I recognize his Southern accent.

Alabama? My thoughts float back to the slavery days in the US and my own situation back home.

"So tell me. Are you really Arabian?" He insistently asks.

"Yes. Why ask?" I know exactly what he means.

"Well, I thought you were Italian, French or even Iranian? It never crossed my mind that you'd be Arabian. You just don't look Arabian at all."

"Well, you know if you don't speak with that Southern American accent of yours I'd never think you were an American either. Remember I thought you were an Arab. You could even pass for an Italian or Spanish with your kind of complexion," I jokingly smile and we both laugh.

"Ya I know. I have Italian blood on my mom's side," he looks at me and feels flattered at my comment.

"O.K., now I know where you get it from," and think with a mischievous smile, *I cannot dare be more specific, meaning how he gets his good looks.*

"How about you, you're not all Arab are you?" He knows exactly what I want him to ask and his eyes are now smiling too.

"No, you're right. I too have some Iranian blood," I smile; you know I've always been proud to announce my grandma's blood in my veins.

"No wonder," he smiles approvingly.

"Well, you see you mistook me for a Westerner and I took you for an Arab, we are after all one big extended family. We do have the same origins, same father and same mother, right?"

"What do you mean?"

"I mean we all are descendants of Adam and Eve," I smile at my comment; he smiles back and says:

"Man, with your looks! Your light hair, hazel eyes, olive complexion and your mouth…"

What are we getting a bit too personal or what? I feel goose bumps all over my body I cannot take this sweet talk, not now any ways I'm not used to it. I interrupt him and look at my watch. "Ten more minutes to go," I say and lean my head back.

"So, what do you…?"

Fast asleep? Or is she pretending to avoid my flirtatious comments? Well, that's what a woman is capable of doing. She can always get out of situations she doesn't like by performing such a small act, he grins and thinks to himself. *Well at least she gets the message that I like her and she is avoiding my looks,* he goes on talking to himself. "Miss," he whispers.

He touches me trying to wake me up; I jump to his touch.

"We're almost there, we're landing," he adds. "We were talking and suddenly you leaned your head back and dozed off. I knew that you were tired, so I just turned my head back to the window," he gives me a cunning smile. He then starts to fiddle with his seat belt and bag, getting ready for landing.

I smile at him and say: "thanks for waking me up." His lovely smile makes him even more attractive. *Don't even go there*, I silently warn myself. Did I actually sleep? Or was the stress too much on my brain and I just fainted? It is like when someone is hypnotized and dozes off, after spilling out all the thoughts. I put the magazine in my bag and put my shoes on, then I check that the seat belt was fastened as usual; I just have to check it and put the seat up. The wheels then hit the ground and we already there. I didn't have time to read or watch a movie as usual; I had my own film rolling throughout the trip, quite a film, too!

Jaddah

June settles in. It's another cold gray day in Newcastle. I'm lying on my bed and reading *Rabbit at Rest* when the phone and the mobile ring at the same time. I drop the book on the pillow pick the mobile with one hand and the phone with the other. I let the mobile ring as it is my friend Jane form Leeds and I can call her back later, I answer the phone and it's Sam.
"Hey Mama."
"Hey, what a surprise! Long time, no hear." Sam is in Florida, majoring in mechanical engineering and I haven't heard from him for over two months. We usually get in touch at least once a month, but I've been so busy with my studies. I remember how Ali sent Sam to Vermont in 1991 but Sam could not stand the freezing weather and moved down to Florida four years ago.
"Mom, I'm graduating in December!"
"You're what? I can't believe that. Are you serious?"
"Yes Mama, why will I joke about this?"
"You know Sam it's been seven years now since you've gone to the US."
"I know, but at last I'm going to do it."
"God I just can't believe it"
"So Mama, I would love for you to come and attend my graduation it's your reward, after all, more than mine."
"Sam, you've really surprised me. I was planning on going home to see your sisters and brothers."
"Mama, what do you mean? You won't attend my graduation?"
"How can I miss it?"
"So?"
"So, let me see what I can do." I won't miss it for the whole world, but I have to see how to fit it in with my studies.
"What do you mean? What you can do?"

"Listen, I have to inform my professor first and then buy my tickets."
"And?"
"Wow! God this is really great!"
"Ya Mama at last, huh?" I can see his smiles coming to me across the phone line.
"Ya and this is a great chance for me too to come to the US; you know I need to get some references and maybe meet the author of the topic of my dissertation. See I've said that I'll never plan for the future. No more planning; I'll just live each day as it comes."
"What do you mean?"
"Well, here I am sitting here on this cold day in June and suddenly I get your call wanting me to come over to Florida."
"Mama, the weather will be great even in December: nice and warm."
"I know. It's Florida."
"So?"
"Give me time."
"Time for what?"
"Hey, listen you crazy one. I have to figure my way down there."
"So, you're coming?"
"Sam, *habeeby* I told you I won't miss it; I've been waiting too long for that. Listen, I'll call you back once I have everything ready. O.K.?"
"O.K. Mama. I love you."
"I know and I love you too. So tell me, now you're a mechanical engineer?"
"Ya I guess?" I can see his smile.
"Oh God that's great then you can fix my car?" I ask teasingly.
"Ya. Ya. Ya," we both laugh.

Whenever we talk we laugh so much. He is the one son who cannot stop talking and he has such a great sense of humor. Actually all my kids have it they take after their dad and me: they are so talkative, but some a bit more than others. "O.K. then I'll see you soon. I love you *habeeby* take care now," and we hang up.

This call came two months after he knew about his dad's marriage and I'm sure that this marriage and the thought of me being on my own, were the strongest incentives for him to finish his studies which had taken so long.

I remember how shocked he was when he found out about his dad's marriage this past April. I had been here for just a month when Kareem came over to visit me. Kareem is such a sensitive person and he just wouldn't leave me in a strange land, all on my own. Sitting together in my living room and re-capping on everything that had been happening with our lives, he suddenly says:

"Mama, I'll call Sam and tell him."

"Tell him what?"

"About Dad."

"Oh no."

"Yes Mama he has to know."

"Please, don't. I don't want him to worry about me. All he knows is that I'm here, studying and will be going back and forth all the time to see your dad and your sisters and brother."

"But I have to. He's part of this family."

He walks to the end of the living-room, picks up the white hand-free phone and dials Sam's number. A few seconds later Sam is on the line:

"Hi Sam."

"Kareem, what a surprise, you hardly ever call."

"I know. Remember I have to pay for the calls."

"So, what makes you call now?"

"Well, Mama is paying," he gives a teasing laugh saying that.

"Don't tell me you're there with her?"

"Yes, I hate to tell you that. He he he."

"Oh, you dirty ugly duckling. You always have your devious ways to get to her," Sam says in his jolly tone.

"Well, let's say I know how to play the right game at the right time," he laughs, never stopping, teasing Sam.

"So, what are you doing there?"

"Oh, I have a few days off of school and thought I'd come and keep her company. You know she's all alone over here."

"You mean you have a vacation? What? In Jordan they let you have vacations if you're messing up at the university?"

"Oh, please. Look who's talking? How long have you been in the US?"

"O.K. Just forget it. So, seriously what's the vacation for?"

"Remember? It's *Eid* vacation. Remember Ramadan? We were fasting for thirty days and now it's *Eid*?"

"You were what? Listen Kareem, you can pull this on Mama and Baba, but not on me," and they both crack up laughing.

"O.K., so everyone else was fasting," he says laughing out loud.

"Ya, that's better you fasting my…"

"Sam. I'm calling you to tell you about something."

"What? Tell me how come Mama is all alone?"

"Well, that's what I want to talk to you about."

"So?"

"Sam, your dad is married," Kareem answers, with a more serious tone.

"I know he's married or else neither I nor any of you will be here now," now he's laughing even more.

"No, Sam stop, I'm serious."

"I'm serious too," he says still laughing so hard.

"Sam. Listen. Your father married another woman, other than Mama."

I can hear him yelling and with a sad look I ask Kareem to stop, but he doesn't.

"What? Kareem that's not funny," he screams.

"Sam, cool down. I know this is shocking. You can't believe how it affected Deema and me when we first found out; then we sat with Mama and planned a way to tell our younger sisters and brother. It is a disaster."

"Oh my God!"

I can hear his sobbing and screaming and tears start running down my cheeks.

"Oh my God, when did this happen?"

"Mama knew about it in September."

"And how come I didn't know?" He is still crying.

"Sam, Mama didn't want to bother you when you're so far away."

"Bother who? Bother…Bother me; me her eldest son?"

"Yes, she thought it would be better to let you get on with your studies. She didn't even want me to tell you and right now she keeps shaking her head asking me to stop."

"Oh my God Mama; I could have stood by her side, instead of leaving her on her own, while I'm over here, having a ball. I can never forgive myself, never."

"Sam, it's O.K. You know how strong she is. Don't worry about her."

He is still sobbing and crying. I can hear him and Kareem is trying to calm him down. I can't help myself and I snatch the phone: "Sam *habeeby*."

"Mama!"

"Sam, it's O.K.," now I'm trying to keep myself from crying, I don't want to make him feel worse, but those stupid tears. "It's O.K. *habeeby*."

"Mama, how can you keep all of this from me?"

"Sam I'm sorry. I just didn't want to bother you."

"*Bother…me?*" Now he's even worse, repeating himself, "*Mama…Bother…me?*"

Now he can't even talk, he just sobs and cries like a baby who has lost his mother.

"Mama, you shouldn't be sorry. I'm sorry I wasn't there for you."

I feel something grabbing my heart. My God, he is sorry? I thought he is really upset because I didn't tell him. I never thought that he is upset because he hadn't been there for me. *Thank you God, my kids are great. They really do love me. Oh, thank you God,* I silently pray and weep; still fighting those stupid tears and trying to keep my voice under control. It is those tears that keep bothering me; I'm so scared I'll break down. "Sam, please…please…Sam…"

"Mama…I love you…," he is still sobbing.

"Sam, if you love me then stop this crying please, it's breaking my heart."

"Oh no…that's the last…thing I'd ever…do to…you."

"So, can you stop?" I know that he is trying real hard. With a little more control he says:

"Mama, I'll come and see you."

"Oh, no you won't." No way am I going to let him leave his school and come to comfort me, though I really need him. "Listen, *habeeby*, I swear I'm fine. I'm really doing so well. I'm happier this way and the only thing that makes me sad is the fact that your sisters and brothers aren't with me. So please don't come and please finish quickly and then I'll see you."

"Mama," more composed than before, "I promise I'll never let you down."

"That's my baby. That's what I really want you to do so I can feel that I've accomplished one of my goals in life."

"Don't worry Mama you'll never feel anything else. All of us will be right there with you, all the way through."

"So, you feel better now? You certainly sound better," I try to laugh, but tears choke me.

"Yes Mama I feel better; as long as you're happy that's all I care for," he is trying to laugh too.

"O.K. then Sam, this call will cost me a fortune." I'm so pleased now that a real laugh is at last released.

"O.K. Mama I'll let you go," he says as he makes a harder trial for genuine laughter.

"You take good care of yourself *habeeby*."

"You too Mama."

"And keep the email coming."

"I will Mama *habeeby*."

That is him, back to normal again: funny talkative and naughty as ever. I feel so good now and know that he is not mad at me and still loves me so I end the call saying: "O.K. *habeeby*, you take care and remember that I love you," I know that these words comfort him most.

"I love you too Mama."

"Take care, *habeeby*." I put the phone down and hug Kareem, who is sitting next to me feeling so worried. I know it's not so simple but it is over and he did right to tell Sam. It was such a hard job to get him to smile and make Sam feel good and back to his own self again.

Sam's call right now added so much hope to my life and at the moment I truly think that what has happened between me and his dad is past and over; all I'm thinking of right now is that at last I've achieved one of my major goals in life. Now I can look to a brighter future, where my kids will each graduate and have their own jobs and families.

I've been thinking of a divorce for a while and finally I've decided that that's what I really want; no way can I go on being his wife any more, it just doesn't make any sense. My brother, Joe, emailed me last Monday saying that he's passing by London on his way to Boston to visit his son Alim and asked me to come and see him. So excited, I called the Midland Mainline and right away made my train reservations.

Mind you this brother was my worst enemy. As kids we used to fight twenty-four hours a day and over the silliest things, like who'd eat the red dates first. I remember at about the age of eleven I used to hide the dates in the back of the fridge. Then one day, during our routine fights, we both ran to the fridge stuck our hands in the back of it; and guess what? Our hands met clasping to the plate of dates. So, you see he is as devious as I am. He too had the habit of hiding the dates from everyone else. That incident is well known in the family and till this day everyone makes fun of it and reminds us how sneaky we can be.

It's true that he was my most awful enemy, but later on in life we became real good friends; well, when I got married in 1969 and went to St. Louis, I really missed him more than any of my brothers and sisters, but I was so lucky, because that same year he got a scholarship and came over. Where else? But to where I am! You know how it is: people usually end up with those who give them the hardest time! So, in St. Louis I became very close to him and my eldest brother, Zahid, who was also studying there.

Anyway, I'm on the nine o'clock train to London to meet Joe and after three long hours the train finally stops at Kings Cross and I hurriedly take a cab to Park Lane Intercontinental, where Joe is staying. I know that he had reserved a room for me over the weekend.

I run to his room and knock like a lunatic! Joe opens the door and we hug and kiss, so thrilled to see one another. He then asks me to come in and we sit on the floral sofa, in his room.

"Girl! You sure look good, happy too!"

"Aha, I feel great."

"So how have you been? We're so worried about you back home and look at you. I wish everyone could see how happy you look and stop worrying."

"I know Mama and Baba are really worried. *Mais c'est la vie*, Joe."

"*Qui*, now tell me what's up? It had been three months since you left."

"Everything! I'm back to my old self again that happy crazy girl who even the devil can't compete with, the girl who drove everyone nuts from teachers to girls and boys," I say and we both laugh.

"Fairooz I can't believe that. I'm so glad to see you this happy."

We chatted for hours never stopping. Well, actually I talked for hours, non-stop and all that poor Joe did was to listen and nod. I didn't even give him a chance to say more than a sentence every thirty minutes! I wanted to tell Joe about my decision but didn't know how to go around doing it and then I started:

"So how's your fiance?"

"O.K., I guess, I don't really know if that was a wise thing to do?"

"What do you mean?"

"Well, thinking of getting married again."

Joe is divorced with three wonderful boys: Alim twenty-four, Wael twenty-two and Ghaly twelve. What more does he want? I advised him not to get married again, but being put under severe pressure from the whole family he got engaged to Hala.

"What? You mean you're not happy about this whole thing?"

"Well, I don't know what to say. I don't feel right about it. I'm so used to having my own ways: no one telling me what to do, asking me where I've been or reminding me how late it is. You know what I mean?"

"Yes I know exactly what you mean. I've been living like this for just three months and I really love it. Freedom's such a valuable thing," I stretch my arms up in the air and take a deep breath as I say that.

"Yes that's it! Why should I give it up?"

"So what are you saying?"

"I don't think this engagement is going to go on any further. We're thinking of calling it off."

"You are?" Looking sad but deep inside me I can hear a voice yelling: *way to go boy! I told you not to do it again.*

"Yes. I'm waiting till I return home then I'll see what happens."

"Just take your time don't rush into a decision," now that is the stupidest thing I've ever said in my life. I know that Joe is the one person, in this whole world, who never rushes into decisions, whether the consequences are good or bad, he always has to think. I now think of what he always says when I used to go to him for advice, *think about it and don't rush. Sleep on it till next week and then we'll talk again.* That is how cool he is. I then discovered later on, that all the kids in the family, used to ask for his advice too, a very cool and amazing guy!

"I won't, don't you worry about that, I'm thinking it over and over and weighing the outcome of such a decision from every point."

"Well, now I can tell you about my decision too."

"What?" He startlingly asks!

"Well me too, I really want a divorce."

"Are you sure?"

"Yes I've been thinking a lot about it and before I call Ali I'll tell the children."

"I think that's wise and make sure you let them know that you want to divorce their dad and not them and that you'll never leave them or stop loving them; that you're doing this because you and their dad just can't live together any more and this has nothing to do with them; that even if they wanted to divorce you, you won't let them do it. This is so important."

"Well, I never thought of it this way but I have decided that they should be the first ones to know about my decision."

"I think that's very smart and thoughtful of you but that's nothing new you're always very careful about others' feelings, especially the people you love most."

I don't know if he really means that or if he is just teasing. He does have a strange smile on his face as he says it, so I say with a teasing tone: "thank you Joe. I never thought that I was, but I really do watch out for other people's feelings."

"No I really mean it and that's what I just said. My God, you are talkative! You just love talking, you even repeat my own words to keep on talking," we both break into laughter.

"But I feel sorry," he says with a sad voice.

"Why?"

"I do really feel terrible. How can you just walk out with nothing, after twenty-eight years of marriage?"

"I don't mind," I answer, happily smiling.

"But that's not fair. You worked so hard to pull that marriage together and you stood by his side all the way along and now you just leave, without even getting a penny off of him. Talking about women's right in Islam? They certainly are distorted nowadays, aren't they?"

"I told you I don't mind."

"You know if you were an employer you would come out of your job with a pension and a huge reward for all those years of service," he now says that with a mix of a laugh and a frown. "I just can't believe it!"

"Hey Joe, take it easy what can you or I do? If our society does this to women, what can we do?"

"Yeah, you're right, society."

"Yes society and not our religion. We both know that in the Koran a divorced woman gets everything she had ever had from her husband, whether it's a house or cars, just about everything. Do you also know that a husband must support his ex-wife and provide her with a maid or whatever means, if he can?"

"Yes I know and he certainly can."

"Well listen just don't worry your mind with that. Can't you see how happy I am?"

"Yes," his face and eyes shine with his wonderful smile.

Joe is considered the most handsome guy back home, in Jeddah. Everyone, who knows him, especially the kids in the family think he is the handsomest bachelor ever. The girls in family all want to find a husband some day like Joe. That is what they call him or else Khalou (uncle). His gorgeous smile reminds me of what used to happen years ago: as a little girl I remember how my older sister Sue's friends used to love going out with her. Well she is a charming girl, but that was not the only reason, they all loved being with Joe, who was just fourteen; and though his friends went along with them the girls were all nuts for Joe only. I thought that he was so handsome, but I believed that Gamal Abdul Nasser and John F. Kennedy were the handsomest men ever! I was only eleven then, but I loved listening to their speeches, their voices and choice of words and the promises they gave their people.

Even at that young age I loved men and my favorite hobbies were and still are: sports, and the company of men. Being close to my dad throughout my life had an immense influence on me, as I truly enjoy that gender's company. However, I discovered way back then that boys were so funny and at times stupid. The reason is that as a little girl I had a lot of admirers in school because I joined them in all their games: I climbed trees, played cowboys and Indians and played football. Then one day I cut my hair. Wow! What a disaster? The number of my admirers went down to one or two. From that moment on I changed my mind about boys' IQ: almost zero, as appearance totally fools them and they forgot how much fun I was to be with.

Joe notices how I'm somewhere else and gives me a strange smile that reminds me that he is waiting for me to talk so I go on: "ah! So just forget all that rubbish. Just feel happy for me."

"You know I do but tell me why did you decide on leaving?"

"Well, that's really strange but you remember when my cousin Noor died four months ago, in February?"

"Yes of course I remember; how can I forget my poor aunt? What does that have to do with your leaving?"

"Well you know how all the family used to spend the whole day at my aunt's, helping her as people came to console her?"

"Yes?"

"Well one day as I was leaving, my aunt asked me to stay and I told her that I had to go and see the kids before they went to bed. Fatma my cousin was there listening and said:

'Your kids? Or you can't wait to go to Ali?'

I don't know why, but I swore to her that I always like to see them before they go to bed.

'Are you sure?' She insisted; 'my brother Hani told me that Ali confessed to him that you are so great in bed and that he doesn't know why he never noticed that fact before?' And she said that smiling.

I got so furious I could have killed her, her brother and most of all Ali. After all those years he goes around telling people about our sex life? Then I thought: that is it. That was the straw that broke the camel's back. I got in the car and said to myself: I won't stay with this guy. A week later I was on the plane and out for good."

"I don't blame you sis, the guy has lost his marbles, but don't worry about a thing. You always have your own mind and you usually take risks and succeed; you are after all, known in the whole family as the nutty girl!" These words broke the ice and we start laughing.

Sunday morning comes, too bad I have to go back to Newcastle and I wish can spend a few more days with Joe, but he has to leave to Boston that afternoon too. Going down the elevator I tell him:

"Oh! I'll miss you!"

"I'll miss you too sis, but my poor ears are so happy you're leaving!"

We laugh out loud as we make our way to the hotel entrance and once again we hug.

"You take care of yourself now Fairooz and remember we all love you and we're with you all the way."

"I know and I love you too. I don't even want to think about what would have happened to me if I didn't have such a wonderful loving family?" I get in the cab and wave to him on my way to the station.

On the way to Kings Cross Station I cannot help thinking of my grandmother: Jaddah. How she too left her house after more than forty years of marriage. I bet that if she had money to buy a ticket or knew of any other means out of the country, I would have had a grandmother and a whole family living in California right now! On the train I remember how I used to tease her:

"Tell me Jaddah, who is your dad?" I asked her idiotically. I heard that story more than a hundred times but I loved hearing it over and over again and I loved teasing Jaddah each time she related it. It's strange but she never forgot the smallest details and I could even hear her voice clearly, as she talked, like she could see him right there, in front of her:

"Oh! Abouya (that's what the older generations called a dad) was a colonel in the army!"

Thank God my generation doesn't say Abouya, Baba is so much nicer, I think. "The army Jaddah? The Iranian army?" I then ask with a wicked smile.

"Girl, what's wrong with you? Are you dumb or what?"

"Then which army Jaddah?"

"It was the Hijazy army then."

"Hijazy?"

"Yes, that was years ago. Al Ashraf ruled the Hijaz region and robbed people of all their rights and even raped their women. Such a totalitarian government! But that was before Al Saud," she enthusiastically tells me.

I read all about that part of history, I'm a book warm and I read anything I lay my hands on. Al Ashraf, were tyrants and people hated and feared them, so they were truly relieved, when Al-Saud defeated them and took over the Hijaz.

Jaddah always spices history events when she adds details to the incidents as she witnessed or even heard about them, so I have to sound really excited too: "God that's outrageous!"

"Yes, it's a nightmare…," she's still talking like she can really see it all.

"Jaddah you know Hitler?" I don't let her finish her words.

"Of course, who doesn't know him? I remember when the war broke your grandfather Youssef, took his family and ours to Aden, Yemen now, because the food was scarce and we had nothing to eat, but your grandfather Mohammad (her husband) stayed in Mecca because of his job."

"Of all the places: Aden?"

"Well Aden is a bit down south, besides he knew his way around there."

"How long did you stay there Jaddah?"

"Oh! I think around three years."

"Three years?" I know that Jaddah is mixing dates up. It was during WWI when all this happened. I heard this story from my mom before. My aunt, Noura, was not born yet; so this incident of going to Aden was far earlier than when Hitler came into being, but I didn't want to correct her, I just love listening to her talking and she is after all, over seventy now, so a bit of miscalculation isn't that bad.

"Yes we had a really nice time in Aden, but were extremely worried about what's going to happen. Anyway, I remember when Abouya ran away from Iran, at the age of thirteen."

See what I mean one minute she's talking about Al Ashraf and Al Saud, then Hitler and Aden and suddenly she jumps to her favorite story: her dad. I know the story by heart. Jaddah's father ran away from his step-mother, who was really mean. He then came on a ship to Mecca and lived there, got married to a local girl and had all of his children there. As soon as he landed in Mecca he made an oath to never teach his children any Persian, so they would never go back to Iran. He wanted them raised in Mecca and prayed that they would stay there forever and apparently his prayers came true: neither Jaddah nor any of her siblings had ever been back to Iran and they didn't even know where they originally came from. Jaddah goes on with a higher tone to grab my attention:

"So when my grandfather died, back in Iran, my uncles sent Abouya a letter and told him to come and get his inheritance. You know that Abouya was a descendant of Salah Al Ayouby: a royalty. So he had a lot to inherit from his ancestors after his dad's death, but he asked his brothers if his step-mother is still living and when he knew that she was, he asked his eldest brother to send him his share, but their dad's will stated that he had to come over there and get his share. Stubborn as he was, Abouya refused to go back and told his brother that they can take his share."

Stubborn? Jaddah talking about stubborn people! In my family everyone is so stubborn; it runs in the genes and guess where it comes from? I've never seen Jaddah's father but his grandchildren have his picture and it is lost some where amongst their things, but I could imagine how handsome he was, by just looking at his daughter. I then notice that she wants me to show some interest in her narration so I say: "oh! That's really sad Jaddah," I wouldn't dare tell her what's going through my little head because I would immediately get one of her fatal pinches.

"Oh no, Abouya didn't think so and he managed and lived till ninety a happy man and at sixty he married Oumy (that's what the older generation called a mom) who was only fourteen."

What a crazy woman she must had been. Or maybe no, she certainly didn't have a say in that marriage. Probably before she was even born, her father had her married off to one of his friends; that is not a joke, but years ago when a girl was born, right there on the spot, just out of her mom's womb, her dad's eyes would tell his friend, *"there, that's the promise I've given you, she's your wife,"* as he would smile and point to that tiny newborn girl. So the girl would grow up already married before she could even open her eyes or move her hands, to a man her dad's age! So inhumane! And this was probably what had happened to my great-grandmother.

"So, Jaddah what was your dad like?" I love that part of the story.

"Oh! Abouya," tears of pride soak her eyes as she remembers her dad. "There wasn't a father like Abouya! Abouya was a colonel," she repeats and goes on; her voice is full of excitement just like a six-year-old, who is relating one of her imaginary tales. "When Abouya rode on his white horse, a little boy, walked by his side, holding his *Shisha* (hubbly-bubbly); right there by his side," she says so, pointing to the middle of the room, like she can really see her dad, his horse and the boy with the *Shisha*.

Now that is all I wanted to hear, over and over again. Imagine someone on a horse smoking hubbly-bubbly holding the pipe to his mouth and a boy walking by the horse holding the flask. Now that is a joke! I can never believe that story and I never will, but Jaddah swears that it was true! Swear all you can Jaddah, but I still cannot and never will believe it. Maybe when I meet him up there sometime, I will ask him for the authenticity of this story, but right now and as long as I'm down here I will never believe it.

I laugh when I remember how bad I was with Jaddah: one terrible, horrible, teasing mean kid, the worst ever and no one in my family could even try to compete: lost hope. I was the best when it came to driving Jaddah up the wall. Poor woman, I sometimes feel that I was responsible for her death, but probably not, she was very old and died at ninety-three, so it was nature's doing and I had nothing to do with it.

I look out of the train and up to the sky and think apologetically with a sneaky smile, *sorry Jaddah. I know you're up there looking down on me and probably saying: "my God this girl didn't change a bit, would she ever? I guess not. I didn't change being up here for over twenty-two years, no one or nothing could ever change me, so why should she? I think that's why I love her; she's so much like me."* Suddenly my trail of thought stops as soon as the train hits the breaks at Newcastle Central Station. Wow! It is amazing what Virginia Woolf did to my brains, through that Stream of Consciousness of hers, it really messed up my head!

Now back in Newcastle, I got on the metro and remembered how when I first came to Newcastle I always took the wrong Metro and had to get down and change it. Now I think I'm an expert, kind of. I can't believe that all I have on me this time is a small Samsonite suitcase. I usually pack so many clothes for a day or two and rarely use them all, but this time I'm a bit smarter.

It's been a light and enjoyable trip and as soon as I get home I walk right into the living room put my suitcase and handbag down next to the green sofa bed, look at my yellow Swatch and notice that it is still early: one o'clock which means that it is three back home. I pick the phone and dial the kids' number. Deema's voice comes across and her heart leaps as I say:

"Deema *habeeby* I miss you."

"Mama I miss you too? Where were you? I tried calling you but you weren't home? Don't you have the mobile on you?"

"Hey, hey, take it easy one question at a time. I was in London to see your uncle, Joe, and I forgot my mobile over here. How are you all?"

"We're all fine. I'm worried sick about you Mama."

Now that is strange to hear a kid, who is worried about her mom. Usually it is the other way around and kids don't even care if a parent is worried or not. I wonder what she wants and say: "I'm O.K. I spent a great weekend with Joe and just got back. So, what's up? What is it you want?" She's a smart girl and notices my high-pitched inquiring voice:

"Mama, you know me better, I don't want anything. I was just worried sick about you."

God that is Deema, she is very sensitive and she always worries about me. Sometimes I feel that I'm the daughter and she's the mother and I fight her for that but I truly love it when she mothers me. So I apologize and go on comforting her, "sorry *habeeby* I know you were worried and you know I'm just kidding," *liar, liar,* I think and go on saying: "listen Deema I would like to talk to you about a decision I'm about to make."

"What is it Mama?"

"Well I'm thinking about what took place between your father and I; at first I thought that his second marriage was a disaster and that it was the worse thing that had ever happened to me and you know how hard I tried to stay, even after knowing about his marriage, just to keep the family together. Now I think it's the best thing that had happened to me, an excellent gift from God. At last, He gave me a good reason to leave your dad, after all those unhappy years."

"Yes, Mama I remember how miserable you were, crying your heart out even in your sleep. I used to walk into your room and find you sleeping and tears falling down your cheeks, wetting your pillow. Why do you think I asked you to leave and not to take any of that? I couldn't stand seeing you so unhappy and for what? He didn't even care. I know Mama what you went through wasn't easy and I'm glad that we asked you to get out and leave him; and you know you shouldn't worry about us we're just fine. We're struggling, but still going, so what did you decide on?"

"What I've decided on doing has nothing to do with any of you. I love you and will keep on loving, till the day I die. You understand that?"

"I know that Mama and I love you more and more everyday; you know we're all so proud of you."

Proud, that is the best word I had heard in a long time. I almost cry and again I don't know what to do with those tears and think, *those tears have no other job better than threatening me all the time!* Then I go on: "Deema I want to ask your dad for a divorce, but you must realize that I'm not divorcing you. Even if you want me to, I'll never leave any one of you and I'll never ever stop loving you."

"Mama you don't have to worry about that and Mama I'm with you all the way, anything that makes you happy makes me feel great. So you just go ahead and do what you want and I'm always with you. I love you Mama, just remember that."

I can tell that tears are choking her and that she too, is fighting them.

"Deema *habeeby* I love you so much. Can I speak to Dalia, Rana and Amr?"

"Yes, hold on a minute I'll call them, I love…," and before I say anything she starts yelling: "Dalia, Rana, Amr pick up the phone. Mama wants you."

Suddenly I can hear the music: I'm put on hold. They don't respond so she is transferring the call to their rooms. Then suddenly Dalia's soft and tender voice travels across miles and miles, to reach my lonely ears, *I wonder how come Joe's ears got tired of listening to some one talking?* I smile to myself.

"Hello Mama. How are you?"

"Hi *habeeby* I miss you."

"I know."

Dalia loves teasing me, she knows that I want her to tell me how much she misses but never does, I think and again smile trying to cheer myself up; then I start, "Dalia I want to tell you that I want to ask for a divorce, but you must know that I'm just divorcing your dad and this has nothing to do with you *habeeby*. I'll never divorce you." I don't take a break when I say that, I just want to get it over with. Dalia is quiet on the other end of the line. I know this is not easy on my kids, I was there myself and it's the hardest thing on kids. I ask her again: "well *habeeby* what do you think?"

"Is that what you really want? Mama you know that if that would make you happy I'm all for it. I'm with you one hundred percent. So don't worry, I know you love me and I love you too and I have to tell you that I miss you, too."

Wow she said it, I tell myself and again I can feel sadness, in her voice and in a funny tone I say: "O.K. *habeeby* let me talk to Rana then!" I'm sure she can see the funny face I'm pulling, too as she chuckles. Rana is right there next to her, I can hear her asking what's going on. They are so close, always together and sometimes say and think of the same things together. Her voice has that naughty and very outspoken pitch and I can see, across the phone, her glittering eyes, which also reveal her character. "Rana, *habeeby* I miss you."

"I miss you too Mama."

"Rana I have to tell you something. You know honey that I never thought of leaving and that I constantly told you and your brothers and sisters that because I come from a broken family I'll try my best to keep this family together. You know too that although I went through a lot, I still tried my best and never asked for a divorce."

"Yes Mama, we all know that."

I can hear her sobbing and wish I can reach out through the phone and hug her. "Hey *habeeby*, I'm sorry I'm making you cry. Please forgive me. I just want to tell you that I want to ask your dad for a divorce, but I'll never ever divorce you *habeeby*, I will forever love you and be with you." Rana doesn't stay quiet for long:

"Mama if you're happy doing that I'm happy for you. I love you and nothing you do can change that. Mama you must know that not only your children, but all of our friends and the whole family is so proud, of what you did. You know that all the women over here think you're so brave?" She tries to hold her tears saying that.

Wow! That compliment and these great words really made my day and I almost cry with joy. I then try to end the call thinking of the expense. I know I could email them and tell them all that, but I wanted to make sure they're all right, when I hear their voices: "oh I love you *habeeby* and take care, is Amr there?" The phone is once again on hold and then a rough manly voice picks up:

"Mama!" I can see his sad eyes, smile with joy.

"Amr I miss you so much." Amr is thirteen, but quite big for his age, he even looks older than his twin sisters, who are actually two years older.

"I miss you too Mama."

"*Habeeby* I want you to know that I'll always be there for you. I'll never leave you. Amr I want to get a divorce, but I want to tell you all first, before I speak to your dad and you must know *habeeby* that I'll never divorce you, I'll always be your friend. You do understand that, don't you? I love you and will never leave you," I sound a bit nervous trying to explain this to him.

"Mama I know. I know you weren't happy with Dad. I knew that a long time ago. I used to see how mean he was to you and how badly he talked to you too. I also have friends with divorced parents and I always believed that this will happen to my parents sometime, too. Mama you do whatever makes you happy; nothing will change my love to you, nothing I will always love you."

I remember myself at thirteen I could never say or even think like this kid! I certainly am the proudest woman on this earth and say these last words: "thank you *habeeby* you take good care of yourself and study hard. I love you."

"Bye Mama I love you."

I hang up and cannot believe what I just heard, Amr my baby noticing what I maybe tried to deny or ignore: the fact that this marriage was a failure. I go to the fridge and pour a glass of orange juice; I need energy, after all I had been through. I look at my watch again and see that it is one-thirty which means it is three-thirty in Jordan. Now my heart beats so fast and I can feel it trembling as I pick the phone up and dial Kareem's number. I don't know why but I feel that he's going to be the hardest of the children to accept the divorce idea; and true enough he doesn't approve of my decision, although I insist and say: "Kareem, you must understand I can't just live with him any more."

"Well Mama can't you see. You're not, you're in Newcastle and he's in Jeddah, so why divorce him? Why let some one else reap what you've grown? Why let her win and get everything you worked hard to build?"

"Listen *habeeby*. I think I'm a winner not a loser, by winning myself back again and remember I have you: my six precious jewels. What more could I ask for?"

"Mama what if after a few years he leaves her and wants you back?"

"Listen Kareem, I don't want him even after, as you say, he leaves her or she walks out on him, even if he comes begging me to get back to him. I'll just...I better stop here. You're getting me upset. Why can't you just understand? Well, I just wanted to tell you what I'm going to do, so you would know. O.K.? Bye," I hang up, before he can say a word. I'm so mad. I rarely get mad, but this time Kareem irritated me so much and made me lose my temper. I need to cool down, before I make one more call; so I go to the kitchen and pour myself a glass of cold water. I start dialing Sam's number; then I remember that it's a Sunday morning and just eight in the morning in Florida and he'll probably be sleeping, so I lie down on the sofa and pick *Rabbit Redux,* to read it, for the third time. Four hours later, I start dialing Sam's number. "*Habeeby* how are you?"

"Mama!" He sounds a bit shocked and asks: "is everything O.K.? Are you worried about me? I'm O.K. believe me."

My voice surprised him, because I spoke to him just a few weeks ago and I usually don't call him that often. I immediately assure him that everything is just fine and start all over again: "Sam I'm getting a divorce, but you too must remember that I'm not divorcing you. I love you and will never divorce you."

"Mama I love you and I'm for anything that pleases you. I'm with you all the way."

We talk for a while about his school, what he is doing now and he tells me that he is working hard to graduate in December. A few minutes later I hang up. I couldn't understand why Kareem gave me such a hard time? But that is the way he is: too sensitive and worries a lot about me, just like Deema; but in this case he is the father and I am the daughter. After Sam's call I cool down a little and get up to prepare something to eat. I have some cooked stir fried vegetables and brown rice, so I just stick them in the microwave to warm them up and start making a small salad. I always kill myself dieting and exercising. As I start heating the food, I once again think of Jaddah. It probably is a Jaddah Day! If she could only see what I'm eating, she would get all sick. Honestly those vegetables, when left over, are not very inviting, I know that, but I just cannot think of cooking every single day and will eat anything, as long as it is good. I see Jaddah up there again watching me and saying: *"girl that looks horrible! Don't you know that the eyes eat before the mouth?"* And I start laughing to myself.

Those are some of her famous words. She was a very wordily person and I regret the fact that I never jotted her words down. I think of what I always told her: *"Jaddah, one day I'll bring a note book and write those proverbs and poems of yours."* The thing is I never had, because she died all of a sudden; but I learned after that incident, that if I wanted to do something really bad I would just go ahead and do it: never postpone anything till tomorrow. You never know what tomorrow holds for you. As a matter of fact, I learned to take each day as it comes and make the best of it; so Jaddah bursting with proverbs, poetry and all sorts of historical events (although messed up at times!) left me, before I could record any of her numerous talents.

There is nothing like grandmothers in the world, nothing; they are a treasure and once they are gone they take something precious with them and life becomes so boring and different without them. You always feel that there is something real important missing in your life and that is how I felt since Jaddah had passed away. I constantly remember her almost through everyday of my life and pray, *God bless your soul, my loveliest Jaddah in the world.*

What my kids just told me on the phone keeps hitting me all the time: I'm strong and brave and they are extremely proud of me. Wow! I have to admit that whatever I sometimes do or say brings flashbacks of the verbal abuse I had taken from Ali throughout the years. His voice keeps ringing in my ears and his harsh criticism echoes around me, like I'm in a cave in the middle of nowhere, in a desert and I remember now and think of what he used to tell me: *"Fairooz, you're too friendly with the children. You must be a little firm. Some day you'll regret that, they won't have any respect for you. You'll see."* Well, I can now sit back and say to myself, *Hey! My kids are my friends too. They love me, listen to me and respect me and they always come back to me for advice in whatever they want to do.* I'm so glad I befriended them at a young age and I never regret it.

I remember how I used to discuss any subject with them, any subject at all and answered all their questions, no lies whatsoever. My answers were always as simple as their little heads could grasp. As a matter of fact this following incident clings to my memory so much: the twins were about eight and I asked them and Amr to come to my bedroom. I had a book to read to them! I loved reading to them and they really enjoyed listening to my lively playful voice and interesting stories. This time I was going to read them a useful and important book, rather than a bed time story. It was a book out of a series I had, that teaches children about different aspects in their life and this one was about sex and the simple facts they needed to know. *It's about the right time to introduce them to some facts of life before they reach puberty,* I thought as I picked it up and looked at all three of them; so I get them all on the bed and start explaining to them the whole process of puberty for both girls and boys, by showing them the pictures and adding: "you, as girls get your period every month," I say pointing to both girls.

"Period?" Rana inquisitively asks.

"Pe...what?" Amr asks.

"Period you dummy," Dalia answers giggling and asks with puzzling eyes: "what's a period, Mama?" She knows it has something to do with that embarrassing subject, but she just doesn't know what it exactly is.

"Oh you know what you see me have, when you're with me sometimes in the toilette and I use those pads, remember I call it Dodo?"

"Oh the Dodo!" They all scream at one voice.

I knew that I had twins, but I never thought that I had triplets. I try to look at each set of inquiring eyes and say: "yes that's it, so when a girl starts getting her period, she has to be very careful with boys. She mustn't sleep with boys, unless she's later on married and even if she is married and doesn't want to have children she must use contraceptives." Now I can see their puzzled faces and before they can say a word add: "yes you know, like the tiny pill I take every night so I won't have any babies?"

"Aha!" Again the triplets say, with a relief on their faces.

"So if she doesn't want to have a baby she takes something like the pill and the inside of her tummy, which is already prepared for the baby turns to a period," I go on. Wow! That is a tough topic and I need to take a breath here. I think that I explained it explicitly and that they understood the whole idea, because if they didn't, they would just keep on asking questions; but poor Amr, this was a bit too much for him to take in, so with puzzled eyes and a shocking look he asks:

"So, Mama I can't sleep next to Dalia and Rana now, because they will get pregnant?"

And all three of us break out laughing.

"No Amr. My God! You're so smart! If all you do is sleep next to us, we can't get pregnant," Rana answers.

Then they both start showing him the pictures and how one could get pregnant and they all start giggling. That was one of my most precious moments, when I sat and talked to my kids and felt their curiosity and happiness. I was always with them, experienced their every move and knew almost all their thoughts and shared all their experiences. I never missed on anything and now I'm so far away, it breaks my heart. Then the phone starts ringing and it interrupts my memories. I look at the Snoopy clock on the wall, it is seven o'clock; I pick up the phone and hear Kareem's voice:

"Hi Mama," he sounds apologetic.

"Hi," I say and don't sound too happy to hear his voice again.

"Mama I'm sorry. I upset you. I didn't mean to, all I want, is for you to be happy; I really didn't mean to upset you. I'm with you Mama and with anything you want to do; all I want is to see you happy," he keeps repeating.

I can hear that his nervous voice has that tender pitch and sounds like he is on the verge of crying, so I at once say: "hey, I'm so glad to hear from you. Listen don't you worry about me. I'm not upset I'm O.K. now."

"Are you sure?" He is happy now.

"Yes, I'm sure," and I am truly happy.

"O.K., I just want to make sure that you know that I'm with you and I also want you to know how much I love you."

"Hey I know. You don't have to tell me that. I love you too." He as usual asks for his kiss and I send it over the phone and he sends me one back and we hang up.

At last I settle the differences and have things cleared with my children. I know that not too many parents tell their kids about such matters but I do and it makes me feel so good and I also know that involving my kids with the most intimate decisions and incidents in my life makes them feel great and important and I'm sure that's why they trust me with their secrets too. I sit down and lay my head back on the sofa, so tired; it was a hectic mission and nothing is harder than being honest, especially when it comes to such delicate matters. Suddenly I jump off the sofa, when the phone rings again. Apparently I dozed off.

"Fairooz did I wake you up? Are you sleeping?"

A British voice disturbs my rest, it's my neighbor and half sleeping I say: "no Karen you haven't;" and think, *I can kill her for waking me up,* and say sweetly: "don't worry I'm just napping." It had been an hour since I've spoken to

Kareem and I woke up with a bit of a headache because of all the psychological strain I had been through, in the last few hours.

"I'm sorry, I think I woke you up," she apologetically says.

"Oh don't worry I'm glad you have. I have so much reading to catch up on." Karen is a typical British girl and very self-conscious about what she does or says. I can see her green eyes feeling sorry because she woke me up.

"Fairooz, I just wanted to remind you of the fortune teller. Remember?"

"Oh, I'm glad you have. I'll call him right away and organize it all. Are the girls coming too?"

"Yes. I told Sandra and Lyn and they are coming. You just organize it and tell me."

"O.K.. So that means we're gonna be five, because my friend Cathy is coming too."

"Okey Dokey, see you tomorrow when I get back from work."

I hang up and go back to the table and this time I pick *Rabbit at Rest* up, I have to find out the importance of Harry's mother in that series. This is the second time I go over this novel, every time I read it for something or another.

I'm so glad though, that Jaddah didn't hear that conversation with Karen or maybe she did and is saying: *"a fortune teller; how many times did I tell you that no one can predict the future but God?"* She knows how much I love this clairvoyance stuff. I can't stop thinking of what Jaddah had really missed by leaving these people out of her life! She could have known what is going to happen to her, but no, she can't evade what fate is about to throw next, whether she believes in them or not and what's going to hit her is just going to happen.

I'm supposed to be reading Updike's book, but I lay it on my tummy and think back and remember Jaddah's life story. A beautiful girl, who got married at twelve to a rich merchant, who was so mean to her, *according to her stories*, I think. She couldn't take his dreadful treatment, but it was too late, because she was already pregnant. Back then, around the turn of the twentieth century women didn't have the means to postpone pregnancies, so Jaddah became pregnant on her wedding night and a beautiful baby boy was born, nine months later. However, God loved her, as the baby died when he was six months old; then her cruel husband divorced her and blamed her for the baby's death. Sometimes luck plays such beautiful games! Then she married my grandfather Mohamed, who was previously married and divorced his first wife, because she too, wasn't a good egg-layer!

My grandfather was extremely handsome: six, two with bluish-gray eyes, hair as black as coal and a nose beautifully drawn by the great artist: God

Almighty, with a full lower lip and a thinner upper lip. He was very keen too about his figure and watched what he ate. By the way, his mother was Syrian and his grandmother according to Jaddah's words, *was one of those people with supernatural powers, who stuck her arm out of the grave!* I always thanked God that I never met her: just knowing that she was a jinni, scares me to death!

My Iranian grandmother was gorgeous too that was why they had six beautiful children. Being married to my grandfather, a prominent man in the Hijazy region, Jaddah had to cater to him twenty-four hours a day; it was true that she had help, but she still worked very hard. When she used to relate her life-story, I remembered fairy tales' characters such as: Cinderella, Snow White and Sleeping Beauty. Her voice comes to me loud and clear now:

"You know Fairooz, I used to bake, cook and sew clothes for about twenty people," she says.

"What? You're kidding Jaddah, right?"

"No I really worked so hard; your grandfather always had guests for diner and sometimes they spent weeks at our house. I also had to sew all our clothes and the slaves', I had six slaves then."

"Jaddah how could you? How could you live with that conscience?"

"What do you mean?"

"How could you buy and sell human beings? Don't you feel horrible now?" I'm always touchy about such matters and cannot stand injustice and don't care what will happen, by my rejections I just cannot. The thought of my family owning slaves: buying and selling them, makes me feel so guilty. I cannot even look myself in the mirror, when I remember that. *Maybe I'm crazy? Maybe I'm over doing it? But that is the way I am. Maybe, on the other hand, I'm simply extremely sensitive?* Jaddah feels my sad tone and tries to explain the whole idea of slavery:

"You know Fairooz, I was born into a society that just did stuff like that and when you're absorbed in such a culture, you just don't see the wrongs. Why would slavery be wrong when everyone else believed in it? But deep inside of me I felt that this was somehow wrong and prayed God that someday this savage business will stop."

It is strange but when I remember the tears in her eyes as she relates that story, I believe that she really wasn't too happy herself about owning people.

From Jaddah's stories and my history books' reading, I again recall that around 1856 the Ottomans had a treaty with some European countries to stop slave-trading. However, the people of the Hijaz region rejected that treaty and the ruler of Hijaz Al-Shereef Abdul Moutalib Bin Ghalib, one of Al Ashraf rulers, helped the people in their revolt against the Turks. So when the Turks found about his alliance with the local people they removed him from his post and assigned Mohammad Bin Oun in his place. Abdul Moutalib tried to fight again, but did not succeed and so he succumbed and set off to Taif, another city in the Hijaz region.

Consequently, the people of Hijaz had no one to back them up now, but they still revolted against the British rule. I remember Jaddah telling me how, after this incident, a famous merchant in Jeddah refused to raise the British flag on his ship and insisted on raising the Ottoman flag. Then the British delegates renounced that and lowered the Ottoman flag and raised theirs again. The people of Jeddah were so furious, to the lowering of the flag of a Moslem state and attacked the British consul in his house and killed him. For a month or two the people of Jeddah heard bombs; they then found out that a British fleet harbored in Jeddah and was bombing the city. They escaped to Mecca and had a meeting to stop this attack on their holy lands, but they didn't succeed in defending their holy city. However, four years later, a committee consisting of the Ottomans, the French and the British was formed to find out the people who were responsible for the British consul's killing. To much of their surprise, no one admitted to the killing, so they didn't exactly know who was leading that move and as a result two of the most prominent merchants of Jeddah were executed, a few more exiled and about twelve of the ordinary people killed, to stop this revolution.

Jaddah's detailed knowledge to all this history always shocked me, but she always told me that her father lived through those times and told her how horrible they were. So the conclusion to that story, according to Jaddah, was that this revolution had affected the outcome of slavery, because when the Hijazy people rejected having strangers interfere in their lives, the great powers thought that maybe they should leave them alone and let them live their lives as they please and stop meddling with their everyday business and so that ended it all and the region went back to slavery, because that was what the locals really wanted.

The memory of those incidents reminded me of Jaddah's excuse of how she had nothing to do with the issue of slavery and how she was born into it and that even if she wanted to change it, she had no say whatsoever as an oppressed member of her society then. Well, the truth of the matter is, until now women in my society have no say in anything either and I once again remember Jaddah's thrill as to how much women had achieved in our time:

"You know Fairooz I praise God everyday that I'm living till this age and time where I can see women getting stronger in this country."

"Jaddah what are you saying? Women getting what?"

"Oh yes, you don't know how we lived then."

"I could imagine, just listening to your stories and Mama's and trying to picture the whole thing. You know Cinderella was better off than you."

"Cin…What?"

"Oh jaddah, it's just a fairy tale," and of course I had to tell Jaddah who Cinderella was.

I used to always read the Koran to her, as she could not read or write. However, she never showed any interest in fairy tale stories or I would have read her all the collections I had. Reading to her reminds me again of the times she and my uncle, Khaleel, used to visit us in Alexandria. Those were the happiest times of our life: the early 'sixties. My uncle used to pack his suitcase with all sorts of candy and stuff we loved and could not find in Alexandria, but that isn't what I actually remember of those visits. When Jaddah used to come over, Joe and I used to fight over which bed Jaddah's going to sleep in. The poor woman was always stretched like a toy: Joe pulling one arm and I, the other. We always fought over her, but if she had henna all over her hands I would be running away from her. I wouldn't even touch her and Joe probably spent nights praying that she would come to Alexandria orange-handed, so he would have her all to himself.

Oh Jaddah, poor Jaddah thinks women nowadays are strong? What a joke? Strong in what sense? I question myself. Women in my country are not even considered second class citizens. No, not even that. The word woman as an entity actually doesn't exist in our curriculums. Our books have chairs, tables, houses, jewelries, clothes, all sorts of possessions and woman is just a part of it all. Women nowadays, if compared to western women or any other women of the world, live in the Victorian Age. Jobs are limited and women can either be doctors or teachers, they are not allowed to work in any place where their preys, MEN, work! Strong? Till this very day, women are totally controlled by their husbands, fathers, uncles or even brothers. Even their younger brothers control their lives. Some women cannot visit their parents except once every two weeks. Imagine? Even if her parents are dying, she just cannot go. Is that strength?

Jaddah has been dead for more than twenty years, but things have not changed much for women. As a matter of fact things are getting worse. Women are not allowed into restaurants without a man: any man. Some women have their drivers eat with them, they are men after all! Women are not allowed either into record shops, they have to stand outside the shop and a man, it doesn't matter who, gets them the music they want. When women go to a tailor they stand in the street and talk to him through a rectangular window. What are they afraid of? That we will jump them? Lay them down? Rip off their clothes and rape them? What absolute nonsense! Women are not even allowed into governmental offices!

I could never forget the day my two younger sisters and I went to a judge's office, in downtown Jeddah, to claim the lands given to us by the government, because we graduated from the university, about six years ago, which was around 1991. God what a day? The humiliation! The insult! The degradation! The way every man in that office made us feel: robbed of all dignity and pride! You had to be in our place to feel all that. When we left the office I told my sisters: "I bet if I raised a goat I would treat her better than those idiots treated us," I was so furious and could never forget that day, never.

What is even worse is that a huge percentage is deducted out of a working woman's salary each month for her pension. However, if she dies her inheritors get nothing of that pension and it all goes back to the governmental institution she worked for. While a man's pension on the other hand, goes to his inheritors; so most of the women at home get their pension before they quit or die and before they complete twenty years at their job, because again, if they spend more than twenty years on the job they get nothing. Oh, there is so much to say. When I think of my life back home I always remember Jaddah. *Poor soul, our life maybe is better than hers, but that's only a proportional matter depending on how one looks at it,* I think to myself as Jaddah's words echo in my ears.

I know why Jaddah thinks our times are better than hers. Around 1933 my grand-father was appointed Minister of Finance in Yemen, where he spent about three years; then on one of his visits back home he nervously told Jaddah that he has a wife and two boys over there. Jaddah almost died. She could not believe what she had just heard, but her Iranian pride stopped her from reacting. He asked her to stay with him, while he gets his other family over, but of course she refused and left, taking her two young children: Aunt Noura and Uncle Khaleel with her; they immensely suffered, because they had nothing, after living in a palace with all the luxuries and help. I recall Jaddah's story:

"I didn't have any money, my father was dead, my mother was poor, my two brothers barely had enough money to support their own families and I didn't want to beg from any one, so we lived in a one-room apartment; one of those rooms that are provided by the rich people for the poor in the country. The food was scarce and your uncle, Khaleel, who was ten only, worked at different jobs and hardly got enough money for our food. One day, your grandfather's cousin saw your uncle, Khaleel, in the street, with patched clothes. She couldn't believe what she had seen and ran up to our place.

'Haleema what's this? Why does Khaleel wear patched clothes? Where are the clothes his dad buys for him?'

'Aisha, his dad doesn't even send a loaf of bread.'

'I can't believe that, but I know you never tell anything, but the truth. You mean his dad dresses up all the kids on the street and his kid has nothing to wear? You know *Eid* is only ten days away. What will the poor kids do?'

Aisha then left our place heart-broken and sobbing and furiously ran to your grandfather's:

'Mohammad I can't believe how a kind tender-hearted father like you, can turn into such a callous person? How can you ignore your own flesh and blood?'

'They are with their mom and she didn't want to stay here; then let her support them.'

Aisha then returned to her house and sewed new clothes for your uncle and aunt and on the eve of *Eid*, she came knocking at our door and gave them their new clothes. Your aunt, Noura, had a red beautiful satin dress, a pair of black shoes and new socks and Khaleel too had a new bright white *Thoab*, a pair of brown shoes and new socks. You wouldn't believe the happiness on their faces when they held their new things!" Jaddah kept wiping her tears throughout the story.

"Jaddah this story is really so gothic!"

"What was even worse was what your grandfather had done six months later! He sent two policemen to our door, asking to take your uncle and aunt."

"My God, what's happened to him? He went crazy just because you walked out on him?"

"Yes a man loses his mind when his wife leaves him. She destroys his pride and dignity."

"Yes but when he leaves it's O.K. no big deal; who cares about her feelings?"

"You're right but that's the way it is over here: a man controls you as a wife and mistreats you or suffocates you till you can't breathe anymore if you leave him, especially if you had kids."

I was twenty-two, when Jaddah was telling me this story and had my first three children, so I could easily relate to all of that and didn't blame her for walking out. How could she just stay? However, her walking out was a courageous move, because at her time, women never left their homes. She probably was the first woman who abandoned her husband and house, because he remarried, at that time women just accepted and even lived in the same house with the other wives.

Strong as she was, Jaddah never gave up. She had strong relationships with the royal family and knew most of the Princesses, who had a say in most of the matters. Two months later, she went to visit Princess Ameera.

"Your Royal Highness, my kids' father took them away from me and you know how I never left them. I can't even see them at all. I hadn't seen them except for the two times Khaleel sneaked by to see me. His father thought that he was in school, which was true but on his way back home he came to see me. I can't believe what their dad is doing to them, their own dad. Imagine Your Royal Highness he let's them sleep in a small dark room on the floor! His wife hides the fruits and good food from them and he never checks on them, never. He always asks about their well-being through his wife. I just can't believe that this is the same man I married; you remember Your Royal Highness how kind he was to his older children, they don't just love him: they adore him. Mariam, Laila, Hala and Amar are so lucky, because they're married and don't have to live with a stepmother, but Your Royal Highness, my babies…" Jaddah was hysterical and cried and sobbed throughout her speech.

Princess Ameera too could not save her tears throughout the story. She offered Jaddah a beautifully embroidered white silk handkerchief, to wipe her tears, of which she had a bundle of different colors, on her right hand side. She then took one and blew her nose.

"Don't worry…Haleema, we don't like…injustice. I'll make sure you get…your children back. Not only that…but I'll also have a monthly allowance…delivered to your house…at the beginning of each month…," sobbing too, she could hardly speak.

"Thank you Your Royal Highness. God bless you, thank you. Thank you God!"

She stood up and went past the huge hall into the street and got into the Princess's limo, which took her back to her apartment. The next morning she heard knocking at her door. She could not believe her eyes. There they were: Uncle Khaleel and Aunt Noura at her doorstep! She cried with joy and hugged them, till they both started to cough, she eventually realized that she was suffocating them and let go. Two days later, she received a letter and Uncle Khleel read it:

Dear Haleema,   *September 23rd, 1941*

I hope you're all right? I'm sure your kids are around you by now. I just want to tell you that there's an apartment, rented just for you and your children. You don't have to worry about the rent or any other expenses. I pray God to keep you in good health and save your children.

Sincerely yours,

Princess Ameera

When Uncle Khaleel finished reading the letter he started jumping up and down the room; screaming and carrying his younger sister along.

On that same day at one o'clock, Princess Ameera's secretary, Soha came to lead them to their new apartment and that was a new happy page in their lives. However, as kids they still needed more money for clothes and sometimes some exotic fruits or vegetables, so Uncle Khaleel worked at different jobs. A few years later at fifteen he worked as a taxi driver to provide them with sufficient money. Imagine his father is a millionaire and he had to work up to twelve hours a day, to get some money and keep them going. It is strange in our part of the world, as the father is totally responsible for his kids until they leave the house and sometimes even after that. Having no education, Jaddah too, struggled to make ends meet, as she sew and embroidered and sold her products to close friends and relatives.

Sitting in my living room on that cold June evening, I feel so depressed remembering Jaddah and the rigorous gloomy life she had led, but I suddenly smile as I think how she reaped her reward, as all her six children turned out to be successful loving men and women. Not only that, but her grandchildren dearly loved her; though some of them gave her a hard time, they still adored her.

I'm so tired and feel that a break is needed so I switch on the TV and keep flipping the channels when suddenly I hear the name Iran. A short-haired announcer appears on the *CNN*. Her gray jacket is lightened by a white top and a red scarf. Her blue eyes sparkle as she announces: "*The Saudi Foreign Minister met with the Iranian Foreign Minister and both signed an agreement to strengthen the relations between the two neighboring countries.*"

I can't believe what I just heard. *"Did you hear that Jaddah? We're becoming friends now. How about that? Thrilled? You know I follow all the news on Iran: for your eyes only, only for you. You know what else? Even when I see one of those Iranian roofless empty buses during the Haj season, I get the thrills and the hair all over my body sticks straight up, staring at the empty bus, smiling to those empty seats and imagining that they are full of Iranian passengers. If any one sees me then they would think I'm mad."* Now I'm literally talking and singing out loud, as I'm watching the news. And I look up to the ceiling every now and then, as if she can really hear me.

Although I felt happy for Jaddah's reunion with her two children I still feel the degradation she had to go through, *that must have killed her Iranian dignity*, I sadly think, to beg a Princess for something that is after all her divine right. As a woman God gave her so many rights and society had forcefully confiscated them from her and all the women in my country. If the laws at home abided by God's laws, then Jaddah would have had her children and she would not have begged anyone for them.

Thinking of Jaddah keeps me so busy all day long! I abruptly jump off of the sofa: *"you have to call Dean, the fortune-teller, and organize his visit,"* my inner voice calls again! I pick up and dial his number, his phone keeps ringing and after about five rings the answering machine starts babbling:

"This is 285 3097 I'm not home right now. Please leave your name and telephone number after the beep and I'll get back to you, as soon as possible."

I don't really like speaking into these dumb machines, but I have to. "Hi, this is Fairooz: F A I R O O Z; please call me at 283 9121. Thank you and bye." That is the best I can do and I even spelled my name for him. I sit back and put my feet up on the beautiful Victorian footstool and this time I watch a movie on TV: *The Devil's Own*, staring Harrison Ford and Brad Pitt. I sit there watching it. Half an hour later I find myself lying down on the sofa my eyes start closing and I keep forcing them open, but as every part of me: they have a mind of their own; no part of me can control the other. I wake up two hours later and the movie is, of course, over.

It was quite an arduous day; my brains were so exhausted, my head drained and my body totally bushed. I was physically and psychologically tortured; in one day I went to London, discussed depressing issues with Joe and my children and to spice it all up, I never stopped thinking of Jaddah.

Jaddah was a resilient workaholic throughout her life and consequently, when I think of her endurance, even now and years after her death, I myself dreadfully toil both mentally and physically. It is strange, but as I remember her I feel my own presence in the stories. I move in and out, bake and cook with her; get mad at my grandfather for leaving such a beautiful woman and remarrying; move from one house to the other; go down a four-story building, because there are no elevators. I even walk on foot down those unpaved streets, carrying a heavy lantern for miles, as there are no cars to take me anywhere; I cannot even lift those feet of mine any longer, they are so bulky with those massive wooden shoes on, that I feel like I have a cast on and the sandy roads enhance all this agony and make it the most burdensome task. I even embroider and sew with Jaddah. Well, that is strange, because I actually can't either sew or embroider. Not just that, but I am even on that white Arabian horse, smoking the hubbly bubbly and completely out of breath. I then find myself thrown on that roofless bus and on the highway, rocking from one side to the other. Through my vivid, homicidal, suicidal fantasy I lived every second with Jaddah; inhaled and exhaled the same air she breathed. Thank God that day is over; hopefully tomorrow, won't be A Jaddah Day!

Mama

I'm sitting next to Mama on this freezing Friday morning in September. She has her feet as usual on the stool, in front of her, and we're both watching the Friday prayers on the Egyptian channel, while she's nodding off. I take a look at her and remember how she was as a little girl. From Jaddah's stories, I know that Mama is the second daughter in her family. Her father loved her dearly; and up till the age of eight, she used to accompany him, almost everywhere he went. This was in the early twentieth century, around 1930 and having a girl accompanying her dad on the streets of Mecca, was out of the question, yet he always let her. However, after the age of eight, she started covering up and putting on the veil and *Abaya*, in other words: acting like a lady, so she was consequently segregated as a woman and could not accompany her dad any more.

Mama grew up to be a strong-willed little girl and accompanying her dad, for those first eight years of her life, molded her obstinate personality; she was extremely naughty and stubborn. One sometimes wonders whether she got her stubbornness and strength from her Iranian mom, or was it because she was too close to her father. It seems that girls raised close to their dads, tend to be strong and have their own minds more than others, but then I might be wrong. Anyway, Mama used to get away with a lot of things, more than her older sister Aunt Mariam or her younger ones Aunt Hala and Aunt Noura. Her dad rarely punished her, as a matter of fact he seemed to enjoy her kind of personality; her mom on the other hand, used to punish her all the time.

Mama's past memories are always her favorite past time talk whenever we're sitting together and that was of course, years after we became parents ourselves, because she wouldn't ever dare tell us her rebellious memoirs when we were kids, we would had driven her crazier than we already had.

She suddenly sits up straight, with a wide smile on her face, fixes the green and white checkered-cushion behind her back as if she woke up from a sweet dream and says:

"Did I ever tell you this story Fairooz?"

I'm sure I had heard it all, but I shake my head wanting her to go on.

"As a little girl I constantly had my black curly hair loose, however when my mean old grandmother visited us and saw me she would beat me up and braid it and even stitched a scarf over my two braids, to make sure I kept it braided and of course covered. Now, that is really cruel, but nothing had ever kept me from doing what I wanted."

No interruption this time, I just smile and proudly think, *you don't have to tell me Mama; no one can ever stop you!*

As if she knew what I was thinking of, she smiles back and continues: "I was just seven and I would get a pair of scissors and cut off those nasty stitches," she stops for a few seconds and takes a deep breath.

I never saw a picture of Mama at that age. Women then, had never had their pictures taken: one of the no no's for women, but I could just picture her black shinning twinkling eyes, her straight nose and long face dimpled chin. She probably took after her mom's Iranian beauty when it came to her looks; but she was five, seven and that she took after her dad, which made her look bigger than kids her age. I look at the picture, pinned on my floral wall in front of me: Mama was around twenty-five, her first picture ever; married then and had my brother Zahid in her arms. My aunt, Hala, was twenty, standing right there next to her; they were both gorgeous! Beautiful eyes, noses drawn carefully, no flaws and very thin lips: thinner than their other brothers and sisters. The amazing thing was their hair: both extremely long and braided. Mama's braids hung down to the middle of her thigh and Aunt Hala had hers down racing to reach the floor. It is a wonder how they kept bathing and combing that hair. You might think I'm describing twin sisters! Well they do look alike till this present day, just like twins and those who do not know them well, do get them mixed up; not only that, but they are still very close, just like they are in that picture.

Mama notices that I'm not concentrating on what she's saying so she nudges me softly, like she doesn't mean it, while fixing her feet on the stool and goes on:

"One day Oumy (her mother, Jaddah) had about thirty of her friends over for lunch," Mama's eyes glitter like a naughty six-year-old. "When they finished lunch they all surrounded your aunt, Mariam, who sat pouring the tea."

Again my imagination takes me to that huge room, where they were all sitting; beautifully arranged mattresses laid on the floor embroidered with green and white leaves; rectangular-shaped beige and brown printed cushions supported women's backs, while small square ones rest under their arms. The floor was covered with artistically designed Persian rugs. Women then enjoyed sitting on the floor, I do not know how they could do it, but then, that explains their bad knees. You see whenever a woman walked in they all stood up to greet and kiss her, one at a time, as she would pass them all and that as you can see is such a destructive exercise to the knee: sitting and standing for say, more than forty times.

I can truly see Jaddah's guest-room right now, where a Spanish mirror with a striking metal carved frame hangs on the entrance wall, paired with a half moon mahogany straight-legged console, which stands right underneath it. Of course no woman in her rightful mind would ever enter into this room without first checking her simple makeup in the mirror, fixing her scarf and making sure her hair looked good; and she would stop right there, on that spot, in front of the mirror, to take a glimpse at the reflection of the room and see who is already in there.

An oak gramophone with a green velvet top and a brass horn is sitting on a 16" x 14" mahogany table, as women loved to dance and listen to their favorite tunes. There are also four Edwardian fiddle-back mahogany tables in each of the four corners of that huge room, topped with four lanterns, which are a piece of art, in their own right.

How could women spend their leisure time either cooking and cleaning or sewing and embroidering? Imagine the fun they had and to think that my rebellious Iranian grandmother was one of those women! But then that was all that women could do then, no careers at all. Her daughters too were raised to be perfect wives and that was all a girl could dream of, as her future totally depended on being an obedient wife to some strange man, I think while my imagination takes me around Jaddah's guest-room.

So, these lanterns are laced at their bottoms, just like belly dancers and the tops too have hand-embroidered lace surrounding them, like a bonnet and all the sewing and embroidery was hand-made by Jaddah and her daughters.

On the floor right in front of those mattresses are small square mahogany hand-painted tables 10" x 11" with spiral legs. The top is just big enough, to put a small stainless steel tray with an ashtray and a glass of tea. The most interesting thing of all of this is the tea cabinet. Pouring tea is a joyous occasion for the people drinking it, but not to the person pouring or to the ones serving it. The tea cabinet is an oak rectangular-shaped piece 16" x 30" with bobbin-turned legs and its four sides are made of clear see-through glass and opens at the front. The inside of this cabinet is full of small tea glasses differently shaped, their saucers and tiny spoons. On top of the cabinet lay the trays again, different sizes and shapes; topped with different sizes of teapots and a well-polished savoir, which is used to boil the water. The trick was in having this transparent view, because everything had to be spic and span, as all those women had nothing but stare!

You can imagine how picky women were then: they each preferred to take their tea separately, which meant that they wanted a tray with a teapot and a certain size and shape of a glass and a saucer that fits that glass; and my poor aunt, Mariam, took care of that all of the time, as she was the tea-pourer.

Mama again notices that I'm ignoring her and ends my unique experience, as she slightly shrieks:

"That day women were a real headache," she goes on. "I was barely eight then and Oumy had me and your aunt, Hala, in charge of serving these women.

'Laila I need some sugar please.'

'Laila this tea isn't strong enough.'

'Laila can you change this glass for me, I don't know how to hold it.'

Laila this, Laila that. They drove me up the wall." Mama laughs as her eyes twinkle with joy and goes on: "Oumy was sitting there and I could see her lips moving; praying that I wouldn't pull one of my pranks but she should have prayed a lot harder. Of all those thirty women, four really got on my nerve, so I went to the kitchen and brought some white pepper in my hand."

Mama stops here, laughing so hard that she has to wipe her tears, takes a deep breath and goes on:

"Everyone was so busy and no one had noticed what I was doing; so I took their four glasses and instead of adding sugar I put pepper and placed all four glasses in a tray and went straight to them, telling each one of them which was her glass and the amount of sugar she preferred; they took a small sip and straight away they all started yelling:

'Ouh...What's in this tea?'

They were continuously coughing and sneezing, with their noses running like a river; it's a mystery to me and until this moment I honestly don't know how they could talk, sneeze, cough and have runny noses at the same time?" Mama chuckles and covers her mouth with her left hand like she's actually eight now.

"Mama you really didn't do that?" I ask, to elevate her excitement, "I know you were naughty but...," and before I finish my words she interrupts:

"Well, if you were in my situation, just think of what you would have done?"

The idea of what I would have done scares me and before I can even imagine; she goes on:

"The only person who knew what had happened to those four women was Oumy. Suddenly she got to her feet and in lightning speed came toward me and of course I was gone, vanished like a ghost! That night wasn't the happiest in my life as soon as the guests left, Oumy rushed to my room:

'Are you crazy? What have you done? You know that they are my best friends?'

Sorry! I told myself, *you just have to choose four different friends,* deep inside of me I was so proud of myself; hoping I would never see those women in our house again. Then Oumy grabbed me by the hand and yelled:

'You stay in this room and tomorrow you'll see what will happen to you.'

That threat alone, kept me so quiet throughout that night; then your aunt, Hala, noticed how worried I was and scared me even more:

'Laila I'm so worried. What will happen to you?'

What could happen? I pretended to be fearless, while I trembled deep inside of me. In the morning I heard Oumy's voice, yelling from the first floor:

'Laila, come down here this moment.'

I have to admit that was the scariest voice I've ever heard in my life. I went down so slowly, pretending that I wasn't scared.

'Laila, what you've done yesterday is unforgivable, and you won't get away with it; come with me.'

Oh my God! What was she going to do? I never heard of a mother slaughtering her daughter or chopping her to pieces. Never heard of a mother whipping her daughter till she bled to death; so I went with her, again pretending to be as calm as ever and deep inside of me I kept praying, *please God save me.* She took me up back to the fourth floor and into the balcony. My God what mothers could do to you? I mean I was up there and my room was right next to the balcony; why did she have to drag me down and take me up again? That alone was a punishment.

'You see this balcony? I want you to stay here no breakfast, no lunch and no diner. Do you hear me?'

Her voice was like the wicked witch of the east. 'What if I need to go to the bathroom?' I asked her.

'If you don't eat or drink you won't need to go anywhere, O.K.?'

So there I was on the balcony, all alone, but that had been fun too! I kept talking to my girlfriend in the neighboring house and had a great time, as my daily routine of sewing and embroidering kept me from that. But then it hit me: I could hear the rattling of the pots and pans and the plates touching one another getting ready for breakfast. The worse thing was what my nose had been doing: smelling Oumy's good cooking and that was the toughest thing of all. I mean you could ignore your ears and eyes, but not your nose when it came to her cooking; and again my pride kept me from even moving an inch from the spot she left me in."

"Mama you were so stubborn," I say smiling, knowing that she needs a break, so she quickly takes a sip of the milk, sitting next to her on the table and starts again:

"Well, I don't think I'm stubborn. I just have some principles and I stick to them," she says with a funny look.

"So what happened next?" I sweetly ask. I know I'm not one of her favorites, so I have to be very careful in how and what I say!

"Every now and then, Oumy would come to the balcony to check on me, come to think of it, she actually stayed in the living room on the same floor, so she didn't have to keep going up and down all the time. Lunch time, she came back again and looked sorrier than me and again peeked, but stubborn as I am, I pretended to be looking some where else. Then around five in the evening, she came up to me and in a remorseful tone said:

'Laila you were very good and you didn't even move from your place, come on now, you're released, come and have diner.'

I didn't even wink and I stayed right there.

'Laila dear come on, let's go down and have diner.'

I didn't respond at all then she started begging for my forgiveness while I insisted on being punished and on her way down the stairs I could hear her say:

'This girl is so stubborn.'

She's saying I'm stubborn, imagine that? You know where I get it from, right? A few minutes later Abouya (her father, my grandfather) was up there on the balcony:

'Laila *habeeby*, come on down and have diner. I can't eat if you're not there.'

That was all I needed: Abouya's comforting words and love, so I went down and had diner with the rest of the family; and that was the last time Oumy had ever punished me."

Whenever Mama remembers her father or talks about him, tears start welling in her eyes. She had been his favorite, or felt that, since he had remarried she had lost him.

"Mama, you were really naughty," I tell her, to get her out of her sudden gloomy mood.

"Oh! That's not all; did I ever tell you about the other time when my sister Mariam had her friends over for tea?" Now she's giggling again.

"No, what happened?" Again, I heard this story before, but I want her to go on laughing.

"Well, a few months after that incident, Mariam had her friends over and I was so mad at her because she always caused me trouble and made Oumy beat me up. At that time, we had a cow and an ox in the yard and while her friends were sitting in the guest-room, I went out to the yard and let the ox loose; suddenly he was in the guest-room and all her friends kept screaming and jumping all over one another!" Mama is now, crazily laughing.

"And again those stupid friends of hers never came to our house again! And guess what?"

Before I try to even answer she goes on:

"Oumy didn't think of punishing me at all and said that the ox probably cut the rope himself and ran into the room!"

I love it when Mama tells her stories and laughs! Now I know where I got my devilish streaks from: both Mama and Baba!

Like all women of her time Mama had a rough life. Her mind then switches to another memory of her past. She was around twenty and noticed how everyone around her was busy, arranging for what seemed to be a big party. I could imagine how excited she was and how she kept running up and down the stairs, looking for her mother, to find out what was going on.

"Oumy told me it was Hala's wedding."

Mama's high-pitched tone brings me back to the living room once again.

"Hala on the other hand, was anxious to know what was going on too and when she asked the same question Oumy told her that it was my wedding, making sure I was away."

Aunt Hala was fifteen then, so there they were: both girls didn't even know it was their wedding night. Marriages were always arranged then, and girls had to marry their cousins and if a girl didn't have a cousin then *tant pis!* She just remained a maiden throughout her life. And Mama's story goes on:

"Your dad and your uncle, Hamid, didn't know either that it was their wedding night. Your dad was on a vacation from his medical school, in Egypt and your poor uncle was in his dad's shop working, when his dad yelled at him in his harsh voice:

'Hamid.'

'Abouya,' he answered.

Your uncle jumped obediently off his seat, looking down at the floor."

I could picture Uncle Hamid's handsome face bent down in total respect, as he replied to his father's roar. He would not even dare raise his head, to look him in the eye.

"'Come with me,' your grandfather told him," Mama's still going on. "They walked down the streets of Jeddah. Your uncle, Hamid, was extremely handsome, with black straight hair covering his head which contrasted with his fair complexion. His dark brown large eyes were wondering where he was dragged and his rounded lips were uneasily moving and praying, *please God, help me.* When they reached their house your grandfather said in a dictatorial tone:

'Now go up and take a bath quickly; today's your wedding.'

God my wedding! Your uncle silently thought. You know, how in those days, if a father points to any jug, in front of him, and asks his son:

'Can you see the donkey in that jug?'

Without even thinking of arguing, the answer would be: 'yes, Abouya and I can see his ears, sticking out of the jug!'

He also told him to ask Alim, your dad," she winks at me and goes on, "to get ready, because he was getting married, too; and your uncle obediently went to tell his brother to get ready for the wedding."

My poor uncle and dad! What a miserable moment that must had been. So they, too, like my mom and aunt, Hala, were completely shocked by the latest news! It was funny but Mama constantly told us that she never even liked Baba, while Baba on the other hand, said that she was always crazy about him and that she would always look through the keyhole to see him and yelled: *I want Alim! I want Alim!* Mama's now exhausted, takes a drink of water and suddenly says:

"Fairooz I'm so tired I'll go in and take a nap."

When Mama relates sad incidents of her life she gets really emotional and tired, plus it is twelve and she knows that she can nap for about an hour, before lunch. As she walks to her bedroom I cannot but think of what had happened to her and Aunt Hala, as they moved to Jeddah to their new house and left their mom in Mecca, *all in tears*. They got married a few years after my grandfather came back from Yemen with his new wife. I guess he just wanted to get rid of his two daughters, to feel relieved and the best way was to get them married off to his nephews. The two newly married couples lived in the family house, where the father-in-law was the head of the whole household and no one had a say in anything; so it had been like Mama and Aunt Hala were married to their father-in-law (their uncle), as he completely controlled their lives.

Now that Mama's gone to her room I lie down on the sofa and reminisce some more about Mama's life and how she keeps repeating the same stories over and over again. My siblings and I can recite those stories by heart. I remember this one day a few years ago in 1973, when we were sitting in her living room and she was relating some of her most depressing experiences about her life with her in-laws.

Her father and mother-in-law were the masters and everyone else had to obey their orders and this was obvious, as they had the whole first floor and each of the married couple had a bedroom, a small living room, a tiny kitchen and a bathroom, on the rest of the three floors. I remember now how Mama's face frowned, as she recalled those miserable days:

"The huge guest-room belonged to my uncle and his wife, so if we ever had guests, which seldom happened, we were supposed to have them in that room. My mother-in-law had also told all her friends, that her newly wed daughter-in-laws didn't like people, so we never had any of her friends visit us. Thank God," Mama said this last sentence with a sad forced smile and continued:

"A month after our marriage Oumy came to visit us, see you couldn't have anyone visit you, not even your mom for one whole year, after your wedding night! So imagine living in a strange place with a strange man and not a familiar face and not even seeing your mom, for one whole year; but I had to thank God that Hala was there and I knew your grandma and your aunts and because we were related, my mom was able to visit us a month later!"

My eyes tear as my imagination takes me back to Mama's past and the narration rolls on and Mama's voice travels through those gloomy tunnels:

"So, here came Oumy, so excited to see us. She went to Khalty's floor (that was what she called her mother-in-law: my grandma) then we heard:

'Laila, Hala come on down. Guess who's here?'

We didn't even have to guess and ran down the stairs. We weren't just excited we were thrilled to see her! It was the first time we were separated from her and when she saw our faces, she almost cried. She was divorced then from Abouya, who had already brought his second wife into our house."

Tears soaked Mama's eyes as she mentions her father's marriage and with her chocking words she went on:

"Oumy hugs and kisses us for so long.

'How are you?' She whispered, 'are you happy?'
Of course that was not the right place or time to ask those questions.
'Alia,' she turned to my mother-in-law and asked her:
'The family and the girls' friends want to come and see them is it O.K.?'
My mother-in-law wasn't very happy with that question and wanted to say NO, but she was embarrassed and spoke with an enforced smile:
'Certainly, but when?'
She just had to know everything! So it wasn't just the permission to come, but also a certain date and time had to be set!
'I don't know it's your decision; you tell me.'
I was so mad at Oumy, why ask? This was my house, too and I could have who ever I wanted over, but I was certainly wrong no one could come not even Oumy without my in-laws' permission," Mama was really upset now as she said that.

Lying in my living room I truly relive through that Saturday morning on September 1973 and could even see my brother Joe and younger sister Samar sitting there around Mama, when suddenly Joe's voice rang in my ears:

"Hey, Mama," Joe smiled, "wasn't that the way people lived then? I mean everybody, with no exceptions? No one could move a finger without their in-laws' permission?"

"Yes," she answered, "but in our parent's house, it wasn't this way; we lived alone in the house and Oumy and Abouya were the ones who made the decisions and they even asked for our opinions."

"Sometimes," I added, "and they certainly didn't discuss your marriage with you, did they?" That was so unkind. I knew right away that I shouldn't have said that and I saw Mama's eyes tearing and immediately said: "Mama, I'm sorry. I didn't mean that," and got up and hugged her, but it was too late: the damage was done and she was hurt. We could all see that in her expressive eyes and all over her face. Later on in life, I learned to really weigh my words before saying anything. I used to speak my mind out, without any consideration for others, but I was too young then, just nineteen, to even think about others' feelings. I regret my straight forwardness in many instances and mostly on that day, but I was a kid then already married for four years, with a four-month-old baby on my lap.

"It's O.K.," Mama said hugging me back, "some day you'll grow up and know what I'm talking about."

"So, Mama what happened then?" Samar asked.

"Your dad had always been very understanding," she replied.

And here approvingly, I released a wicked smile. I always love to hear positive comments coming from her about Baba.

"Yes, he really was and he used to get upset when I'm upset," she stared at me, to show me that she knew what my smile meant.

"That's strange," Joe added, "wasn't he a tyrant? Weren't all men dictators then?"

"Yes, but I guess because he was attending university in Egypt, he was different and very open-minded, just like my dad."

"Was your dad open-minded?" Samar asked.

"Yes he was very well-educated and he was in contact with people from different countries and you know how that changes one's mentality. You know when you meet different people with diverse cultures and traditions other than yours, you tend to absorb some of that and my dad was constantly very observant and knew what suits his culture and what didn't; and that was how he was at home: extremely open-minded for men of his time."

"Mama, I didn't know that Sido (grandpa) was like that," Joe said with bewilderment. "I only know him now: always quiet and doesn't say much just asks how I am and that's it and most of the time he doesn't even remember who I am," he added.

"Yes, it's too bad you didn't know Abouya then; that was actually what happened to him when he remarried: he totally changed. You know that his wife is twenty-seven years younger than him and it had been so hard for him to communicate with her, as they don't mentally or intellectually meet; there is a huge gap between them in every imaginable sense," tears in her eyes, as she spoke again: "I know what you mean and it's horrible to see him this way now. Anyway, I told your dad that I wasn't happy living in this house and that I wanted to move to our own house, even if it was a one bedroom apartment and he asked me to give him some time till he finished his studies, so I just waited."

"That was fair enough," Joe said. He was always careful of what he would say even as a kid, though Mama thought otherwise; to her Joe was too blunt and never weighed his words *like me*, especially when he talked to her. It's funny, but Joe and I lately thought that, because we weren't Mama's favorites, we had to be very careful in what we say to her. We were both always playing the board game: *The Snake and the Ladder*; and felt that it takes us forever to climb up those ladders to win Mama's love, but then the smallest mistake would slide us down the snake, all the way down to the very bottom: the pit!

"But I just couldn't absorb the idea of having my friends visit me downstairs," Mama went on right from where she first stopped: "I wanted them to come up to my place, so I told your dad and we both agreed that I shouldn't have them down there and the next day right after breakfast I told my uncle:

'Ammy (that was what she called her father-in-law: my grandpa), I want to entertain my friends in my place.'

'Have your friends where?' Your grandmother furiously asked, almost choking on her words.

'Have your friends upstairs?' asked your uncle, Hamid. 'What's wrong with my mom's guest-room?'

You know your uncle, Hamid, was so different from your dad. He totally believed in patriarchy all the way through: a man was the master; and that was how he was with your aunt, Hala. Poor girl she never objected to anything, never; and Hamid was also a Mama's Boy and did what ever his mom wanted him to do, without even thinking twice."

"I thought Uncle Hamid was a very understanding person?" Joe inquired.

"He certainly wasn't, you've never seen him when he gets mad at your aunt. I know. Remember I lived in the same house for four years and Hala always told me everything; that is if I didn't hear his yelling across the corridor, which happened all of the time and just this last week I witnessed one of his furious and most outrageous tantrums, remember Samar, you were there?"

Samar nodded, with a puzzled look, "yes, how could I forget his red face and bulging eyes, as he was screaming and waving at Aunt Hala?"

"Well, any way, Ammy didn't say a word," Mama went on. "He just waited for your dad's reaction and of course, your dad just sat quietly and said nothing, he then asked him:

'Well Alim what do you think?'

It was strange because your grandpa never asked for anyone's opinion; but when it came to your dad, his eldest son, he almost always sought his advice. See your dad was very observant too and very well educated, so his dad listened to what he had to say.

'Well Abouya, I think Laila has a point there, if she wants some privacy with her friends, I don't see why she can't have it?'

'Alim you're spoiling her by treating her this way. You should be the man of the house and the decision-maker, not her!' His mom jumped in.

Your uncle, Hamid, was nodding, blindly in total agreement with his mom, but your dad was so cool, that the comment didn't even move him and he calmly declared:

'Oumy things are changing in this world. A man doesn't have to treat his wife like a maid, she is after all his partner and she's going to be the mother of his children someday…'

'Well, I didn't hear that she's pregnant. You've been married for more than a month now,' she interrupted him.

She didn't even let him finish his sentence. She was a very domineering woman, but the best thing about your dad was that he always stood by my side and never gave her a chance to interfere in our life. I couldn't ever deny the fact that your dad really helped me in asserting my point of views; not like your poor aunt, she had no one to support her. Well, I was her only support in that house, but that wasn't enough and she really suffered."

"So what happens then Mama?" Samar once more asked.

"Ammy, furious at his wife's comment shouted at her:

'Alia, why don't you just shut up and let him talk.'

Basically, that is the way a husband spoke to his wife, but not your dad he was really different."

"We know," both Joe and I said with a pleasing smile and in one breath, we are after all, Dad's strongest supporters, and again, with Dad we're not worried about sliding down the snake: we're always on top of that board!

"Yes he is, although I'm not married to him any more, I just can't deny this," Mama bashfully added.

We know how honest Mama is and we all thought that because she never loved Baba, she wouldn't say anything nice about him, but we were totally wrong, as she always tells the truth and never denies anything, and her story goes on:

"Well, Ammy got really mad and to embarrass his nosy wife and put her back in her rightful place, he gave his consent to my wish.

'Laila, I don't see why you can't have your friends in your place they are your friends, and after all, it is your choice.'

I then took a quick teasing glance at Khalty to see how upset she was and discover that her face was darker than the black veil she had on and I almost jumped with joy. Wow! I couldn't believe that! But then your grandpa was always good to me, although I *was* very obstinate, he still loved me. I never took or did anything I didn't like and I always spoke my mind.

The worse thing about your grandpa was that he always sided with who ever complained first, even if the complaint was a complete lie, so I learned that; and I was always there first with a list of disputes. You know that though he had tried throughout our marriage to change me and turn me into what he believed a woman of his time should be like, he never succeeded. I *was* too stubborn to abide by the tide," she proudly smiled and continues: "Your aunt, Hala, on the other hand, never objected to anything. She was stupidly obedient…"

"So, your friends came over to your house?" I interrupted.

"Fairooz, can't you just keep quiet? Why do you always have to interrupt?" Mama said.

She tried to shut me up by placing her left hand against my mouth, but she still answered my question and went on:

"Yes they did and I never received my guests anywhere else. Then, when your dad's vacation ended, he had to go back to Egypt to finish his studies and wanted to take me along with him, but his dad totally rejected the idea and wouldn't listen to reason. He thought that if I went with your dad we would never come back home and we would live in Cairo for good. Remember he was the Man of the house, the one person ruling and running it, and certainly your dad was just part of that household."

Suddenly, the phone rings in that small Newcastle living room and I jump as my thoughts are interrupted. A man with a Jordie accent is on the line. It's Dean, the fortune-teller, and after a few words of introduction he apologizes, because he was abroad and had just returned. *It is almost three months since I had left my message on his phone,* I think. He then asks how many are we going to be?

"We're five and we're wondering if you can come on Friday, September the eighteenth?"

It takes a few seconds and I can hear him flipping his diary pages before he answers:

"Yes, Friday is fine. I have nothing. What time?"

"Well, we prefer the evening time, as most of my friends work in the morning."

"Great! The evening is better for me too. How about six then, I'm busy all day long, but I have a three-hour slot free and that's more than enough for the five of you. So we'll be done by nine."

"That's great. See you then, Friday September the eighteenth at six," and I hang up. I have to be very careful with British people's accent, because I find it hard to understand, especially those with a Jordie pronunciation. It's strange, but during this twenty minute conversation, I used 'excuse me' ten times; 'can you repeat that please?' Five times; 'can you come again?' Twice; and 'can you speak a bit slower?' Three times, as I find it extremely tough to grasp that Jordie accent.

Now as I'm revived back to the present, just a few months from the year 1999. I look at the pictures of old Jeddah, hanging on the walls in the living room and suddenly, I remember that Mama is here, visiting me and is actually sleeping in her bedroom. Around two o'clock I go to her room and wake her up, to tell her it's time to eat. We sit at the small table in the kitchen and have our lunch. After lunch I fix some tea and we both move back to our posts taking the same positions we've earlier had. I then look at the pictures of old Jeddah, hanging all over the walls and for a few minutes I was living in Jeddah during the 1940's. Mama notices my wondering and interrupts my imagination before it even starts:

"You know Fairooz those pictures bring it all back to me," she then points at one picture and says: "this was your grandpa's house; it was where I lived with your dad when we were first married,"

Once again Mama's memories won't leave me alone. They're so depressing Snow White and Cinderella can't even compete! At least they were characters, drawn from fairy tales, not real like Mama and the women of her time. As I stare at the houses on the walls I see myself on Grandpa's roof. This house was built in such a way that it had a nice breeze throughout the year, no matter where I stood; however, this time the blustery wind is blowing each section of my long brown curly hair all over my face and with both hands; I try to hold it back, but then the wind forces my skirt up and I find it really hard to fight that wild blowing wind, so with my right hand I hold the skirt down and with the other hand I pull the hair off my eyes; I want to get a good view of what is happening to Mama then. Although the wind is blowing, the tiles are really hot, so I run back into the bedroom and fetch a pair of slippers. I see my parents sleeping on the bed and I suddenly cover my eyes with both hands, too embarrassed to watch what they are doing. Mama sitting next to me on the sofa notices how my hands cover my eyes and pulls me back to reality, as she shockingly asks:

"Fairooz, what's wrong?"

"Nothing Mama," I answer. I daren't tell her where my imagination had taken me. I once again look at the wall and see another picture of a big balcony and a *Zeer*, a clay container, where people kept water for their own use. In Sido's house, each couple had their own *Zeer*; I also remember how my grandmother knew when any of her sons made love to their wives! Mama again disrupts my imagination and it's funny, but she starts where I am now, as if she knows what I'm thinking, staring at the *Zeer*, and asks me:

"Do you know that my mother-in-law had always known when we made love?"

"What?" I pretend to be shocked, as if it's the first time I hear this story.

"Yes believe it or not, she really did. Why will I make up stories?" She asks with a sarcastic tone.

"No Mama you never do, but this is a bit over the board," I reply with a tease. I think of what Zahid my older brother had always told us, *Mama is one of **Les Miserables**.*

"Make all the fun you want, but honestly your grandma had never put a glass to the wall to listen on us, nor peeked through the key-hole to see us, but she would check and literarily measure the water in the *Zeer*. So whenever we made love she knew it because the water level went down. And can you believe that she used to check the water level before your dad came back from Cairo? And then when he was here she would check it all the time to see how much had been used. You see, the amount of water differs if we just washed our hands, used the toilet or took a bath. Hey, I can see how shocked you are but this is exactly what happened, you can even ask Aunt Hala and Uncle Hamid about the authenticity of my story," she laughs as she adds the last words and goes on with sad eyes this time:

"Oh! If I would tell you how we lived then, it would take years and years to tell it all, a book wouldn't be enough and that's only my life story, what if I tell you about your aunts and my friends? Remember I had been very lucky because I was a strong person and I had a very understanding husband, but imagine how oppressed other women were then; their life stories are just too much to even relate. We women led a tormented life and you might think that things didn't change for you now," she says looking at me with comforting eyes and goes on, "I know that you are still suffering and trying hard to gain your robbed rights back, but you are a lot better off than us."

These last sentences reveal how much psychological pressure Mama's going through, as tears well in her eyes. I move close to her and hug her and now my tears start rolling down my face, but I forget about them and I reach out to wipe her eyes, to avoid the tears from running down. "Come on Mama, this is all over now Mama. Look at all of us, we love you so much and no matter what we do, we can never repay you." My eyes sadly caress her as they say, "*nothing we do now can repay you,*" and I hug her even closer.

"I know this is my reward: my seven children's love to me is the greatest reward I have from God for my patience. You know all this time I never tried harming or even thought of doing any malice to anyone, never; all I ever did was pray and remember: patience pays well and thank God it certainly had. I'm so happy, having you with me and all of us being in good health; what more can I ask for?"

She tries to avoid the tears from running down her cheeks but can't avoid them and starts crying; I rub her shoulders, kissing her hands and caressing her and instead of wiping her tears off, they mix with my own.

It is September the fifteenth and Mama's going back home today. At nine in the morning she is looking around my flat praying: *God bless her and her place until we meet again,* she prays while blowing air out of her thin-lipped mouth. Two weeks passed so fast, I wish she could stay, but she has to go to Paris where my brother Zahid and his family are waiting for her and where she'll spend another two weeks with them.

We get in the car, both really depressed. On our way to Heathrow we hardly speak, *how can I leave her all alone? Please God help her out and let her come back to her country soon,* Mama is still praying. We stop at a rest area and have a quick sandwich and a cup of tea and then head on to Heathrow and I keep thinking, *I miss her already, she's still with me and I already miss her. I wish she can stay longer.* As she goes into the gate we hug and kiss and I really don't want to let her go, but she has to. *I know that she means to leave me alone so I'll miss her and go back to stay, I know Mama,* I think as I kiss her, before she disappears. I then drive back to Newcastle with a broken heart: a heart that longs for Mama and home.

I get back home around four, so exhausted mentally more than anything else, that I drop dead on my bed and fall asleep, without even taking my boots off. Then the loud ringing of the doorbell wakes me up and I rush to open the door.

"Fairooz, how are you?"

Karen is standing there with her back half turned just about to leave; apparently she was both knocking and ringing the bell for some time, while I was snoring.

"I thought you weren't in, but then I saw your car parked out on the street! Are you all right?"

"Sorry, I just didn't hear the bell I was sleeping. Come on in."

Since I had moved into this flat, Karen had passed by everyday for a coffee and a chat, right after work. I go to the kitchen to get the kettle to boil and she follows me and starts talking:

"So, tell me Fairooz how was your day? You don't look so happy. Oh, your mom's gone! I'm sorry."

"Yes I took her to the airport at nine and I came back around four."

"I'll miss her so much. So tell me you haven't been to the gym?" She changes the subject to take me out of my sad mood.

"No time for that today," I answer and still feel so low.

"Oh, you Skinny Jim look at you. I don't know why you even go to the gym?"

"I just have to go, I feel lost when I don't."

"I know, wish I did the same. Look at my fabulous tummy."

She stands up to show her tummy, smacking it alternatively with both hands. "Look how fat I am." Her blue eyes are waiting for confirmation that she doesn't really have a big tummy.

"Really Karen all you need is little exercise. You must make time for that and maybe, just maybe watch what you eat."

"I know, but I can't diet and you know I'm just too lazy. I'm so tired getting back from work each day at six; though it's a bit slow it is still hectic to be out all day and it's so hard making business these days as you rarely have customers."

We come back with two smiley mugs. I like my coffee black but make sure Karen has two spoons of sugar in hers. I smile at her comments, I know that she envies me for not having to work, but studying is even more strenuous on the brains and makes me physically exhausted too.

"So tell me Fairooz did you call the fortune teller then?"

"Oh yes. I'm glad you asked; I forgot all about him?"

"So you haven't?"

"No I have and he's coming on…"

"When?" She too cannot wait.

"This coming Friday, the eighteenth."

"My God today's Tuesday and he's coming in three days I must call the girls and tell them."

"Yes, I have to call Cathy too."

"Okey Dokey! So that's it for today, nothing new to tell me?"

"Nope, I guess not."

"No emails?" She inquisitively asks.

"Oh, just the regular emails from my family." I know what she is hinting at and just want her to spell it out and of course she cannot wait any longer.

"No emails from America?"

"Oh Karen you know Randy sends me an email everyday and you know that we chat everyday too!"

"So? How's he? Isn't he ever coming to see you?"

"Well, now that you asked, yes he might come over."

"Never! When? He's coming all the way from America? He must really love you? So? When is he coming?"

I can barely answer and quickly say: "he has a business trip in November, to Geneva and might pass by England." She is sipping her coffee real slow so she can talk and ask more, but now the cup is empty and she knows that I'm not saying any more, so she looks at her empty cup, puts it down and stands in a hurry.

"So I'll run off, I have some messing around to do upstairs."

This is almost what is said every day. She grabs her coat, purse and keys and heads to the door.

"Well, see you tomorrow. If you want anything just give me a buzz. You know I don't sleep till ten," and off she goes.

It is great having a caring neighbor and twenty minutes later, the phone rings.

"Hello," it's Karen again! "Fairooz tell me when will your mom get home?"

"Remember she's going to Paris and she just called five minutes ago, telling me that she's already there and that my brother and his family were waiting for her at the airport and she says hi too."

"Oh I'm glad to hear that. Tell her hi, next time you call."

"I will! Bye now."

I pick *Rabbit at Rest* again and try to concentrate, but missing Mama so much, I can't get a word through my blocked brains and I start day-dreaming or shall say evening-dreaming as it is seven o'clock.

I was back to a hot Thursday afternoon on June 1987 where all seven of us were sitting around Mama in her living room around four o'clock. I had all my six kids then, just thirty with six kids! Gosh, I probably felt that I was in a marathon, to have so many kids at that age. Zahid had four girls, Sue four boys and a daughter, Joe had three sons, Samar a daughter and three boys, Yasseen two girls and boy; and Sunny a daughter and two sons. So that is a large family, but all the kids were either playing in the garden or the basement. Hazim, Sue's eldest, son came in for a quick drink and saw his mom and uncles and aunts listening to Mama, so he rushed out and five minutes later, all the older children were in the living room, with blaming expressions and in one breath asked:

"Why didn't you tell us Sitto is telling her stories?"

They were so exhausted, after playing soccer in the sun for two continuous hours, but they wouldn't miss Sitto's stories, to them it was like Jaddah's stories to us: they were a bunch of fairy tales and wild imaginations and of course devious smiles covered all their faces. You really have to grow up to believe some of those strange weird stories, but no matter how much I grow, I still could not believe Jaddah's story about her dad, the horse and the hubbly bubbly!

Mama didn't even notice that the children had come in she just went on with her story, so absorbed, narrating the events of the day she and Aunt Hala had decided on running away to their father's house and how they had to plan for that escape. Mama told us how they had packed their clothes and went up to the roof and threw them over the wall, to their neighbor's house. Mama then told her neighboring friend's mother that they were going to run away and asked her to keep their clothes till the next morning, when they would pass and pick them up; she also begged her not to tell any one. She and Aunt Hala trusted these neighbors with their lives, so they were certain that they would never tell on them. Mona, their friend's mother didn't even ask why they were running away, she had always known how unhappy they were.

Mama's grandchildren could not believe what they were hearing. They just sat there and stared at one another with amazement, not a word said, *Sitto a runaway?* They were probably thinking, looking shocked and again asking silently, *Sitto, a fugitive?*

"The next day we told Ammy that we're going to visit our next door friend." Mama started again. "We put on such innocent faces, that no one suspected anything at all.

'Don't be late,' his wife said.

We knew better, we could never be late and knew that if we weren't back before sunset, the door would be locked, and we would be out of the house. That was what Ammy did: anyone who came after sunset could just spend the night on the streets, not only that but the next day he/she might get a beaten or even whipped."

The children knew that Sitto was the one who had always beaten them, but they could never picture her getting a beating so Laila, Zahid's eldest daughter, startlingly asked:

"Sitto, you got a beating?" Laila was named after Mama and had some of her characteristics too and she even had that naughty streak, just like Mama.

"No, not me nor Hala; one time Ammy tried to beat me and I didn't let him, I also stood for Hala, but everyone else did: your dad's uncles and aunts married or not and even his wife. One day your dad's grandfather hung Uncle Ahmad and whipped him with a belt, until he started bleeding, then Hala and I took him to my flat and tried to heal his wounds; and believe it or not? It took us two weeks to get him back on his feet again. You see, your great-grandfather was very cruel with his children and he even hit children of the neighborhood if they misbehaved, but he wasn't exceptional, men of his time were forced to act in such a brutal way."

I took a glimpse at the children's totally dumbfounded faces and laughed to myself, I know how they exactly felt and what they were exactly thinking, *Sitto's fairy tales!*

"You know I'm strong," Mama spoke again, "I just won't take anything I don't like and I certainly didn't like being beaten, not when I was already a mother: Zahid, your dad was a month old then," she said, looking at Laila, who was thinking, *believe me Sitto we all know that you're Super Woman!*

This story was new to the children they were so excited and didn't even blink while listening to it.

"Sitto, why did you run away?" Alim, Joe's eldest son, asked.

Alim, on the other hand, was named after my dad. This whole idea of running away was a bit too adventurous for them all to understand.

"Ah!" Mama sighed deeply and continued: "that was the sad part about the whole story; Ammy and his wife forbade us from visiting our mom; we begged forever, but all our efforts were futile. Then I told Hala, 'Listen, I'm running away. Do you want to come along or stay?' And to my surprise she responded:

'No, I'm coming with you.'

This was the first time she would make such a decisive decision, without thinking of her husband, Ammy or his wife; so two weeks later we instigated our plan."

Mama was hoping someone would interrupt her, so she could take a break, but no one had. She looked at Joe, then at me hoping we would say something as she said her last sentence; then she gave up, stopped to take a deep breath and a sip of water from the glass set on the table in front of her; and as she was about to start again, I asked:

"But Mama, fill me in on this. I thought it was during *Haj* and you were already in Mecca, where your dad lived, right?" I heard this story before and knew all the details, too!

"You're right," she said, "thank you for reminding me. Yes we were in Mecca performing the rituals of *Haj* and we had our clothes with us and didn't throw them over the wall to our neighbor's. So Hala and I woke up early in the morning, just before dawn; and when everyone was still snoring, before they even turned in their last minutes of sleep to get up and pray, we sneaked out of the tent. It was still dark, but we already planned it all and knew the way to Abouya's. We were out of breath by the time we reached Abouya's house, which was just two blocks away, but we were so scared and could hardly breath. Abouya was totally shocked at our hysterical state.

'What are doing here?' He asked.

His rounded-shaped glasses fell to the floor, he couldn't believe his eyes!

'Abouya, we ran away,' Hala answered.

I didn't want to speak for her, so I let her say it.

'You Hala? There must be a hideous reason, if you're involved.'

Abouya knew that I would do something like that for no reason whatsoever!

'So? What's the matter?' He looked at me and asked her.

'Ammy won't let us visit Oumy,' I then cut in, 'and not only that, but so many strange things are going on in that house!'

'Things?' he said, 'like what? Well, first come on in and rest, you seem out of breath, are you hung…'

Hala was famished and didn't even let him finish his sentence:

'Yesss!'

He hugged us and said: 'O.K. you just take a seat over here.'

He led us to the living room.

'I'll ask the cook to prepare you some breakfast; meanwhile I'll have two rooms prepared for you. You can then take a nap and I'll hear what you have to say when you wake up.'

That was how calm he was, he didn't want to upset us more than we were; so the cook brought us some cheese, refried beans, pita bread and all sorts of traditional plates. I could still taste all of that! Abouya then came back and saw our empty plates.

'You were really hungry!' He said smiling.

'Abouya you can't even imagine the kind of food we have to eat there,' I told him.

We didn't want to nap; we wanted to tell him the whole story.

'What does she mean?' he asked Hala.

'Well, we had a choice of soup with either flies or lizards!' Hala answered with a wicked smile.

'What??' He almost died."

I can now imagine Grandpa's lips falling to the floor! Like Rasputin's lips the revengeful wicked sorcerer, in the animated film **Anastasia**, *I quietly smiled to myself.*

"Abouya never repeated his word," Mama went on, "yet this time he surprisingly inquired:

'You what? This sounds like a witch's potion, lizards, flies and snakes? Come on put, some sense into your words.'

It wasn't the right time, but we broke into a loud laughter. Abouya was shocked and this time I didn't let Hala speak, no I had to verify her words.

'Yes, Abouya Hala is telling the truth; the kitchen is so dirty. We once had a bowl of soup full of flies and Ammy told us that all we had to do was to remove them and go on eating and he even told us that we were simply so spoiled; and of course we didn't touch it or anything else and left the whole meal.'

Hala then told him about the lizard:

'And you guessed right Abouya, two weeks later the same incident occurred, but this time it was a lizard and again we couldn't touch our food.'

Abouya was flabbergasted and couldn't find an excuse for his brother's cook's carelessness and just said:

'But that's not a good enough reason, for you to run away.'

We knew that he was so wise, trying to cool things down: a lizard and flies in a bowl of soup? That was unheard of, even in his wildest dreams.

'So, tell me dearest why did you really run away?' He inquired looking at me.

'Abouya if I would tell you all that had happened to us in those past two years, I would need another year,' I responded.

'No just tell me the most essential episodes,' he said with an extremely agitated voice.

I never saw him in such a state and his face started to turn red."

Grandpa's face is red hot, as Tom's (of the **Tom and Jerry** *cartoons), when he eats fiery burning chili pepper! I know that I just have to stop this imagination of mine, as it keeps cutting Mama's story all the time, but I can't help it, I thought to myself.*

"Abouya's patience was fading," Mama was still talking. "He could control his words and calm the situation, but he certainly couldn't do anything about his senses; he was awfully disturbed and I didn't wait for Hala to say a word I immediately went on.

'Well Abouya, my mother-in-law always fights with us and causes problems between Ammy and us, not only that, but she lies and lets Hala get into trouble with Hamid.'

He then turned to Hala:

'True?'

Hala nodded, unable to prevent the flood of tears rushing down her eyes. I then carried on:

'One day she argued with us about cooking for the whole family and told us:

'Hala, you cook two days a week and Laila you have another two days and Hafza (the nanny and cook, who was bought into the family) cooks the rest of the week.'

I couldn't tolerate such discrimination and jumped in: 'why don't you and your two daughters take turns too? How come we alone cook and help Hafza?'

She was shocked and hesitantly said: 'my daughters have bad backaches, you know that?'

Well, I never knew that they had any health problems, so I looked at Hala and leaned my head against the wall, pretending to have a backache too and Hala did the same, then she got so furious and yelled:

'Who do you think you are? You just do what I ask of you; you are my daughter-in-laws, I won't treat you like my own daughters.'

Now I was really upset and shouted: 'what makes your daughters better than us?'

It was just a big mess and when Ammy came home I was downstairs by the door, waiting to complain first and we won! So we didn't have to cook two days each and we all chipped in the kitchen. Abouya couldn't say a word and Hala made him even angrier as she reminded him:

'And how could they restrict us from going to Oumy?'

Now Abouya couldn't keep quiet: 'O.K., don't you worry, you don't have to go back you can stay here, this house is big enough for you my dear; I'm so sorry about all of this.'

And so we stayed at Abouya's for six months."

Mama again looked around for interruptions, but she received none so she excused herself and went to the toilette: she needed a break. Five minutes later, she returned to find all the faces awaiting her, in enthusiasm. She sat back in her place and continued:

"During these months our father-in-law had tried to get us back. He drove to Mecca several times and begged Abouya to ask us to return to our house and husbands, but Abouya obstinately refused and told him over and over again:

'Remember Youssef when you asked me to let you have my daughters for your sons?'

Ammy just looked at the floor and raised his bluish-gray eyes every now and then, in extreme politeness. Abouya was fourteen years older than Ammy and raised him when their mother died, so Ammy really respected him. There was so much resemblance between the two brothers and you could tell that their mother was Syrian, as they both had colored eyes and a fair complexion.

'Remember Youssef, I asked you to take good care of my daughters to treat them like your own daughters too, remember? You are after all their uncle, remember?'

Ammy just looked up and nodded.

'It seems to me that you didn't keep your promise,' Abouya added.

Ammy was so ashamed of himself and admitted to all the horrific stories we had related. However, he really wanted us back and he even asked other people to interfere. So, Abouya's friends and relatives came to Mecca, asking him that we return; and at last he asked us:

'What do you want to do? Do you want to go back? It's been six months now, but I want you to know that I don't mind you staying with us here, not at all.'

Hala immediately jumped in:

'Well…'

I was so mad at her; I could kill her for her submission. Go back to that hideous house? But I knew how much she loved her husband; as a matter of fact she couldn't live without him and neither could he. Also your dad and your uncle, Hamid, were really upset and wanted us back," Mama said looking at us.

"I knew that Hala would go back and I didn't want her to go back on her own, so I decided to return; I also thought of you Zahid and how hard it would be on you, to grow up without a father," Mama's sad eyes were fixed on my brother Zahid.

"So we returned and Abouya asked us to write him a letter if anything upsets us again and that he would just come to Jeddah and get us. Although women were illiterate then, Abouya made sure that we got the basic education. You see, most women our age are illiterate, but Abouya was really sharp: a clairvoyance."

"A what?" Alim asked.

"Clairvoyance or in other words, one who could speculate about the future and in a sense he was," Mama answered with a cunning smile; she knew that her grandchildren were now making fun of her dad, *the magician;* she could see it in their smiles.

"See he always looked into the future and when we were kids he insisted that we get a proper education; proper education basically meant: to just read and write. I know what you're thinking the education we got is nothing compared to what you get now," she kept on going, "but for girls to just learn that was unthinkable of in our time, and Ammy was one of the first men who tried to talk Abouya out of it:

'How can you teach them? They'll start writing letters to their lovers later on. That's just the beginning and later on they'll read love poems and stories.'

Yes it was inconceivable then to have educated girls, but Abouya just answered him and all the other men, who approached him with the same attitude:

'I want them to learn how to read and write, so if they get married and God forbid, have problems they can just write me; I don't want them to go to strangers to read their letters and know about their most intimate secrets.'

And I'm so happy he let us learn how to read and write; and I can see your eyes asking how come I didn't have a higher education? And you're right I should have, but your *grandfather* totally rejected my going back to school," she said that to the children, with extreme emphasis on each word, while looking at Sue, Joe and me: Dad's devotees.

"Your grandfather had always told me," she said, looking at the children:

'Laila, you're too smart the way you are. I can't deal with you as you are and you want to get an education?'"

The children all nodded, they knew how right their grandfather was. They also knew that their grandma was too smart the way she is without even a secondary degree. However, we the girls were really sorry she didn't get a higher education, because had she done so, we would probably have a female minister in our country by now. Not only that, but she would have easily changed the whole system, as she is absolutely strikingly intelligent!

"So I just didn't finish my education," Mama continued with her naughty sparkling cunning smile.

"And you know what? One day after your dad had started working at Al Riyadh Hospital we had guests for diner, all medical doctors and their wives; and while we were talking, one of the ladies asked me which university I graduated from? My answer was: the university of life; and they were all shocked.

When they left your dad was really mad and told me that I embarrassed him by saying that," Mama said that looking at me.

The children weren't paying any more attention to the education issue they were still so excited about, *Sitto the fugitive,* so Kareem (my son) jumped in and asked:

"'So Sitto what happens then?"

"Well we went back; Abouya took us back and whispered in his brother's ears:

'They are back. I hope things change around here? If they ever leave again they'll never return.'

Ammy just nodded, doubting his two eyes; he couldn't believe that we were back.

'Don't worry I'll make sure they're happy,' he answered.

And since that day he did try really hard, but my mother-in-law wouldn't give up. By then, your Sido had finished his studies in Cairo and came back home and I told him I just couldn't live here any more and that we had to move out. He had two job offers by then: one in Bab Mecca Hospital, here in Jeddah and the other was in Jiyad Hospital, in Mecca. He knew how I felt and chose the one in Mecca. We both wanted to be as far as possible and ever since that move, we never lived with my in-laws again and always had our own place."

"Sitto, this is your house, right?" Deema (my daughter) asked pointing to the floor of the living room.

"Yes when we moved back to Jeddah, three years later, I once again wanted to live alone. Sido then found this house, bought it and put it down in my name."

"Wow! He must have really loved you?" Laila asked and straight away all seven of us smiled and shook our heads and in one breath said:

"Yes!"

"He really did," Mama said.

"*Did?*" Joe said, "we all know that he still *does,*" he emphasized his words with a teasing smile.

"So why did you get divorced?" All the children asked alternatively, with puzzled eyes.

"You know love has to be a two way thing; he loves me yes, but I on the other hand, never loved him," she answered their bewilderment.

"Oh!" they all sighed once again together, in a sorrowful expression.

"I had everything a woman could dream of, but I was just so unhappy and insisted on a divorce and when it happened he remarried."

Sitting in my living room, on 29 Willowfield Avenue and looking at the flowered wall paper ceiling remembering all those stories, especially what Mama went through was the most exhausting burden on my poor brains, but she was not the only woman, who suffered in her life back home, as she admitted. *Thank God I didn't have to live through Mama's or Jaddah's time,* I think, looking at the ceiling as if I'm praying; however, I have to admit that there is just a trivial difference between their lives and ours, as we still suffer to achieve our basics everyday needs. Imagine we're almost in the twenty-first century and are still unjustly treated!

I'm so exhausted of living in the past, it's time to let go and think of the present and that is my true concern. I'm so worried about the future of women back home, so anxious about my daughters', nieces' and all the girls' future. What do they have to look forward to? Nothing, simply more *oppression*; yes that is the right word: *oppression*. However, being an optimist and a fighter I just have to dream for a brighter future.

Fully recovered from the past, I suddenly remember that I have to call Cathy and tell her about the fortune-teller. It is only a few days away. I look for the portable phone and go to the bedroom, but it is not there; I then move to the dining room, but it is not there either. I usually take it wherever I go in case anyone calls from home, but the thing is no one ever does and if I accidentally leave it on the sofa and go to the toilette, it rings and I have to run to it and sometimes it's too late and I miss the call. At last, I find it on my floral bed duvet in my tiny white bedroom. Straight away and without even returning to the living room I dial Chathy's number. I'm certain that by the time I get back to the living room, I will forget calling her and that is how deteriorating my memory is getting. Now I can really feel for my poor children and how sick they get of my repetition.

"Aloo."

"Hello," it is a man's voice probably Mike her husband.

"Hi, is Cathy there?"

"Yes who is speaking?"

"Fairooz."

"Just a minute please," I can hear him calling her name out and a few minutes later, two to be exact, she is on phone.

"Hi Fairooz," she replies in a soft tender voice.

"Hi, Cathy I don't mean to disturb you, just wanted to tell you that the fortune-teller is coming next Friday at six," I mean to be quick because her husband is at home.

"Great! So tell me is he the British or Chinese guy?" She asks with a thrilled voice; her Spanish accent never left her tongue though she lived in England for over eighteen years.

"Oh! He's the British guy his name is Dean."

"I'm so lucky, I'm free then but mind you, even if I'm doing something I'll cancel it, I can't wait to see him. Just let me write it down," she is too thrilled.

"O.K. Cathy I have to go I'll see you then."

"Thanks Fairooz bye now."

I can imagine Cathy' petite figure, swinging with joy from one side to the other and her beautiful blue eyes sparkling with excitement; however, I cannot stop thinking of how miserable her husband is to her. Her childhood memories keep flashing before me: another abused child, it is so sad. Enough of that I don't need any more sad memories of any human being on this crummy earth.

If I'm an optimist and I truly am, then I'll think of the beaming part of my life: my kids. They are my torch in this new life I'm leading, they are what keeps me going and the thought of them looking up to me waiting to see what I'll accomplish keeps my wheels rolling. I can never let them down and whatever I do has to honor them and make them feel proud; but my true light and inspiration throughout my life had always been Mama and Baba and whatever I do in my life I always think, *I wonder if they're pleased at what I'm doing. Not just pleased, but truly proud too.* It seems that I never grow up or maybe I do, but I always think and wonder, like a child whether my parents are content with my actions and life.

Anyway, I had some great events happening to me during these past few months: first Kareem's visit in April, then Mama's visit just these past two weeks and to top them all: knowing that Sam's graduating in December.

Now I get up and do a little cleaning around the house and think of what I have to prepare for the girls, when they come over on Friday. Well, really not much, just some drinks and crackers, that is so simple. As I tidy up the living room, I sit back and wonder as to when it is ever going to be warm around here. The heaters had been on since March, non-stop and now it is the second week of September and I never experienced a warm day yet. Scared to even think of the winter in this city and mentally exhausted, I sit back and tilt my head on the cushion thrown on the sofa bed. Then I remember that I have to check my email for the second time; I usually check it about four times a day, but I was so busy today and didn't have much time. I start my laptop and find lots of junk mail, an email from Joe, Deema, Sam and Randy. Then the greatest surprise of my life! I find an email from my best friend Mary. At first I assumed it is from her son or daughter, because that's their address and I keep in touch with them, but I never thought it's her! It is almost nine years since I last heard from her. That is a lovely surprise and it certainly changed my mood. She is probably in Boston, attending her son Amir and her daughter Samira's graduation; they had told me earlier that they were graduating soon. Wow! Now Mary that is your reward in life; I'm so elated with joy and feel like my own children are graduating. Well Amir and Samira are, after all, my children and I never felt anything other than that and cannot even describe the feeling of euphoria and optimism that hit me! Now, at last, I can go to bed, with a true overwhelming ecstasy that filled my heart, my rooms, every bit of my flat and my new bright future.

Mary

It's a blistering freezing Thursday morning on October eighth. I didn't read Mary's email yet, for two reasons: first I was so busy with my dissertation and had to send the second chapter in two weeks; second and more important was that, on that evening of September fifteenth, after seeing Mary's email in my inbox list, I went to bed full of hope and joy. However, my sleep was interrupted with a dream of Mary, her ex-husband and their children. In the dream they were each dragging the children to a different strange place. I woke up before knowing where the children ended up. That nightmare made me decide to leave her email till I finish my assignment and pull my hopes back up again. Whenever I start my laptop, I debate over checking that one email and today at last, I thought that I cannot put it off any longer, so I start opening it at eight o'clock, after having my green apple and black coffee.

∽

Subj: Long time no see!
Date: 15/09/1998 1:01:43 PM Eastern Standard Time
From: MaryK@aol.com
To: FairHoura@hotmail.com

Hi Fairooz—I came across your email to the kids and thought I would surprise you. I can't believe we're in touch again. This is really great; email is the best thing man's ever invented and I tell you it is cheap communication, I mean a lot cheaper than phone calls.

The kids apologize they didn't get in touch with you for the past five days, but we were in Newport and had a great time. We still have a week before their graduation party, I can't wait.

I really can't believe that two of my children are graduating. Fairooz it's such a great feeling! I hope that some day soon you'll be in my shoes and feel it.

When I sit back and think, I don't know why all this had happened to me? I just can't understand it all. I was so good. Is that a punishment I'm receiving? But why? I was always a true believer. I love God and never, I think, did anything that upsets Him, so why me? Sometimes though, I think this is His sign of loving me. I don't really know. Well, they do say or it's believed that, if God loves someone He tests his/her faith by pouring miseries onto his/her platter; then He sits back and watches one's reaction to His catastrophes. I hope that's really true.

You know what I went through; you're my best witness. The two of us had been through a lot together, right? Oh, Fairooz, I'm so sorry telling you all this, I'm really sorry but it had been so long since I said this to any one.

I hadn't seen you in so long, but boy, am I glad we're together again? Well almost, but don't you worry now that we can keep in touch, I'm sure we'll meet soon.

I'm so sorry, I know you have your own problems and I know I shouldn't be adding to your burden, but hey, girly don't you worry about a thing. Look at me now! Two of my children will at last graduate from Boston University, not just any school!

Fairooz someday soon, you'll live through that great moment of extreme ecstasy. I hope you're still as strong a believer as I know you to be? Keep clutching to that faith of yours, never let go and girl just keep hanging on. You take good care of yourself now. I hope I'll see you soon. Mary

P.S.: Thanks for your invitation, the kids told me, but I don't have the money to come over to visit you: you know I'd love to.

I cannot believe what I just read: no hatred, no disappointments, no anxiety or heart rupture and certainly no wars. I smile to myself and think; *the kid went through enough, she only deserves happiness now*. I have my Arabic satellite on and I'm trying to watch my favorite football team *Itty* play, but instead of concentrating on the game I find myself roaming around in the streets of St. Louis. My eyes are set on the screen of both the laptop and the TV, but my brain is scattered some where else.

My wicked imagination takes me back to 1969, when I first met Mary. Poor girl: an American, who married an Arabian and lived in Jeddah for more than twenty years. I just cannot believe how any foreign woman can live in my country: Westerner or Arab? As for my fellow Arabian women and myself it is probably, because we do not have a choice; it is after all our country and we just cannot take off and leave. Our ancestors, roots, childhood, adulthood, loyalty and love belong to the land, mine at least; but we are, after all, the living dead and what Eliot hints to in "The Waste Land", is certainly applicable to our lives over there.

That was a long time ago, around August 1969, when I got married (at fifteen), left home, my family and went all the way to St. Louis, Missouri with my husband, who was studying there at St. Louis University. I remember that day like it's just yesterday. Now I know how it feels when people never forget, like Jaddah or Mama, relating their own stories like they're living it right now.

Driving down the busy streets of St. Louis, during the rush hour and heading back home, after picking me up from my school, Ali stopped at the traffic lights gave me a quick kiss and started to speak, when he noticed how I was staring at him. I looked at him and thought how gorgeous he looked; tired or not, he was beautiful for a man. He smiled at me and his full lips made his large round hazel eyes wink and caused his extremely long eyelashes to almost touch the lower part of his cheeks.

"What is it honey? What's wrong? Why are you staring at me in this way?" He asked teasingly, when he actually knew that I just liked looking at him. Still staring, he went on:

"hey by the way Omar and his new girlfriend are coming over for dinner tomorrow."

"Oh!" I answered coolly, I knew that I didn't have to worry about anything; Ali always did the cooking, whether we have guests or not; so all I had to do was toss the salad, open the dressing and pour it on. Ali usually dropped and picked me up from Xavier High School, which I attended as a junior and which was right next to his university; so the next day he picked me up from school and said:

"Hi honey."

"Hey," I jumped in and with my pink lipstick, stamped a little kiss on his right cheek "so what are you cooking tonight? We have some chicken and rice at home," I excitedly told him on the way home.

"Yes I checked that yesterday while you were taking a bath, but I want to buy some zucchini, tomatoes, bell peppers and minced beef."

"Wow! You're making stuffed vegetables?"

"Yes you like it the way I cook it, right?"

"I love it. You know I love anything you cook," he was a great cook and he had lots of recipes and spices and all, but that was not the only reason I said that. If I ever told him that I didn't like his cooking guess who was going to cook next time? I never even tried to learn because again, if I ever learned, we'll have a new chef around the kitchen, "so, you're also making that delicious roasted chicken of yours, with the rice at the bottom of the pan?" My eyes sparkled with excitement! I could see how my tongue dropped to the floor.

"Yup," he was really thrilled now, I guess the smallest compliment made anyone's day and this certainly made his. "We just have to pass by *Liberty* and buy the meat and vegetables; I think we have enough rice."

"Yes we do." So we drove to the supermarket and bought everything we needed. It was about four and when we got home I asked him: "Ali, do you have enough time to cook?"

"Oh plenty don't worry, remember they're coming around eight and we won't have dinner till ten, so there's plenty of time. Did you tell Zahid and Joe, too?"

"Yes and they'll be here earlier on, to help us out."

"That's really nice."

My brothers lived in the same complex, just two apartments down the corridor, so we were always together and as soon as they got back from their university, which was St. Louis U too, they would come over. Now it was around five, and I was in the kitchen rinsing the lettuce, when the bell rang.

"Hello Fairooz," Zahid and Joe were standing there.

"*Ahlan* (that's welcome or hi in Arabic)," I welcomed them, always so happy to see them. We hugged and kissed. Zahid walked into our one bedroom apartment and straight into the living room and Joe followed him. Joe's inquisitive self made him look around the living room every time he would come over, to check what was new or what was moved from its place.

"Where's Ali?" Zahid asked me.

"Where else, probably stuck in the kitchen?" Joe, my smart aleck brother answered him, not even giving me a chance to wink.

"Well we're both stuck in the kitchen, come on that's where you should be too," I grabbed Joe by the hand and all four of us were cooking now, imagine? They say that a ship with more than one captain sinks, and we did have one captain: Ali. We were just his aid: cleaning, chopping, washing and even tasting; and that was the best part of it all: tasting. I'm always hungry and I always fought to do that job in particular. By seven everything was on the stove almost ready. All it needed was some cooking and Ali would do that around eight-thirty. So I went to the bedroom and brought a few games: *Life*, *Risk*, *Monopoly* and *Clue* and with a smile I showed them to Ali and my older brothers and they returned my smile approvingly. I then sat on the floor next to Ali, as the sofa was enough for two only. At exactly eight the doorbell rang and I ran to open it.

"Hello," Omar said introducing his girlfriend, "this is Mary."

"Come on in I'm Fairooz."

"Hi everybody, this is Mary," Omar said.

"Hi Mary I'm Ali, this is Zahid and that's Joe, Fairooz's brothers, come on in please."

"And they are your cousins too," I said jokingly, to remind him.

They came in and had a seat. Omar was a handsome, wonderful, kind person, whom I really liked and felt was part of our family and he too, believed that he belonged to the family. He was not only one of Ali's best friends, but Zahid's too and as kids they all grew up together in old Jeddah and played football everyday after school, in the narrow street of *Harrat Al Mazloom* (a well-know area in the center of old Jeddah). They even did their homework together and sometimes spent the night over in each other's house. Omar was Ali's age and Zahid was four years older, so they were always together in and out of school. Joe, who was a year younger than Omar and Ali, was sometimes left out: he was a kid anyway, to them of course; so the three of them were always together. Again, when they came to the States they chose to be in the same state and even attended the same university. Now Joe, considered a grown up like them, was included in their activities and life. When everyone sat down I found that the boys have left a place for me, on the one sofa in the room, next to Mary, so I walked and sat there. The real reason, I believed they left that space for me was that they wanted to sit away on their own, to feel free and say what they wanted; you know how it is: once men get together they just talk and forget that us women even exist.

Mary was a gorgeous redhead, with clear complexion. When I meet some one for the first time I sit like a dummy and just stare. That day, I tried not to gaze but I guess that was the only way I can learn more about her. Finally, her almost yellowish-eyes looked at me as she started talking:

"You have a nice name."

"Thank you but do you know what it means?"

"No but Omar told me all Arabic names have meanings."

"It's the turquoise gem, I think it is called: aquamarine in English?"

"Oh I don't really know, I'm no expert on precious stones," she said with a sweet smile, drawn on her pink thin lips.

"So I hope you'll remember it now," I felt that I had known her before this meeting and kept on inquiring, "so do you go to school?"

"Yes I'm at Cleveland High how about you?"

"I go to Xavier. Are you a sophomore?" I asked.

"No I'm a junior. How about you, are you a sophomore?"

"No I'm a junior too. I thought you are a sophomore," that was a talent we women possess: asking so many questions to find out how old the other woman was. She might be between fifteen and sixteen then.

"I can't believe that, so you must be sixteen and married?" I could see the shock in her tone.

"No I'm fifteen I skipped a year when I enrolled over here," I happily answered. Now she knew my age, she got me first.

"And you're fifteen too?"

"No I'm sixteen"

At last I was relieved, now my worry was over and I knew her age too.

"So Fairooz what are you doing in a Catholic school? Xavier is Catholic, right?"

"Yes but it is the closest to Ali's university. You know his school is right across the street from mine."

"Ya, but how can you deal with the nuns and girls in school? All the mass days…"

I cut in before she finished her questions, as usual, "well, actually when I enrolled I told the head of the school that I'm a Moslem and that I had enough religion of my own to last me a life time," I said with a smile, then went on, "I also showed her my transcripts and so she exempted me from any religion classes, which was great! I also asked her if I could be excused from attending mass and she didn't mind that either, so when the whole school goes to mass I sit around and do nothing."

"Aha I see! She must be really nice and understanding. See I'm a Catholic and I never attended Catholic schools, because they're so strict. How can you manage?"

"Well, actually everyone is so nice to me. I know I have to study so hard to keep my B average, that's the only bad thing about it."

"Ya you know Cleveland is a public school and it's a lot easier in public schools than it is in the private ones, like yours. I'm sure you do a lot of studying?"

"God it's a killer, I tell you I have to really work hard to keep that B. See when I enrolled the headmistress told me that I should be a sophomore, but when I showed her my transcript I asked her to give me a chance to prove that I could work hard as a junior and make it through and if not to move me down to a sophomore and luckily she agreed.'

"Gosh, Fairooz that is a lot of work!"

"Ya I know but I'm stuck now and there's nothing I can do about it." We carried on talking and talking, never stopping and the men went on talking forever too.

"Ali I can't smell anything cooking. What is it? We have nothing to eat today?" Omar smiled worriedly, it seemed he was very hungry, too.

"Man! I'm glad you reminded me," Ali said looking at his watch; he then stood up and rushed to the kitchen.

The kitchen was not that big, but very convenient. The upper right hand cabinet was just big enough to store our yellow set of plates; the left lower cabinet had all the pots and pans, which weren't too many: just three pots and a pan. The cabinet next to it contained all the electric appliances: a blender, a can opener and the coffee grinder. Ali liked to roast and grind fresh coffee beans. The only machine that was set out on top of the cabinet was the coffee machine, as we used it all the time. There were also four drawers for the utensils and bits and pieces.

Ali was shocked because he totally forgot about the food and it was already eight forty. He had to quickly put the vegetable pot on the stove and heat the oven. He was so precise about time, very punctual. I walked in behind him into the kitchen as if I was responsible for the cooking too. It was the first time I meet Mary and I didn't want her to know right away that I was useless around the kitchen: I was all right with that fact around my brothers, Ali and Omar and I had never been bothered, but I just didn't want Mary to know yet; as a married woman I assumed that I had to be a good cook, too.

Zahid walked into the kitchen a few minutes later and asked if we needed any help. I asked him if he could take the newspapers to set them on the floor. We sat and ate on the floor then, as we didn't have a large enough dining table. Joe, Omar and Mary came into the kitchen too and it got too crowded, so I stepped out and waited. A few minutes later, the plates, forks and spoons, vegetable pot, pan and salad bowl were on the floor and we all sat down and started attacking the food.

"This looks so good, what is it?" Mary asked.

"That's stuffed zucchini, this is stuffed tomatoes and that's stuffed bell peppers," I answered, "what would you like?"

"I don't know; I never tried any of it."

"O.K., let me serve you half of each and I'll take the other half and if you like it, we'll share some more."

"Thanks."

So I split each vegetable in half and gave her one half and took the other. Mary with an astonished tone looked at me and said:

"Gosh it's so delicious! I can't believe how good it is. Fairooz you're a great cook."

Everyone looked at me then at Ali and laughed. I was staring at them, hoping they wouldn't say a word.

"Fairooz, is a good what?" Joe, the wisecracker asked.

We were always horrible rivals and had great fights throughout our lives.

"Hey Mary, Fairooz doesn't know how to boil an egg."

"I do too," blushing, I jumped in and said; it was so embarrassing and he just couldn't keep quiet.

"I don't believe you," Mary answered "is this ready made, a TV dinner or what?"

"No, Ali cooked it," Omar knew.

"My God Ali you're a great cook. I guess Arabian men are great cooks! Omar is a great cook too, he does the best Bar-B-Q fish ever," Mary said with surprise.

"Oh, no don't you get fooled; some men can't cook at all, right Joe?" I looked at him teasingly as I said that; now was my chance to get back at him.

"Oh, shut up," he angrily replied.

"What is it? Now I want to know," Mary inquisitively asked.

"Well if I can't boil an egg, which is true I might as well tell on some one else's cooking..." I started laughing and tried to swallow my food to avoid choking.

"Fairooz you wouldn't dare?" Joe furiously shouted.

Fearless of what Joe could do I went on, "well, Mary two months ago, my dad came to visit us with his wife Hiba. It was the first time we meet his wife, and it was almost five years since we had seen him last; so Joe suggested that we throw them a dinner party. We all helped in the preparation of different dishes.

I did the salad as usual, Zahid made a lovely lamb and vegetable casserole, Ali his famous chicken and rice and Joe cooked this great turkey, but guess what?" I knew that Zahid would defend me all the way through, as he was always on my side, so I said that with a funny tone.

"What?" Mary couldn't wait.

"Fairooz you better stop," Joe put his hands on my mouth, but I fought and almost bit it off.

"Well, as he was carving the turkey for serving, guess what we discovered? Well, it seemed that Joe forgot the giblets and neck wrapped inside it."

"Fairooz, I'm gonna kill you," Joe said, now trying hard to hide his laugh and pretending to be real angry, because we always mentioned this incident and laughed.

Zahid cracked up laughing and looked at Joe to remind him that he couldn't touch me. Joe then admitted that he didn't know that you had to clean the inside and that he never thought there was anything inside anyway. It takes a lot of courage to admit to one's faults and Joe always had: when people had already found out! I explained to Mary how my dad just teased him about how good the turkey was, because the giblets and neck were still wrapped in a piece of paper and how we all laughed till tears rolled down our faces.

"That must have been really funny?" Mary looked at Joe and said with a wicked teasing smile and I knew from that moment on, that Mary was going to be a great friend: she was after all, on my side against Joe.

"Ya very funny Mary, welcome to the family," Joe added.

Then we all started clapping and couldn't stop laughing. When we finished eating we cleared the food and dishes off the floor and thanked Ali for his delicious meal. We all complimented him on how great a chef he was. I didn't know why we thought the food was great? Was it because we didn't know any better? Or was it because we were famished? But it was really good and we had a great time eating and talking. Again, we all helped in clearing the food and washing the dishes and putting everything back in its place. Then I put the games out and we all chose Risk and went on playing for four hours, until one o'clock! Good thing it was a Friday night, so we didn't have to worry about getting up the next day for school. Suddenly, we all started yawning, Omar smiled at Mary and they got up to leave, then Zahid and Joe followed them and Ali and I headed to bed right away.

From that day on, the seed of a true friendship had been planted and all four of us were always together; actually six of us, because Zahid and Joe never had steady dates. Mary and I sometimes went out for lunch or coffee, or even for our favorite hobby: shopping. Well, we didn't have much money then, so we usually didn't buy anything, but window shopping was still fun.

A year later, Omar and Mary moved to Milwaukee, where she found a job as a waitress and Omar went on with his studies, but we still kept in touch and they came to St. Louis to visit Mary's family who lived there.

About a year later, on a snowy day in January they came to visit us, so I bought a Gooey Butter Cake, which both Mary and I loved and I also got a small yellow cake for Ali, Omar, Zahid and Joe. Mary looked a bit worried, or should I say too worried. She came and followed me to the bedroom, where I had gone to get some cushions.

"Fairooz I want to ask you a question and I want an honest answer. Please don't think I'm getting too personal."

"Don't worry Mary. What is it? You know you can never get too personal and you know I'll try to be as honest as I can."

"See…Omar and I…Well…We're thinking of getting married."

I didn't know whether she was shy or scared of the idea, but she could see how shocked I was and immediately admitted that her mom was all against it and was fighting them all the way through and that her dad too, was not very pleased with the idea of his daughter marrying a foreigner and going to an unknown country. I let Mary talk and was thinking to myself, *I know how it is with Americans: they hardly ever heard of Arabia and some don't even know that such a place exists. Most Americans don't know where anything is, except the USA. Well, I'm talking about kids my age the ones I meet in my High School, who unrelentingly ask me whether we live in tents? Have cars? Wear clothes or just cover our private parts with leaves? I enjoy these questions and always tell them that we live in tents and we have different sizes of tents; like their houses here: either a one, two, three bedroom tent or even more and we even have two or more floors; some people live on top of the trees, though; and that we don't have cars, we have camels and that's what we use for our transportation, but I tell them that they must know that we have various models of camels: Cadillacs, Mercedes, VWs, just all sorts of camels! Just like their cars. I really pull their feet and those poor kids really believed me. They know nothing else, who'll ever tell them that I am a big liar and a cheat. I'm the first Arabian they had ever seen and probably the last. I love days when I can pull such pranks.* Probably that was what Mary had ingrained in her head; though I was sure Omar had told her all the truth.

I didn't know how to tell her what I truly thought, but she wanted me to be sincere and it was a very delicate subject that required complete honesty so I said:

"Mary to be honest with you I think you should listen to your parents."

"What?" She probably thought I just didn't want her to marry a guy from my country, "are you serious?"

I tried to explain my point of view, as I told her that I didn't think that she could live there and that even I, a native hadn't been able to live there and was married at such a young age to get out; but being as stubborn as she was she insisted that her happiness was with Omar. I knew I had heard that rubbish before from people who were blinded by love: *I'll be happy where ever I am, as long as he's with me. O.K....O.K....Enough!* I was talking to myself and didn't know what to tell Mary, I had really disappointed her with my response and I could see her expression probably thinking, *I wish I never asked you,* and we just kept quiet for a while then we heard Omar asking Ali the same question as we were going out of the bedroom. I knew what Ali's answer would be, as we both agreed on that issue:

"Omar, don't ever do it, it will never work."

Again Omar insisted that they were totally in love and it had to work, but Ali asked him to be practical and reminded him that life was totally different over there; and to take an American and expect her to adapt, was plainly unrealistic. However, Omar thought that Ali was again just jealous, while Ali relentlessly repeated that we had different culture and traditions and even though Omar explained almost everything to Mary, when she would go over there to live, it was going to be a completely different experience. He then noticed that we walked in and with his sad eyes pointed at me, trying to tell Omar, *look at her a native, yet she's dreading the day she returns.*

But Omar's insistence made Ali tell him that Mary might act like she likes it there, she might even try real hard to, but she never would and that one day she will look around and ask herself: *what am I doing here?* And that there were so many examples of such marriages back home and that ninety percent of these cases, ended up in either divorce or separation.

"Come on Ali, this marriage won't be like all the others we hear about, this one is different, this is going to be a success."

His persistence made Ali just reluctantly nod. I looked at Mary and she sadly looked back at me and that was the first and last time we ever discussed this matter.

This incident took place in 1970 and a few months later I finished High school, but I never had the chance to finish my studies. I was dying to do so and to go to university, but the scholarship that was sponsoring Ali didn't sponsor women; *they didn't think that it was worth their time and money to sponsor women then,* and because we didn't have enough money, I enrolled in a beauty school and seven months later I graduated and worked as a beautician for about a year; and in 1972 when Ali finished his studies we packed our stuff and headed back home.

I had not heard from Mary since I had come home, because phone calls were very expensive and they didn't have this new great invention: email, yet; and to call someone you had to place your name in the telephone-company and when ever it was possible they would call you and connect you. So I had no news from her at all for over two years.

Omar would not dare tell his family that he was marrying an American. That was unheard of in his family. Well really that was the case in almost all of the families back then. Omar as a matter of fact, had a fiancée then, almost a wife. It all started when his father's old driver, Mahmoud, asked him if he could bring his two little girls from Yemen. Omar's dad immediately sent for them and they joined their father, in Jeddah. However, Omar's mother a very smart woman got so panicky; she knew that she was the third wife and that someday when these girls grow up her husband would marry one of them. So, there goes an intelligent woman's head to work! She suggested that they would marry the two girls to their two sons: Omar and his younger brother Tameem. As a wife it was an extremely smart move, but as a mother and a human being it was disastrous and so inhumane. She had after all, destroyed her sons' and two innocent girls' lives. Omar was just eleven then and Tameem was about five and the girls were about the same age too! So they had a small engagement party and were announced married and this way the father could not ever marry any of the girls.

Tala, the eldest of the girls, had black curly hair, braided all the time as Farah, Omar's mother, never allowed her to show off her beautiful hair, so she could never let it loose. Her big black eyes always had the saddest look, with tears continuously welling up in them. She knew that Omar didn't love her and never would; such a horrible feeling for a girl her age, *now eighteen*: to be in love with a man who never thought of her as an equal. She was after all, only a maid in his house and she always stuttered, especially when he was present.

One day when Farah was out shopping, Tala thought she could get some attention out of Omar, so she put on her short red sleeveless dress and her red high heal shoes. She then glued herself in front of her mirror, put a bit of red lipstick, defined her beautiful eyes with some black kohl and powdered her cheeks with a bright pink blush. She pulled the rubber band off of her hair and let her curly hair loose; swaying her slim body she walked right out to the living room, where he was watching his favorite program: soccer. She came close to him and asked:

"Ooomar, wwwould yoou liiike a ssssnack? Mayyybe some peanuts and a coo...ke?" She said stammering all the way through and of course Omar paid no attention whatsoever, he didn't even hear her, so she repeated her stuttering: "Ooomar...," and before she even finished her sentence Omar turned around to her and yelled:

"You silly thing, can't you see I'm busy? How dare you talk to me now?" And a loud slap over her face swung it from one side of the room to the other! "My God," he carried on, "what did you do to yourself? You look like a clown, go and look at yourself in the mirror. You look like you just ate someone with that sloppy red lipstick all over your huge lips. Didn't any one ever teach you how to wear make up?" He looked at his palm smeared with the pink blush and rubbed it with a Kleenex tissue. Tala couldn't believe her ears as he continued, "and what do you think, letting your fuzzy hair down like that? Get out of my face, you make me sick."

Tala ran to her room sobbing, her tears were running down soiling her red dress: a river let loose. She went straight to the bathroom and looked at herself in the mirror over the sink; all she could see was a clown, a clown with a print of four huge fingers all over her right cheek. She couldn't believe that any human being could be as cruel as that, but she still loved him! She washed her face with her rough loofah, trying to get rid of those palm prints and that clown she could see; her tears never stopped and her sobbing brought Soraya, her younger sister, to the bathroom.

"Tala what's wrong? My God who hit you?" Soraya angrily asked her.

"Nothing, no one hit me."

"Come on Tala; don't tell me those fingers are your doing? Who hit you? Was it Amaty (Madame) Farah? Or was it Ammy (Sir) Mohammad? Tell me," she looked at her awaiting her reply, but Tala insisted on saying:

"No one, nothing," she was so hysterical.

Suddenly Soraya held her sister by the shoulder and started shaking her, trying to get the truth out of her lips.

"I won't let you go until you tell me what happened?" She stared at her sister, who could not look her in the eye and screaming, she asked again, "was it Omar? I know it's him! Was it? That bastard I can kill him. How many times did I tell you to ignore him, he's not worth it. How many times did I warn you that he'll never ever love you; he's a selfish arrogant ass-hole. Why even pay any attention to him? Tell me why?"

Soraya was younger but a lot tougher than her sister, though she was petite and skinny, everyone in that house feared her; and they knew that she didn't want Tameem and didn't like anyone in that house; no one was nice to her or her sister, except the father, Mohammed, yet he too, treated them as maids, so she really disliked everyone.

"Tell me was it him? Tell me," she shook her sister vigorously and with more anger now, "Tala, answer me."

"Yees," Tala at last replied, "I thought I caaan let him just looook at me and tell meee something nice and all he did wasss make fun of meeee, I haaate him," she went on, stammering even more than before.

"Hate him? Yes I believe you. Ten minutes later you'll be right there underneath his feet trying to please him. Tala, how many times did I ask you to run away with me? This family won't ever let us go and these boys will never marry us. How many years had we been in this house? It's almost eight years now and look at us we don't have any rights or money, nothing! They treat us like slaves. I just can't stand this any more. We cook, wash, clean and iron and do all the stinking work around this big house." She was so mad and rushed out to the huge floral wall-papered living room.

"How dare you hit my sister?" She pulled her arm up, trying to hit him, but he clutched it back.

"Hey! Who do you think you are? You know who you're talking to? You're nothing but a maid around here; do you hear me?"

But that didn't stop her from yelling at him:

"You're so mean, I can't believe you. I know I'm a maid, but remember I'm human too; me and my sister do have feelings and the only thing that keeps us in this horrible place are your parents, who never want us to get away. Your dear mom tries to convince herself that my sister and I will marry you and your brother; well I have to tell you she's living in a dream world! How can she even think that? Treating us like maids? As for myself I'd rather marry a beggar off the street, than anyone in this family!"

"Yes she's dreaming and so is your stupid sister, to think that I would ever marry her?" He yelled back at her.

She again raised her arm ready for a slap and again, he pushed it back.

"You're really crazy, you want to slap me? And your sister thinks that I, Omar Hamid would marry her? A member of the Hamid family, one of the most prominent families in the country, would marry some one like her?"

"You? Prominent my foot! Who cares who your family is? Don't you know the proverb that says: *don't ask who my dad is, ask who I am and what I can do?*

You're so silly you can't come down from your precious ivory tower, can you? I know that your family *was* once even rulers of this region, but what does that have to do with you? Tell me please! You make me sick!" She walked out, not even caring for his reply; furious, he got up, ran behind her, trying to catch and beat her up, but she swiftly hurried to her room and locked the door.

As a result, the two girls, who lived as maids couldn't even think of marrying anyone else, because they were already engaged; and an engagement in my country is actually a marriage contract and to get out of it, you had to get a divorce. So that was how messy their life was, all four of them: boys and girls. Omar's mother on the other hand, was smart indeed in protecting her family and keeping her husband to herself and her kids, but then where were her motherly feelings? How could she do this to her sons and those two innocent girls?

Consequently, Omar had to wait till his father died, before he could even think of taking his American wife-to-be to his family, but fate stepped in faster than expected! In 1971 Omar received a telegram informing him of his dad's sudden heart attack. He immediately went home to attend the funeral and five days later he returned to St. Louis; however, he didn't tell his mother of his plans and as soon as he arrived in St. Louis, he sent her a letter.

"Aida!" His mother called her eldest daughter. "Come over here quickly please!"

A few minutes later Aida, a beautiful seventeen-year-old girl came to her and asked:

"What is it Mama? You scared me; you sounded so worried, what is it?"

"I received this letter and it has an American stamp, I think it's from your brother Omar." She handed the letter to Aida. "Is it?"

Her mom couldn't read or write so she always asked Aida to read for her the letters, sometimes the newspapers or magazines and always the Koran.

"Yes it's from him."

"O.K. open it quickly and read it, I'm so worried, is he O.K.?"

"Mama, please just let me open it," she noticed how worried her mom was, so she tore the envelope and a small piece off the top of the letter too, but she held the top together and started reading, in her soft delicate voice:

Dear Mama,

How are you and my brother and sisters? I miss you all so much. I miss my dad too. I feel lost without him. You know that as long as you have a father you feel that you're a kid and then suddenly you lose that father and you feel that you're a grown up and responsible for all your actions. Anyway, I'm sending you this letter and I hope you don't get upset and can understand the way I feel.

Remember how I always refused the idea of marrying Tala, but you know too that I didn't have a choice; Dad ruled and controlled my life and my most intimate decisions. Well I know you're different and I know that you'll always stand by my side, but when he was alive (God bless his soul) you couldn't do anything. Now Mama I want you to really understand what I'm trying to tell you...

"What's wrong with him?" Her mom interrupted, "why does he keep on repeating himself over and over again? Why doesn't he just come out and tell me what's bothering him?"

"Mama, hold on, just wait. If you let me read we'll know what he's trying to say." Aida stared at the letter again and went on reading:

Mama I want to divorce Tala...

His mom choking with tears, "what divorce? We never have divorces in this family," she said out loud. *What's wrong with this kid? Is he going crazy?* Now she asked herself, more than she did Aida.

"Mama, please let's see what he has to say O.K.?" Aida answered and suddenly folded the letter, hugged her mom closely and at the same time, tried to wipe the tears off her cheeks and in a sad voice continued: "O.K. now. Stop this. I won't read any more if this is going to upset you. You already have a weak heart."

Aida knew that after her dad's death her mom had heart problems. She had lost one parent and she was not willing to lose another. "Mama, please enough crying," she sobbed, still hugging and rubbing her shoulders.

Her mom wiped her tears with her sleeves and told her that she wouldn't cry anymore and to go on reading. Aida, being as sensitive as she was, could still feel how upset her mom was and insisted that she would finish reading it tomorrow.

"No please Aida, go on."

Reluctantly, Aida unfolded the letter again and started for the third time:

> *If you really love me you'll let me divorce her. You know that I'll never be a happy man if I marry her, and she too would be the most miserable woman on this earth, marrying a man who detests her. I also have to tell you that I have an American girlfriend, whom I'm in love with and want to marry.*

Again her mom stopped her: "American? Since when do we have boys who marry foreigners? No way is he going to marry a foreigner!"

"Mama Omar is twenty-one and you have to let him live his life. When Dad was alive he controlled the whole family: sons and daughters and their husbands and wives and of course their kids. You can't be like that too; you yourself suffered a lot from his dictatorship. I know I sound harsh and you probably think I don't love him, never. You know I adore that man and will forever adore him, I'm just being realistic as we each have to live our own lives."

Her mom looked at her and thought, *for a girl her age, she certainly is very wise!* Then declared: "I guess you're right; I did suffer with your dad a lot, but I had to go on accepting his ways to keep this family together and no I don't want any of you to suffer. I lived and will forever live for the four of you. Nada, your younger sister, is just nine and I will raise her differently. I'll teach her how to make her own decisions and if she needs my help, I'll be there for her; I'll be a different person with all of you. I don't want you to live the kind of life I lived," she smiled at Aida, as she said that and pulled her arms out to hug her, "so please Aida do go on reading."

Aida once again read:

> *Mama if you don't mind I'll be coming when I finish and I'll bring my girlfriend Mary, with me. We'll be married by then. Mama, please understand my point of view. I'm waiting for your reply; your consent will make me the happiest son to the best mother in the world. Lots of kisses and hugs to my lovely mom.*
>
> Love,
>
> Omar

Aida smiled as she read the last two sentences; she knew how her older brother Omar could steel her mom's heart with some soft flattering words. She looked up at her mom, waiting for her consent too.

"Aida, get your pad and pen and come back here again please," she smiled at her. Aida ran to her room and rushed back with her printed flowery purple pad and her favorite green Parker pen; she sat next to her mom and looked at her waiting:

"O.K. now start with:

Dear son,

You know that I love you and anything that makes you happy makes me happy too. Whatever your choice is, I'll always be on your side and whenever you need me, I'll be there for you. I'm sure that Miry (I hope I say it right) will make you happy, and I know that you'll make her happy too.

I'm writing you this letter to tell you to go ahead and marry her and come back and when you come I'll give the two of you a nice wedding party. You just don't worry about a thing, finish your school and come back. I miss you so much. Take care now habeeby and remember that I love you a lot and God bless you.

Love you.

How's that Aida? Do you think it's O.K.?"

She awaited Aida's approval, so Aida got closer and hugged her saying:

"Mama you're the greatest mother in the world. Of course it's great. We love you so much." Aida folded the letter and went to the office to get an envelope. She knew that her mom didn't pronounce Mary's name correctly but she still put it as her mom said it, kept all the repetitions in the letter and structured it in the correct form she had learned in her writing class; she just hoped it was right! She was so thrilled; her mom was a new open-minded woman.

Two years later, Omar came home with Mary. They were both so excited to be home together and Mary felt that she was at home, with her new family. Omar's mom also kept her promise and started the preparation for the wedding party. She asked Mary to do whatever she liked, so Mary was in charge of the whole wedding: the party itself, the seating arrangement, the food catering and even the dresses of her brides' maids. She couldn't believe this was all happening to her.

And the wedding party turned out to be a great event in town. The huge garden accommodated more than six hundred invitees, and the famous Arabian singer, Zaina, who was so talented, never stopped singing except for a few minutes every now and then to take a drink of sweetened water (water with sugar) or a sip of her tea glass. Her songs were a combination of folklore and modern songs. The diner was so delicious, a buffet from the five star, Al Hamrah Hotel: hors d'oeuvres, salads, seafood dishes, white and red meat dishes and the desert was a huge variety of Arabic and Western delicatessens, everything was just so great!

The excitement of meeting my best friend in my own country was above description; no words could express my happiness to see her, although I had never wanted this marriage to take place, seeing her in Jeddah filled my chest and heart with ecstasy. Now I could once again sit and talk with her forever and could bring up any subject with no fear or shame; she too could sit and tell me anything and everything she wanted: we were secret keepers!

I was always amazed at this girl: the things she could endure through her marriage to Omar and her unhesitant acceptance of our customs and traditions, when I myself could not! I was a kid when I got married just to escape such a place and look at her! I mean she had gone through so much and never complained, so strange! I used to look at her in astonishment and ask myself, *Why is she taking all this? I a native won't.*

One day, when I visited her, I found her sitting in her white shorts and black top in front of the largest bowl I had ever seen, chopping and cutting lamb meat. Her slim white translucent body was sweating from head to toe! Her red hair tied up in a ponytail, her frail hands clutching to the bones and her thin long fingers looked so tired of this whole ordeal! The first time I knew about this was on a hot day in July 1975, her son, Amir, was two months old then. We spoke everyday over the phone and that day I called her, but she was busy and said:

"Omar brought this whole lamb and I have to cut, chop and bag it."

I almost fainted and couldn't believe my ears I asked myself again: *a whole lamb to chop and bag?* She then explained to me that he usually bought a whole lamb, because it was cheaper and let her cut and put it in bags and in the freezer. I still couldn't believe that! Someone buying a whole lamb and letting his wife cut it, just to save a few Saudi Riyals? Of course I didn't say a word to her and just hung up. I was so furious that a man from my country could do this to a poor foreign girl. Then a month later, I was there in her house for a chat, on my way back from the *souk* (the market). I had taken her by surprise, because I didn't call her, but it was normal in our friendship: she passed by without a call too; but this time I found it hard to chat, because she was too busy with her lamb! She had her pink printed apron on:

"Oh Fairooz, come on in, I am just busy in the kitchen. Come on in."

I followed her to the kitchen, where I sat on the square glass diner table.

"How about a cup of coffee? I just made some," she asked with a sigh.

"Sounds great, you know I love your coffee; it's always fresh."

"Ya I'm like you, a coffee buff," she poured two cups of black coffee and sat for a break, "so where were you, Fairooz?"

"Oh shopping, the kids needed some clothes and on my way back home I thought I'd drop in and say hi. You know I haven't seen you this whole past week."

"I know I'm sorry, but I was so busy cleaning, cooking…"

"And chopping and cutting," I couldn't wait for her to finish her sentence; I was so upset to see my best friend going through this.

"Ya chopping and bagging," she gave me a faint tired smile.

"Mary, I don't want to tell you this, but why do you do this horrible work? Why don't you ask Omar to buy the meat chopped, cut and packed?"

"You mean it's possible? Omar told me that that was how people buy it and that I'm just a spoiled American girl."

"Oh no, you know if Ali ever buys me a whole lamb I'll just leave it to rot. Or I'd put it outside my apartment door, it's not my job, I'm no butcher!"

"You're kidding?"

"I wish I am, but I'm not. You know Ali used to bring the vegetables and fruits in huge boxes that can feed a family of twelve. I mean he did that every week that I couldn't walk: boxes were lying all over the kitchen! And you know there's only me, him and our two kids! And I did tell him over and over again not to; that he should only buy what I had written for him on the paper: just a few kilos of this and that. But no, he insisted on buying whole boxes of everything and always said:

'How could I go to *Al Halaga* (fruit and vegetable market) and just buy food in small quantities?'

So one day he came back from *Al Halaga*, I had to spend the whole day in the kitchen, separating and putting things in bags and in the fridge; then the next time he did that I got really fed up with it all, I took what I needed of each box and put the rest in front of the apartment door."

"Fairooz, you're really brave!"

"I don't think so I've just had it, so when he got home he couldn't get to the door. Boxes were all over. He rang the bell and when I opened the door, he was so mad, but did I care?"

"I know better," she said giggling.

"Well of course I didn't give a damn, excuse my language.

'Fairooz! What's this? What did you do? All these boxes out here, all my money wasted?' He yelled.

And I just said: 'sorry Ali I told you several times that I didn't want all of this and it all got rotten and thrown in the garbage by the time you went to *Al Halaga* again; hey and don't you worry, Ahmad (the guard) took it all, so nothing's going to be wasted and your money isn't wasted either. Some poor man will eat it all.' And believe it or not, that was the end of it; I never saw those boxes again, everything he buys now is in kilos and already bagged and all I have to do is stick it in the fridge."

"You know what? You are really something!"

And that was that: Omar too never bought a whole lamb again; all his grocery was packed and ready to be put in the fridge or freezer. I bet that Omar wasn't too happy about me telling Mary things like that and I hope that she didn't tell him that I sometime advised her.

Thinking back at the way Mary took it all, is torturing my peace of mind, but today is a nice day in October and I really want to put my mind off of Mary's miseries: my children are coming over to visit me tomorrow! I can't believe it! Deema, Dalia, Rana, and Amr are coming? Is it a dream? I have to make sure I have the exact details of their flight. No one can believe that I already called Saudi Airlines more than five times, checking the flight number and the arrival time, fixed the beds, arranged the rooms, made sure each cupboard had enough hangers and all the drawers were empty for them.

Tomorrow's the big day. Sleep can't find its way to my eyes, especially tonight. I'll just stay up watching movies on TV, or just any silly program; I don't want to shut my eyes and miss their flight.

In the morning I took the train down to London then I got the Metro and arrived at the airport an hour earlier. I couldn't stand still, moving around all the time, grinning, humming and smiling to myself, I honestly didn't know what I was doing. People around me were staring all the time probably thinking I'm crazy, remember I'm in England, but I don't care! Ten minutes before the flight landed, I had my camera out and ready.

Oh my God, there they are "Deema!" I shouted out in my loud voice, "Rana, Dalia Amr!" They couldn't miss my voice. Once I saw them tears started lingering in my eyes; I couldn't stop thinking that in a month's time they would go back home.

They came rushing toward me, carrying their back packs. I know that I can't go in and squeeze them to death, but again I just walk to the door and they come close and we kiss and hug forever. Then they go back to fetch their luggage and my camera doesn't stop flashing pictures; they too start making poses, silly poses of course for the pictures. I love those kids they too act the way they feel, not bothering with what people think, as long as they're not harming anyone. On the train home Deema asks:

"So, Mama what are we doing next?"

"My God you just arrived. Give me a break," I know that the word *break* doesn't exist in their dictionary; they probably have a special kind of dictionary! I know that from this moment on I won't get any rest until they get back on the train, heading back home.

"Mama you know we only have a month? So what are we going to do?" Amr asks.

And the twins shake their heads in agreement; their eyes sparkling with excitement.

"Well I do have some nice brochures about different amusement parks around here and we can go to Blackpool for a weekend," I assure them that I have it all planned.

"Blackpool, what's that?" Deema asks.

"It's supposed to be a lovely city by the sea. I heard it's really nice."

"Great!" They say at one breath.

"So what's in Blackpool?" Dalia asks.

"A lot of amusement parks and a pleasant atmosphere," I answer and my face looks as excited as theirs, but my head is thinking, *am I really up to all of that?*

"Mama and what about London, aren't we going to come back here again?" Deema asks, "you know most of my friends are here now."

"Yes, Mama ours too," adds Rana and right then Amr smiles and says:

"Ya, mine too."

I know with that kind of smile *a Fairoozian smile* that he probably has some devilish plans in his head.

Time passes so fast. I don't have time to rest and the only moments of solitude for me are when they go to the gym for an hour. Then on the tenth of November we take the train, for the sixth time, down to London, but this time I'll come back without them! We spent five days in London, again never taking time out. On the fourteenth was the twins' sixteenth birthday, which we celebrated in Paparazzi, an Italian restaurant. I bought two cakes, ornaments, hats and two sets of candles for each cake and we had a really good time.

Then the dreaded day comes: the fifteenth, both Karen and I take them to the airport. I think of how lucky I am to have such a friend, *Fairooz I don't want you to be on your own when the kids leave.* I hold my tears back and try to pretend like I was fine, but I guess they have to go back, they have already missed too much of school. Their dad was really nice to let them skip a week of school, so the twins could celebrate their birthday with me. And that's a first! But I guess he was trying to be very nice, since I had asked for a divorce five months ago; and he even asked Amr to buy me a card and a bouquet of flowers on the tenth of October, a day after their arrival, for it was our wedding anniversary. When I told Amr that I didn't want him to buy me anything, he was really hurt and I had to explain why: "listen *habeeby*, I would love anything from you, but because it's from your dad I don't really want it, plus the occasion is irrelevant to me. Please don't get upset, you know that I want a divorce and if I accept this gift, it will make your dad think that I have changed my mind, which I haven't." I hugged him and he kissed my head, showing me that he understood what I was trying to say.

"Don't worry Mama, if that's what you want, I'll do it."

As we walk down terminal three and on their way into gate twenty-four, I keep repeating, "hey kids, remember to call me as soon as you get home, O.K.?"

"O.K. Mama, we promise we will," Deema says and thinks, *I can't believe how much you can nag. I have really forgotten,* and smiles.

On the way back to Newcastle, Karen notices my sad expression and even feels the tears, which I'm holding back:

"Fairooz, you're so lucky. You have such wonderful kids. I can't wait to meet Sam! I met your second son, what's his name?"

"Kareem," I know it's hard for her to remember our Arabic names.

"Ya, he's so sweet when he was over in April, so loving and so nice to you. You are one lucky girl," she smiles.

I can feel her heart broken too, as she touches my hands to comfort me and I tell her: "Yes I'm so lucky. I always thank God for giving me such great kids, a wonderful loving family and the best friends ever," I'm not just being nice, but God never leaves me alone. He is always with me wherever I go; He is the best of my best friends and if it hasn't been for Him I would never have such a loving family and great friends.

At four we get home and I ask Karen to come in for coffee, but she is too tired and goes to her flat and as soon as I get in and change my clothes I get a glass of water and try to keep myself from crying and feeling depressed. Although I had checked my email everyday in London at the Internet Café at Whitley's, I still can't wait to get on line. So I run to my laptop and in a few seconds I'm already there. Now that my kids are still on the plane I know that I won't have any emails from them and I had already read Sam's and Kareem's in London. Ah! This is one of the emails I wait for everyday: Randy's. Oh! I know I never did tell you who Randy was. Well, it's like a fairy tale. Randy was my friend at Roosevelt High School, back in St. Louis. Oh, I'm sorry I don't mean to get you mixed up, but yes, I spent the first year at Xavier High and then the second year I moved to a public school, which was Roosevelt and attended that for a semester and then I took summer school and got my high school degree; so it took me a year and a half instead of three to finish high school. Don't think it's because I'm smart, no, high school there was really easy; what Mary said was so right: there was no comparison between the two schools I attended. I mean at Roosevelt I didn't have to open a book and when I just slightly studied I got straight A's. Anyways, Randy really liked me then, but remember I was a married faithful wife, *stupid me!* Anyway, he used to make passes at me and I ignored him and even his friends used to tease him whenever I passed by. Again it's funny how fate plays its game and it's amazing how small this world is! One day as I was checking my email in April '98, *when I first came over here,* I found this strange email:

Subj: Is it really you?

Date: 12/04/1998 5:01:43 PM Eastern Standard Time

From: RSmith@hotmail.com

To: FairHoura@hotmail.com

Hi Fairooz—You probably can't remember me, I'm Randy. Remember Roosevelt High? Yes I can't believe I found you again! I'd been trying to get in touch, or even locate you for so long.

You know it'd been twenty-six years. Yes, since '72; anyway, I just got a new computer and I'm on hotmail, so I thought let me try locating Fairooz. I looked for your name through the directory and when I was asked for your address, all I could remember was that you're from Jeddah, Saudi Arabia, so I put that down; and I never ever thought, not one in a million, that I'd ever find your email address.

I still hope this isn't just an illusion and that it's you I found and not some other Fairooz. Please keep in touch and tell me what you'd been up to all these years. Take care now. Randy

Randy? How could I ever forget him? He was so nice to me and I know that he really liked me then, but I never thought he would still think of me, after twenty-six years. My God! Twenty-six years ago and he still remembers me; so of course he found the right Fairooz after all these years and so we kept in touch since! Now, seven months later we are still keeping in touch through email, chatting everyday or even talking over the phone once a week. We made a deal: he calls one Thursday and I call the following one, so we really got to know one another pretty good, that is considering it was overseas. Randy was married too and had two boys; he got divorced two years and went out with different girls, but never found his soul-mate. He also admitted that I was his soul mate and I have to admit that, he is my first true love. Before knowing him, I always thought that love never existed: it's some fantasy out of a book or a movie, but now I know that love is the best thing that has ever struck me. After reading his email, I went back to check my emails and make sure that I had replied to each and everyone. It had been a month since I had answered any of them: I just read and saved them.

Well, my eyes drop to Mary's email again and I re-read it one more time and my movie reel starts rolling. I remember the hard times she had to go through, when she found out that Omar was cheating on her in 1986. She accidentally stumbled over his Visa receipts then and discovered huge amounts paid on his trips to Paris, Morocco, the US and other places; enormous amounts spent on purchases and clothes; unbelievable phone bills and some expensive fancy restaurants. *I can't believe my eyes,* she thought while flipping the papers over and over, to make sure she was reading the right thing! She went back to the name of the cardholder checking, hoping to find a mistake and frantically ran to the phone, dialed my number and asked me in a hysteric voice to come over right away.

It was a good thing I already had my cooking done, cleaning and all and my three kids were still in school. It was nine in the morning and I had to get home around two, before the kids or Ali were back; so I quickly got dressed and didn't even know if I had the right clothing on; who cares! I could always go out in my nighty as far as I was concerned; I had the *Abaya* on anyway! I rushed to the lift and thanked God that I remembered taking my keys along, at that time I didn't have any help, just a driver who stayed in the guard's room from seven to two, then he went to his house and came back at five and stayed till I asked him to go, so if I locked myself out of the apartment that was it; I would have to call Ali and then you know what would happen; I ran down to fetch Majid, the driver, who was not in the room.

"He's buying a pack of cigarettes and will be right back," Ahmad the guard told me. Ahmad was from Yemen and always dressed in a *Fouta*, his traditional clothes, which consists of a cotton material that is put on as a skirt or a *Saree* wrapped around his waist and tied up in a knot at the front. It does look like a woman's skirt and the top is a simple T-shirt. His big belly made the *Fouta* look tight and short. His shaved black hair matched his black eyes. So here I was instead of being in the car on my way to see Mary, I was standing there staring at Ahmad! I hate the fact that I can't drive! You get out stressed with time and in a hurry, then you find out that Mr. Driver isn't there.

When he got back five minutes later, which seemed like an hour, I was so furious: "Majid, how many times did I ask you not to go anywhere without telling me?" Of course that didn't mean a thing to him, as he still did, "take me to Mary's please and if you can step on it." It usually takes twenty minutes to get to her house, but today it just took thirteen and if I was driving it would probably take eight. As soon as the car stopped I ran out, forgetting to tell Majid what to do whether to wait or go and come back later. I ran to the lift and pressed number 12, as I reached over to ring the bell, I found out that the apartment door was ajar.

"Mary, Mary," I dashed in; I was so scared I would find her dead!

"Over here Fairooz in the living room."

I went to the living room and found papers all around her. Omar's suitcase was lying on the floor too. She looked a mess, her hair was all over her face and her face was soiled with her mascara, as tears ran down her cheeks.

"What is it? What's wrong? And why is your front door open?"

"I left it open for you. Oh Fairooz look at this, just look!"

"What?" I looked and couldn't see anything there, just papers scattered all over the place.

"Fairooz Omar's cheating on me."

"What? No, he can't be."

"I tell you he's cheating on me," now she is crying.

I tried to comfort her and got up to bring a glass of water.

"Look at all those statements! They're different bills to hotels, restaurants, department stores and flights. I tell you this…"

"Oh Mary, maybe you're wrong?"

"I thought I am and forever prayed that I really was, but then I called some of those hotels and found that a Mr. and Mrs. Omar Hamid stayed there."

"How did they give you this information at the hotel? They're usually very strict."

"Well I told them I was his secretary and that he wanted me to check his bills."

"Mary you're so smart."

"Smart my foot, me smart? I was taken for a fool, look at him cheating and I'm here being such a good wife and taking care of everything around the house; plus I have to keep taking whatever shit his sister throws at me, all this and what for? Is this what I deserve?"

"Mary, I'm as shocked as you are and all I can say is take it easy and wait until he comes home and then see what he has to say. Maybe there's a terrible mix up there?"

I myself was the stupid naïve one; I never thought something like this would happen; again you read about betrayals and all, but you never think it would hit so close to home. However, Omar denied everything and Mary just let go.

Then a few years later, we moved into our own house, or should I say Ali's house, as I own nothing! And Mary and Omar moved into a nice villa too. Problems never quit visiting their house, always fights quarrels and sometimes a lot of rage was involved in their disputes; many times Mary threw Omar's clothes out on the street and broke dishes and glasses. I was always there present to calm her down and settle things. I was considered Mary's closest family member, since the poor thing had none of her own family around.

Early 1988 Joe called me and told me that Mary was in the hospital; I felt so bad, because I was so busy with my schooling and didn't speak to her for the last four days. I rushed, got dressed and ran down the stairs; I called out to the most important person in my life, my driver and asked him to take me to Siha Hospital, it was the best private hospital in Jeddah and its emergency room was very efficient.

When I saw her I almost broke up in tears, it was the worse state I had ever seen her in. Needles were sticking in her right arm, bruises under her left eye and her hair's a big mess, with her white roots about an inch long and cut in such a bad way, like some one had just picked up the scissors and chopped it off.

"Fairooz why are you here? I didn't tell you because I know you're busy with your MA; who told you?"

"Joe just called me; Mary, what do you mean you didn't want me to know? Mary you must know that you're my sister and no MA is more important than my sister," I reached out and touched her left hand, as I couldn't touch her right needled-hand.

"Oh! Fairooz! You know I feel you're more than a sister to me too, I love you."

"I love you too Mary," I didn't want to ask her what exactly happened and she didn't let me wonder much longer.

"Fairooz, Omar tried beating me up, when I knew for sure that he had a Moroccan mistress. I tried to hold his arm up and he pushed me, then he suddenly hit me on the face. Yes he has a mistress! I noticed how he always goes to the guest-room and sits for hours whispering in the phone and one day I heard him mention her name in such a soft erotic tone. I tell you this bastard…"

"Mary, please don't upset yourself, so what? Let him be. You don't deserve this; he must be crazy to look for another woman!"

"Fairooz you can say all you want, it would not be the same if you were in my situation. How could I let him be? He was the first man I ever knew. You know he was my first date? You know that, right?"

"Yes, I remember it all as if happening right now, before my eyes," and I was not making up stories; I could see how they met, right there in front of me.

"When I confronted him earlier he denied everything, but now he cannot deny it any more. He told me that he's going to keep me, just to drive me crazy and that he's never going to stop seeing her. Can you believe that?"

No I couldn't believe it, that nice guy, turned into a beast? But I think that is what my environment does to men; being in a segregated society and having a lot of temptations and a lot of money drives them insane, I mean really insane. Who would believe that he would ever cheat on his true love: Mary? Wasn't she the one he insisted on marrying and escorting all the way from the States?

"Mary…" She didn't let me finish my sentence and I was glad she cut through, because honestly I didn't have the faintest clue as to what I was supposed to say.

"When he left to work this morning and after telling me off I just went to the kitchen and got the big knife…" Before she could say another word I felt faint and stopped her by shouting out:

"Mary?"

"No, wait, I just went to the kitchen, held my arms out and look at what I tried doing?" She wildly went on!

Thank God I couldn't see a thing, the story itself and the bandage really made me feel sick and I almost fainted so I sat down right away.

"My lovely friend, why would you do such a thing? Believe me no man is worth killing yourself for."

"Fairooz, I wish you can feel this burning feeling inside here," she put her right arm to her heart. "You don't know how I feel. You never can, unless…," noticing my shocked face, she stopped right there.

I was glad she stopped there because I thought then that, *Ali is so good to me, he does have a horrible temper but then he loves me and he would never cheat on me, never.* I can't believe how dumb I was! This incident was the first suicidal attempt by Mary, but unfortunately it had just been the start.

After four more attempts I called her and told her that I was coming over for coffee and a quick chat. A few minutes later I was ringing the bell and her Philippino help, Mila opened the door for me. She was about forty-five, with short black hair, that covered half her rounded face and black eyes that showed how much she loved Mary and her kids. She took my *Abaya* and hung it on the wall:

"Madame I'm so glad you're my Madame's friend. You know she needs some one like you, as she has no one around her over here. I feel so sorry for her, but when I think of you I feel a lot better," she whispered those tender loving words into my ears, as she didn't want Mary to hear her.

"Oh! Mila, Mary is so lucky to have you. You're really a great friend, too. I myself feel so soothed, to know you're always there for her," I touched her right shoulder. I do love touching people, I love expressing my feelings and that's why my heart is on my face, all the time. People will immediately know if I like or dislike them, my face shows it and my heart never keeps it a secret either.

I then went in and found Mary cooking her favorite meal: honey roasted turkey, for it was Thanksgiving. Mary still celebrated her American occasions, as well as ours; unlike some American girls I knew, who refused mingling with our customs and insisted on staying purely American. She is a very smart girl and had taken advantage of our culture and mixed it with hers. She even learned how to speak Arabic and is still awfully fluent at it.

"Hello there! How are you today?" I came in and kissed her.

"Hi Fairooz, I'm fine and you?"

"*Pas mal!*" I sometimes tried to sound funny.

"Come on, Fairooz stop twisting your tongue, what's that you just said?"

"Oh! It's not bad in French, come on didn't you say that you're going to take French classes? You're fluent in Arabic now, so?"

"No I'm not."

"Hey, I tell you, you really are, you speak like a native and even my mom and aunts say that all the time, so I'm not just being nice."

"I admit I do try real hard. You know that I tried so hard to fit into the family and society, boy it's so difficult!"

"I know that Mary, I tell you, you're one brave kid."

"Do you know that when I go home to visit my family, they think I'm getting to be too much of an Arab and over here people still consider me a foreigner, so where ever I am, here or there, I feel out of place: an outsider and honestly I sometimes think to myself who am I, really? I don't fit anywhere."

"Hey, kiddo, cool it! Don't make this sound so depressing, you're doing just fine," I tried to cheer her up, but I knew what she was exactly talking about. She felt lost trying to fit into this place and doing so she lost some of her natural origin too; it's so hard, *but I warned you, and you just didn't listen,* I thought to myself. "So tell me are you or aren't going to go for French?" I said trying to change this whole gloomy topic.

"I will. It's the next thing on my schedule. I promise. So next time you try sounding smart, I'll out smart you!"

We both laughed; I was so glad she felt cheerful today. It had been so long! She had a beautiful smile. It's horrible how some people can deprive you of everything, even the simplest things in life: a smile. I then helped her with her cooking. "Mary I can't believe how great a cook you've turned out to be?" I said this, awaiting a compliment too.

"Oh Fairooz I'm not as good as you. You're the best cook I've ever seen."

She knew that I expected a compliment back and said it with a teasing grin, as we laughed and on our way out of the kitchen, I turned back to her.

"Mary you can't believe how happy it makes me to see you that cheerful."

"Ya when I see you I feel great. I know we passed through a lot of bad times, but we had some great times too, right?"

"Are you kidding? We've been through the best of times."

"Remember Fairooz the sting ray?"

I laughed out loud just thinking of the incident. We used to go snorkeling all the time, all four of us, Omar, Ali, Mary and myself. We each had two kids at the time, so we used to leave them with my sister Samar for the day.

"How could I forget that? You mean when that sting ray attacked you?"

"Ya," she nodded choking on her laughter.

"Ya your white short and white top attracted that poor huge thing and it came plunging towards you."

"Ya, you remember? That was oh, how many years ago?"

"Can't remember, around 1976 maybe? All I remember was how Ali and Omar dived after it and shot it with their spear guns and the huge thing kept swinging them from one end to the other, it was so funny!"

"Ya and we two were so mean, we just stayed up there, watching them and laughing our hearts outs," she added taking a breath, laughing and relating the incident.

It is funny how sometimes we remember incidents like they've just happened yesterday, I thought to myself and then looked at my watch and knew I had to get going, so I got my *Abaya* and on my way out we were still talking about those days. We knew this would take forever, so we just sat down on her front stairs. I still didn't tell her what I wanted: the real reason for my visit; I was still waiting for the right moment to start. We sat on the steps and we were back like old times: talking and laughing.

"How about the time we went canoeing in the Mississippi River, do you remember that?" I asked, still laughing.

"My God Fairooz, you really remember a lot? That was so long ago, when you and Ali still lived in the US, no kids yet, around 1970."

"Well, ya. How could I forget that day?"

"I could never forget it either. How you and Ali were in one canoe and Omar and I in another, and how the two canoes were tied with a rope at both ends and you and I were sitting in front of each canoe, making sure the way was clear."

"Ya, and of course we started talking and you know what that can lead to."

"My God, we suddenly hit a huge tree trunk and...," I had to stop for a breath and went on, laughing and remembering. "Then the two canoes flipped over and all four of us found ourselves in the water."

"Ya, the coolers, our cameras, our wallets just everything," she too couldn't stop laughing; "I could never forget how mad the guys were and how much we tried hiding our giggles, but of course they noticed that we were cracking on the inside.

'Stop this,' Omar told us.

'It's not funny, let's get ashore,' Ali angrily added.

God, that was so funny; the two of us, just looking at one another and then we suddenly cracked out loud, laughing and apologizing."

"Mary, that incident could never leave my memory."

"Mine neither, we really had some great times together, right Fairooz?"

"We certainly did. Great times, whether they're sad or happy, they still were great."

"Oh Fairooz I don't know what I can do without you?"

"Don't even think; I'll never leave you alone; I'll always be on your side, where ever you are."

"What do you mean?" She asked, with a puzzled face. Now both of us stopped laughing and had a serious look on our faces and I knew that, now was the right time.

"Mary, you know I love you and you are my best friend ever. You know that I didn't see you this happy in ages? I just can't stand the thought of you being unhappy. Mary, I think the time has come for you to leave."

"What? Are you crazy? Leave?"

"I know I sound horribly mean, but I really think you should go back home."

"Home? What do you mean? This is my home!"

"No Mary I think you should go back to St. Louis. You think I just want to get rid of you, right? You just don't know how hard it is for me to even think of this, but I just can't see you hurting yourself any more and I honestly think that if you stay here you'll just lose everything."

"Fairooz are you crazy? How can I lose everything? I still have my kids and I'll never lose them. You told me that so many times, so how can I lose everything? I have my kids and they're everything to me in this world."

"Mary! Oh Mary! I know. I've never seen a mother as loving as you are to your kids, but Mary if you stay here Omar will drive you crazy and by trying to hurt yourself you'll lose yourself and in return your kids. You know one of your suicidal attempts could succeed or you could even lose your sanity, then what do you think would happen to your kids?" She started weeping so I drew her close and tapped her back. "Listen Mary if you go away you can pull yourself together again and then your kids can join at any time. They'll grow up and come to you, but if you stay here something bad will happen to you and if you kill yourself or lose your mind, people will just tell those wonderful kids of yours: *your mom was crazy*. These nasty words will stain their life forever; now you don't want that to happen. Do you?" Now I was crying too, trying to wipe my nose with my top. "Mary! Oh, Mary! Please understand what I'm trying to tell you! It's so hard on me, to ask you to leave, but I'm doing it, because I love you and I can't see you getting hurt."

Two weeks later school was out, it was summer vacation, I picked up the ringing phone and it was Mary, her happy voice came to me over the phone; she sounded a bit sad, but there was a pitch of optimism in it. At last she decided to go back to St. Louis. She was going to tell Omar that she would go and visit her parents and take the kids along and just stay there.

A few months passed and Mary was still back in St. Louis. She put her four kids in school and told Omar that she was going to stay for a while and then come back. Omar immediately married his mistress, without telling anyone and rented another house for her. However, he felt defeated: his pride, selfishness and arrogance couldn't let him stop right there; he couldn't even face himself in the mirror, every time he looked into it; and by now had a plan of his own: to get his kids back. He called Mary and told her that he would go to the States for a visit, because he missed her and the kids a lot and my poor innocent friend fell for it.

So he went over to St. Louis and after two weeks of being extremely sweet and nice he told her that he wanted to take Jana and Karam to Six Flags. He noticed that she had some work around the house and he also knew that he couldn't fool his older kids: Amir and Samira; so the next morning Mary kissed them as they were leaving. In the car, Omar cunningly questioned them:

"Hey kids. Do you miss home?" They looked puzzled and didn't know what he meant, so he explained: "I mean our home in Jeddah?"

Karam jumped with excitement: "yes Baba very much; both Jana and I always talk about how someday we would go back."

"So what do you say if we do? We'll go to Six Flags today and tomorrow we'll go back to Jeddah. I just told your mom we'll go to Six Flags today, to tell you about that great idea."

"But how can we leave Mama?" Jan asked, with tears in her eyes.

"Listen Jana, I can't live without you and your mom likes it over here and doesn't want to come back with us, neither do Amir and Samira, so as long as they're happy we can, I guess, leave them and go."

"So are you going to tell her?" Karam asked.

"No. We'll just leave tomorrow morning without them knowing, you think we can do that?" He asked with a grin on his face, pretending to be desperate for their consent.

"I guess we can?" Karam answered, looking pleadingly back at Jana. "Come on Jana please," Karam nagged and Jana at last, nodded approvingly.

"O.K. then we're all set; today when you get to bed just pack a few things in your bags and tomorrow I'll wake you up and we'll leave around five, when everyone is still asleep," they shook their heads. Poor kids didn't know what was waiting for them back home!

Around six in the evening they were back from Six Flags and told everyone how great a time they had, but Jana had a very sad look on her face.

"Jana, dear come over here; what is it? You don't look too good to me?" Her mom asked.

"Oh. She was sneezing a lot. I think she's coming down with something," Omar answered, before Jana could even blink.

"Oh! I'll get you some Vitamin C that will make you feel better."

And so the plan went on! The next morning Mary woke up and went to the kids' rooms, to check on them. They usually woke up around nine, and it was eleven and they were still sleeping; she thought they were probably too tired today. She went to their beds and found them fixed and empty. Suddenly, she had a funny feeling in her heart, Omar was not around either; he would usually go out for a walk and come back around this time to shower. She ran to the bathroom, slammed the door open, but no one was there:

"He took my kids away! That bastard took my kids!" Amir and Samira came running to her hysterical screaming.

"Mama what is it?" Amir asked.

"What's wrong?" Samira cried, as she shook her mom, she hadn't seen her mom in that state since they had been over here. She at once felt what had happened.

"Your dad has taken your brother and sister."

"Mama it's O.K., don't cry! Maybe it's better for you; they weren't too happy over here, you know that and they always talked about going back to Jeddah, to live with Baba, so?" Amir said, not too convinced himself about his dad's mean action.

"Mama please, you still have the two of us, so don't do this to yourself," Samira tried to hold her.

Now Mary was tearing her shirt off, pulling her hair out and slapping her whole body!

"My God, how can I be so stupid?"

"No Mama. You're not stupid, not at all. Baba fooled us all, it just happened, so please don't start blaming yourself again; remember we need you around us." Amir answered hugging her tightly, making sure he avoided their mom going back to that horrible state of hers.

The film keeps rolling. And while I'm physically sitting on my sofa in Newcastle, my thoughts mentally take me back to Jeddah, a few years later: it was

August 1990. The Gulf War just started and it was a critical time in Saudi Arabia. Saddam Hussein invaded Kuwait and the States moved its bases to Saudi Arabia, to protect it; the whole country was against such a move and a strong feeling of resentment filled each house in the country. We didn't want a foreign force, building bases on our land.

In October the American army had their women drive around the country and some Saudi women thought that it was not fair that they could not drive in their own country, while American girls could. So they wrote a letter to Prince Mouhsin in Riyadh and asked him to allow them to do drive, but his delayed reply made these women feel like it was a waste of time and they just got in their cars and drove through the streets of Riyadh. I remember so well, what happened to those poor innocent women, Sohair, my friend worked as a Professor at King Saud University in Riyadh and she told me all about it. She thoroughly explained to me how as she walked down the university campus collecting her stuff, ready to leave, everyone pointed at her and whispered:

"Oh look at Dr. Sohair! Guilty as a…," said Salma, a girl in her History Department.

"Look at her. As if she's done nothing," added another of her students.

Sohair looked back at them, she could feel and sense that they were giggling and pointing at her. *Listen you idiots, I did this partly for me yes, but I mostly did it for you, to provide you with a brighter and liberated future,* she thought to herself, *are you happy living like cows on a ranch? No, not even cows; at least cows have the right to roam around as they like. What do you have?* They could see her angry face, but no words came out of her mouth.

Sohair and other women were condemned by the most religious-fanatics in the country; and their names were posted along the well-lit streets, where most of the mosques were located. Lights were everywhere, such lights that reflect the inward darkness of the hearts of such people. In those beautifully constructed mosques, mostly white, God's words were associated with the cruel discrimination of those scrupulous women! Just imagine the immense influence those sick-minded sheikhs have on people, as they brainwash oblivious minds every Friday!

"Kill those Sinners," cried one of the sheikhs at the mosque, in the holiest place, in his Friday prayer's speech.

"Expel them adulterous bitches; exile them," shouted another.

"Shoot 'em bitches," yelled someone else, in another mosque.

"Get rid of those harlots," screams and more screams.

People just repeated what was said, just like brainless parrots. Stop, think for yourself! Did they really deserve this? But no, all you could hear all over the country were those words floating all over, festering the filth-filled air. Markers smeared street walls with such accusations: *whip and lynch those culprits, banish' em whores, execute those lecherous broads.* Mosques all around rotted with the burning flesh of those innocent women, floating all over. There was a stale smell evaporating from every inch of those buildings; molds and smudges of their inculpable blood soiled the floors and walls of the well-arranged expensive marbled-tiles of those mosques.

At the entrance of each and every mosque in that town, the names of a good number of open-minded well-educated women in the country were posted; women who helped in raising millions of students, women who were so loyal to their country and people. They were named the most horrible names ever: whores, prostitutes, atheists, communists and any nasty name one could ever think of. Why? All they ever did was drive along the streets. Was that their crime? Oh! Those suffocating customs and traditions! When will they release those chains and locks off of women's hands, feet and thoughts? The Klu Klux Klan would have been more merciful! How could they do that to such innocent women? How could they accuse them of such horrible acts? That was not the religion I was raised to believe in! Not the God I could never live without!

I often wonder if the word woman really exists in any dictionary, back where I come from; I'm only sure that the word MAN does! It's a man's world after all and man sets the rules and laws. The most religious Moslem country in the world, is not a God abiding country and does not follow God's law, as set by Him in the holy Koran, its laws are MAN made!

It was another warm day in October in 1990 and here I was back in Jeddah, sitting on the floral sofa, in the burgundy-colored living room at home and watching the nine o'clock news, when the phone rang and a very familiar voice said:

"Fairooz, it's me, Mary."

"Mary? Oh my God. I can't believe it's you. Hey, you sound like you're just across the road, so close; where are you?"

"I am across the road; I mean I'm really close. Well, I mean I'm over here, in Jeddah!" She sounded as excited as I was.

"What? You must be kidding? Here, in Jeddah?" She could feel my astonished thrilled voice.

"Ya I'm here to see my kids and to renew my *Iqama* (visa). Hey, when can I see you? I miss you so much, it's been so long."

"Actually I have nothing right now, shall I come over, or you wanna come over or meet anywhere?" I was so happy I couldn't even talk.
"How about in an hour, can you come over?"
"Where are you?"
"What do you mean? I'm at home."
"Home, where's that?"
"Hey kid, what's wrong? You sound so nervous. I'm still in the same house off Tahlia Street."

I was actually extremely nervous. She probably didn't know what happened since she had been away. I knew and the whole city knew by now, that Omar had brought his new wife to live in that house, with his two kids, but how was Mary there now?

"You're in that same house?" I asked her again.
"Yes Fairooz that same house? What's wrong with you gal?"
"Oh nothing, I'll be there at eleven then," I put down the phone, went right to the kitchen to check on the food and thought, *I wonder what's happening? Mary won't stay at the same house with his wife? I bet she doesn't even know about this new wife?* Well, I knew a lot about Mary although she was away, as Sam, my son, was at university there and he was always in touch with Amir, Mary's son. So I knew that she had a job and was happily living with her two kids. I was also sure that she knew nothing of Omar's marriage.

At eleven I was there by her front door, waiting eagerly. We kissed and hugged jumping like kids. We never thought we would ever meet again. She pulled me by the hand, like a seven-year-old pulling her friend to show her, her new toy. I missed her coffee so much and before sitting on her red sofa in the living room, I looked at her and just as I started asking her if she was making some, she walked to the kitchen, *I know she read my eyes,* I thought to myself and just followed her. We sat at the same table and talked and she told me about her kids back in the States and how happy she was over there. That she went to this therapist, who helped her put her feet back on solid ground. I couldn't believe how strong this girl was! She went through so much in such a short time and came out on both feet! Then she started talking, with a worried expression all over her face:

"Fairooz, please don't think I'm going nuts again."
"I never thought you ever have! What is it?"
"Fairooz this whole place feels and smells different. Remember how when I was back here, I used to call you to come over and see…"

I cut her short. "Ya and I did see that black stain all over the walls, behind the cabinets, under the mattresses and everywhere?"

"Exactly well, I never thought I would see it again, come with me."

She took me to her living room again and she turned over the sofa bed and there it was all over again; I couldn't believe my eyes either black blotches covering the bottom of that sofa. She kept turning her whole living room over and she could see my surprised face and hear the shrieks I made every time she turned something, then we went up to her bedroom. We moved her cupboard and right there like I had seen it a million times before: those black blotches were back again; she then took me to the kids' rooms, I couldn't believe it, this stuff was all over the house! That witchcraft thing was back! I remembered how I used to ask her to put a cassette with some recitation from the Koran and this I thought, kept that witchcraft out of her house. She looked at me with that old doubting look in her eyes, I didn't like that look at all, it brought some horrible memories to my mind and at last she said:

"I tell you Fairooz, I feel something was going on while I was gone, these two past years, tell me please. Do you know anything?"

I wouldn't dare say a thing. I was not crazy and I didn't want to drive her crazy, I knew that she was here for one or two months and was going back home, so I just had to keep what I knew to myself and save my friend's sanity.

"Know what? Hey gal, don't you even start this," I answered with a smile on my face, trying to be funny, but it didn't work this time.

"Fairooz I tell you something real big and horrible is happening in this place, this country! I tell you there's a group of men who're involved in this whoring business, so many, I know. Fairooz you take care of yourself and be cautious. I mean take care of your husband. I don't want you to go through what I had been through, but I know for sure that Ali is part of that group; so please be careful. I even have a list with all those men's names. You just won't believe who else is on it!"

She's really losing her marbles now. Ali? No way, he is acting very strange these days, with terrible rages all the time, but no way. I never want to even think about that and I dismiss this whole discussion; I just delete it from my memory, I think, staring at her.

Suddenly I sit up straight on my sofa in Newcastle and realize how true her words were: all that rage had a reason, which I never suspected, but now I know that he put on those tactful madness acts, so he could leave to his mistress.

It's strange, how a small thing like a simple email, brings years and years of flashbacks! I honestly feel like I was lying down on a chaise longue, totally hypnotized, relating all those depressing past years and though I tried so hard to slip out of them, I really couldn't. However, when I accidentally find myself back in the present, those horrifying strenuous sessions completely cease. Now I feel so much pressure, so stressed out and my head can't take it any more, it hurts so bad, that I feel dizzy and once again I lie down and put my feet up on the cushions.

Sam's voice comes rushing into my ears, reminding me that he's graduating to boost me up and make me realize that I have after all, accomplished part of my task in life. The score is one down and five to go; I still have to reap the fruits of five more kids. I worked so hard to just sit back and reap. I'm so happy and glad too, that Sam's voice had brought me out of that miserable recollection.

Now when I think of Sam's graduation I feel so relieved. How can I go and attend his graduation? I start making arrangements to go to Florida. I can't believe I'm going to the US and I can't believe that I'll attend his graduation. *December nineteenth will be the best day of my life,* I tell myself.

Deema will also come over from Jeddah, to attend the graduation and complete her Interior Design degree in Irvine, California. So the plan is: go to Boston on the seventh of December, to get some references from Harvard and on the sixteenth go to Sam's; then on the eighteenth pick Deema from the airport. And then on the nineteenth, the happiest event of my life will take place: the graduation ceremony.

December the seventh at last comes and I again take the train to Heathrow to take the one o'clock flight to Boston. It takes six hours to get to Boston from London and after spending strenuous days, at Harvard Library, I finally go to Sam's. Two days later, Deema arrives; it was great seeing her again, I missed her so much.

Then the big day arrived. I felt like I had wings, flying above in the sky, I don't remember walking at all while moving from one spot to the other taking his pictures. My heart still beats when I remember that day. Then five days after his graduation, Sam asks me:

"Mama don't you want to go to Boston to see Tant Mary and maybe spend New Year's Eve with her? It's the last year of the 'nineties so go and enjoy it with her, before it is 2000."

I know what he's trying to do; he and his two cousins are trying to get rid of Deema and me, so they can have their privacy; so we go to Boston and stay at the Holiday Inn on Beacon Street. I then call Mary and forty-five minutes later I hear a knock at the door: Amir and Samira are there, to pick us up. I can't believe how they have grown. Samira is a beautiful young lady, nicely dressed in black pants and a gray coat down below her knees and has a colorful scarf and matching gloves on. Amir too, has grown into an extremely handsome young man. His baggy jeans are half hidden with his black cashmere long jacket and his neck is covered with an orange scarf and again matching black and orange gloves. We hug and kiss so happy to be united again and they take us to their place: one big family. Again Mary and I are there sitting at the kitchen table and talking forever, never stopping. Her kids and mine know how it is like when we get together.

We spend most of the time at her kids' town house. It is a nicely furnished three bedroom town house, which their dad had helped in furnishing and is still paying the rent. We talked about the ecstatic feeling we both have as our kids graduate. She had two down and two to go and I have one and the other is on her way and still more to go. On one of my visits Mary asks me:

"Fairooz, do you know that Omar is married?"

I try to get out of it this time, but she doesn't give me a chance to answer.

"Don't deny it now; Pat told me that he married as soon as I got back to St. Louis, in 1990. I told you then that I had this weird feeling, I also told you that there was a strange smell all around the house: it was her scent! Do you know that she lived in that same house and when I went away for a visit that year, he set her up in a furnished apartment, till I left?"

I think to myself, *she's got me and I have to admit,* so I nod.

"Fairooz I know why you didn't tell me then and I really appreciate it, I know that you thought I would lose my marbles, again."

"Listen Mary, I never thought you have in the first place. I think you're the wisest and bravest woman I know."

"Don't worry I got over that and I'm filing for a divorce now. I've been asking him for one since I've heard about his marriage, but this guy is so strange; I don't know what he really wants? Why doesn't he let me go?"

"Well. You know how men are: so weird. I got my divorce after begging for it for almost four months, but I'm so glad I have it."

"O.K. enough of that shit! Mind my language," she smiles at me.

"Don't worry; I have the same vocabulary, remember? No big deal!" We both laugh.

"Hey guess who I ran into, four months ago in St. Louis?" Again she has that teasing devilish smile.

"Who?" I can't wait.

"Guess."

"Come on tell me, you know I don't like to guess?" I reply with a look of unease.

"Oh yeah, but you certainly love having other people guess, right?"

"O.K. O.K. is it Sharon?"

"Sharon?"

"Oh! You don't know her. She's a friend of mine. We went to beauty school together, a very nice girl. O.K. Is it…" She can feel how stuck I am. "Listen, Mary, I really can't think. Tell me, who is it? Come on. Please, I promise I'll never let you guess again," she certainly succeeds in her game. She let me promise not to let her guess again. How can I say such a thing? But I promised and it's too late to change my mind now and think, *I just can't believe I've done so!*

"Promise," she insists.

"Yes…," and before I finish my sentence she jumps in, it seems that she too can't wait, she had to say it.

"Randy! You devil. He says you keep in touch."

"Randy?" I try to lie, but she knows me more than I know myself.

"Come on Fairooz, I know you too well. I can see that look on your face. Randy Smith, remember him? Rings a bell? Your friend from Roosevelt High?"

"Oh! Randy? Well, yes you're right we do keep in touch, through email. When I first moved to England I found this email from him. Can you believe that this guy was looking for me all this time? And he at last found my email address, through hotmail directory."

"Really?" She says, teasingly.

"Ya, I have to admit that he promised to come and see me, over here."

"You mean in Boston and?"

"Well, he's here…"

"O.K. you don't have to say another word, that's why you're always busy everyday since you've been here and that's why I don't get to see you before five everyday?"

"No that's not true I go to Harvard everyday to get some references for my work," and her look makes me admit right away: "well I did meet him a few times, but I still got work done."

"Got some work done my foot Fairooz," now she's laughing out loud. I feel so embarrassed. I feel like a teenager. Me? Falling in love? Never! But I guess it's true. I'm so glad that Mary is the first person to find out about Randy.

"It's funny Mary, but all those years I was married I never felt the way I do now."

"It's called looove kiddo," she says, with her devilish grin.

"Ya, I guess you're right. I'm so damn in love with this guy."

"So what's next, are we ever gonna hear the bells ringing?"

"Me? Are you crazy? Marry again? I never think of marriage again."

"Ya I know, I really believe you. You know Fairooz, they say, never say never. So tell me what are you going to do for New Year's Eve? Are you spending it with…?"

God! I can't believe how much she knows me, I think and then say: "cut it out Mary! No I'm not. I'm spending it with you and the kids. What are your plans?"

"We wanted to go to this nice place, but then they don't allow kids under eighteen and you know Jana is seventeen, so we can't go. So what if we all spend it here together, at home?" She asks me, with that begging look.

I forgot to mention that Jana and Karam are with her now, so it's really one big happy family. At last she has her kids with her and they're so happy. Omar told her that she could keep them when they came over for a short visit, five months ago. *Some day we'll be together,* I secretly sing to myself and I finally answer: "great idea! Let's ask the kids what they want to do." The kids love her idea too; so Amir, Samira and Deema immediately leave to buy some champagne, crackers and nuts; and we have a great time: dancing and jumping around; complete lunatics, like we never had a sad day in our lives.

Two days later Deema and I move to Irvine. Deema starts school and I get real serious with my thesis. However, the crash of the Egyptian plane and the death of JFK Jr. disrupted my work for about a week; and all I did was sit by the TV and watch the news.

Nine months passed by and I had a great time, all alone with Deema. We got to be more than a mother and daughter. Deema was at times, my best friend and I could talk to her about anything, as we sat for hours discussing a lot of things: what upset or made us happy, we even fought a lot over the silliest things and to make up, we end up going to the movies: our favorite pass time.

September nineteenth 1999 was Deema's graduation; and again I go around the house singing, *I'm flying without wings.* It's a lovely day in Irvine and the sunshine fills my heart and lungs with warmth, love and extreme elation, *another victory,* I delightfully smile to myself and think over and over again, *the counting goes on: two down and four to go!*

A Taste of Freedom

Stepping out of my car I notice the beauty that surrounds me! Where ever I look I discover more and more of nature's allure enhanced by the morning dew. Never had I driven through as wide a variety of trees and flowers as these, such green grass: *green, green grass of home,* I sing to myself and think, *where is Whitman to see it all?* Enormous areas of nature adorned, with endless splendor, which mirrors a heaven on earth. Can this be it? Is this it? Heaven at last! I always wonder: is there really a heaven or even a God? *Dangerous thoughts, but stop don't even think, just believe, there's no room for doubt,* I remind myself.

The streets are so clean and soothing to the heart. Oh the heart! That tiny, delicate and essential part of my body, that was so bruised, cut and wounded down to every vein of its bloody soft tissues; all the way across its arteries, to each lit-road of its generous paths. A real cruel exertion was performed to that poor heart. Oh how I awfully miss my children and my seventy-eight-year-old dad. *Oh please God keep him alive and healthy till I see him again,* I feel a painful pinch in my heart. I may never see him again.

Throughout my life I was so sensitive. My tearful eyes remind me, "*remember Fairooz, since you were a kid you never asked your dad for anything. You just cried and asked him to return from his trip as soon as possible.*" Then with a quick wink they go on, "*and remember how you always fell sick with fever, when he was away and didn't put anything in your mouth; and as soon as he was back, you were back to your lively devilish self!*" Strange life this is, no concern for others: sensitive or not, who cares? Throughout my life I was and still am so careful as to hurt nobody, so no one would hurt me. What else could I do? No one can evade fate. Man eats man! No mercy, I'm all alone in a different place. No family, no children, no friends, abandoned and deprived of my own country; me, of all the people and all that love I have for my country.

Oh how I miss the sensual Red Sea, as I see myself right now walking along its coast; touching and tasting its water, smelling the fish from the bottom, and feeling the wind blowing and piercing tiny holes through my slim body, regenerating every cell in it. There is nothing like diving in that sea: an absolutely gorgeous experience! I can almost observe the corals, weeds and the multi-colored fish down there; then I imagine myself fishing all day long. Probably that's how I learned to be so patient: fishing for endless hours. The last thing I ever thought of was leaving all this behind. I adore and worship the soil I step on back home, but wasn't that what fate wanted? I didn't want that, it did! I always advised people against abandoning their own country; and look at me now, as tears well in my eyes.

I get in the car again after getting some groceries for Mama and head back home. As soon as I get there I go around to the back yard, set the grocery bags on the floor and move around on this November morning. I touch the apple and pear trees, I then empty one of the bags into the others and pick some strawberries and raspberries and place them in it. I walk by the flowerpots and smell the different flowers and roses; and I intentionally hit them with a swaying movement of my body, to acknowledge my presence. I then take off my shoes and step bare-footed on the icy grass, which is like a wall to wall carpeted-floor. Walking on that freezing grass cooled my sad nostalgic heart. I then put my shoes on again and move right to the vegetables to check on them. *Oh! Maybe I can eat green beans, lettuce and tomatoes next week, right out of my garden,* I think. "Oh you're all so beautiful and great," I then say out loud. I love talking to my plants. I make sure I touch and speak to them whenever I'm out here and I feel that they enjoy that too. If my neighbors ever notice me they'll probably think I lost it, but I don't care, I still do it anyway. I always wanted to grow fruits and vegetables in my garden, but I was never granted that wish, because it never was my garden to begin with: it was always Ali's. Throughout my life I never asked for much, I'm the type of person who is satisfied with the simplest things in life, like a touch of tenderness implying, *I love you,* or even a flower, just any implication of caring is all I ever wanted. How simple is life?

However, nature provides me with my utmost needs and all my senses come to life when I'm close to it. I never let anything pass by without acknowledgement: a bird chirruping on a tree, kissing and rubbing against its lover; a cat running up a wall, chasing his next door gorgeous Persian cat; a dog sniffing around the pavement, searching for the scent of his mate; pigeons getting so close to me, ten maybe fifteen of them, never scared; that is how I certainly wish people were: loving, cuddly, honest and fearless of one another. Is that a possible dream? Yes, it's only a dream, and dreams don't always come true. If they did, what else will we live up to, dream or fantasize about? Or even imagine?

I leave all this beauty and go into the kitchen's back door into the living room, where Mama is sitting on my favorite green sofa bed and forever glued to the TV set. When she visits me I let her choose her favorite spot. She smiles at me as I walk towards her and bend down giving her a kiss on both cheeks. The last time she visited me was in 1998, now she's once again visiting me in the same flat in Newcastle.

Mama is seventy-seven now, still beautiful with short gray hair tucked under one of those netted-bonnets. She is here for four weeks and I want to be with her all the time. She doesn't like to feel left out: involves me in everything she does and wants to be involved in whatever I do.

The US Presidential Nomination is taking place live on *CNN* and Mama is watching it with extreme enthusiasm. Mind you she doesn't speak English, yet she can follow any English program and just asks a few questions every now and then, *just a few!* Mean me talking to myself.

"Fairooz I'm so glad you're here, tell me what's happening over here?"

Being out in the garden, I really don't understand what Mama is talking about. "What is it Mama?" I ask knowing that she certainly realizes that I wasn't following the news for at least the past two hours, but she still asks!

"Well I was watching the news where they had Bush's picture on the screen and his supporters were so thrilled and then suddenly, the whole scene changed and all the faces looked puzzled and grim. What's wrong?"

Of course I don't have a clue about what's happening, so I sit next to her and try to concentrate and then I grasp what's going on and say: "aha! You're so right Mama. They announced that Bush has won the presidency and Al Gore congratulated him, but then they found out that there was some discrepancy in the ballots in Florida and they're recounting the votes again and that's why the Bush campaign looks so excited!"

"Ya and look at the faces of Al Gore's supporters, they're so happy and anxious at the same time; some are screaming with joy, some are shocked with excitement and some are crying and praying that he wins."

"So, who are you supporting Mama?"

"I don't know. You know it really doesn't matter who wins, as long as they are just."

"So why bother with all the details?"

"Well. I just need to know who wins. You know America is the greatest power now and the outcome of its elections affects the whole world! How about you Fairooz, whom are you backing up?"

I look at Mama with amazement! *No education?* And I laugh to myself. "Well, I actually want Al Gore to win. He's more experienced, as he was in the Clinton's administration for eight years."

"Ya you're right. I have to admit that, that administration was one of the best the US ever had!"

Now I stare at Mama and can feel my mouth falling to the floor, *Rasputin's lips,* again come to my mind. What would have happened if she ever finished her education? Too bad she never got the chance to do so! I secretly smile as I think, *why did Baba prevent her from getting a better education? Maybe he was right! No I don't really mean that; things would have been different if Mama, at least got a university degree: maybe she really would have been the first woman minister in my country!* She does after all have that hot Iranian blood in her!

Each of Jaddah's offspring takes something after her. Some look like her, some take her taste in food, others have her hot temper running in their genes and certainly we all have her extremely tender heart. *Oh, Jaddah, how I miss you so; life is never the same without you,* I keep thinking of Jaddah's house, the one she died in, so simply furnished as usual, to fit her simple needs in life. All she ever wanted was to be loved and needed. As long as her loved ones were around her, she nurtured all her essential needs and emotional fulfillment. Oh! Let's not forget God! I can literary feel His presence right there, sitting next to her on her colorful mattress and all I remember is her praying: in her room, in the living room and even in the garden, everywhere.

Everything about Jaddah is always clear in my mind. Her house, especially her living room, which had a few mattresses on the floor, lined across the rectangular room; hard cushions ran all the way across the back of those mattresses, to support my back leaning on the wall. Softer hand-embroidered cushions, topped with a small beige lace divide each couple of mattresses, against which I could rest my elbow. An old-fashioned radio in one of the corners, was sitting comfortably on a small antique brown table; small antique hand-made and engraved colorful square tables, were placed in front of those mattresses, with a plastic ashtray on a tiny white laced cloth on each one of them. Mind you, she never touched a cigarette, but she loved people and made sure that she provided all their needs.

Pictures of her children, grandchildren and even her great-grandchildren covered every inch of the walls. A Citizen clock squeezed itself right in between those memorable pictures. Funny enough, but her clock was set in Arabic timing. Don't ask what that is? I never understood it. The brown cabinet leaning on the wall, had so many boxes and empty baby food jars. She fancied collecting empty boxes and bottles and my worst nightmare was asking her:

"Jaddah, where can I find a small spoon?"

"Open the cabinet there," she would point to the brown cabinet, on the left hand side of the living room, "and you'll find a white box, open it and there are the spoons," was usually her simple answer.

You would think it was that simple, but it never was. I would open the white box to find a smaller box within, and after opening five boxes I would find the spoon; all this trouble for a spoon! *Next time I'll just bring my own utensils' drawer along with me,* I would think smiling.

My yearning to feel Jaddah's presence once again takes me to her house. I see her, always sitting in that living room until it is time to sleep. Around seven in the morning, she gets up and goes to her bedroom, where a double bed faces the window overlooking a beautiful garden. The chest, in the center of the room, has all her beautiful memories. The handkerchief she embroidered as a seven-year-old girl, pictures of her six children and her twenty-six grandchildren. She wouldn't dare bring her pictures out when I was around. *That thief! That little devil!* That's me of course, as I could feel her thinking; but I have to admit I am a photo thief: I look around me and make sure that no one sees me and in goes a picture at a time, into my pockets, *oh how I love pictures,* I smile to myself.

There are also two side tables on both sides of the bed. One has her favorite son's picture: Uncle Khaleel; and the other has an alarm, which is always set to five o'clock so she can get up to pray before sunrise. Framed pictures and portraits are all over her walls, in this room too. Across the hall is the guest-room, where she has some nicely arranged sofas and two light brown tables, topped with all sorts of antiques. A beautifully multi-colorful printed teapot, *her mom left her some thirty years ago,* my eyes say as I imagine staring at it, surrounded by four tea glasses are placed on one of the tables. I usually call this type of glasses belly dancers, as they have a waist right in the middle and remind me of a belly dancer, who has a scarf wrapped around her hips, to show the precise movements. The other table has a box full of what is supposed to be cigarettes, the kind people smoked fifty years ago. Actually, the box is divided into two sections. One has pieces of square white paper and the other has what I thought to be brown chopped straw.

"So how do people smoke this? You say they're cigarettes?" *I truly feel myself there now!*

"Yes, and that's how people do it," Jaddah's voice travels through the tunnel of a contented serene past, as she starts to demonstrate.

Her thin bony hands reach out and her skinny almost flesh-free fingers pick up a piece of the square paper and a pinch of the brown chopped straw.

"This is the way it's done: put some of this tobacco on one of these papers and wrap it really fine," she eagerly shows me. *I suddenly move forward trying to reach her and touch the tobacco through that tunnel, forgetting that she is gone!*

So that's what this chopped straw is called, I think and while poor Jaddah is putting a lot of effort and energy to illustrate the accurate method, my mind just cannot stay concentrated, it has to wonder.

"Then lick the end of it to have it, stick and off go the matches," she still explains.

Mind you, she always has them right there, waiting for her chimney guests. A wooden ashtray engraved with the tinniest flowers one could ever see, lies next to that box. What delicate tiny fingers could have done such craft? The cigarette box, matches and ashtray are all spread over a small silver tray, which has Turkish engravings as well. The edges of that tray also have tiny prints and no handles on its sides; this tray is the most beautiful piece on that table. To finalize the exquisiteness of this exhibition, two crystal chandeliers hang from the ceiling; however, dear old Jaddah never liked sitting on those fancy sofas in that guest-room; she always had her bottom glued to the floor in her living room.

I could never forget that warm-smelling house! Jaddah was a woman who was so full of love and could certainly shower the whole world with it. She had helpful tender hands which could extend to touch every misfortunate human being on this earth and tears that could warm each miserable soul. *Oh Jaddah! Save all that love, kindness, touch and tears. Extend your arms and touch me, be with me and soothe my aches. Please leave everyone else and come to me or else let me come to you. I am your dearest most annoying granddaughter. I know you can see me and I am sure that you can feel with me. No one else can. Oh how I miss you,* I almost speak out loud as tears and more tears run down my cheeks. I get into these gloomy moods whenever I think of her. I get up quickly, so Mama doesn't notice my tears and walk to the kitchen; and with a tissue I wipe my eyes, blow my nose and clear my throat.

Though Jaddah passed away more than twenty-two years ago, I could still feel her presence, hear her old stories, proverbs, advice and even her jokes, riddles, poetry; and of course, lots of history. Suddenly I feel her pinches, *Ouch!* If they ever had a competition in the Olympics for the best pincher, she would have certainly won the golden medal.

No one in the whole family could joke and tease her as much as I did and surprisingly enough she loved it. One thing that I can never forget about Jaddah was her lethal bite, though she has lost her teeth more than thirty years ago, her tough as steel gums were strengthened by nature! I could never forget this incident when I was about twelve, and one day Jaddah threatened to bite me if I didn't stop teasing her. "Oh come on Jaddah, how can you bite me? No teeth!" I asked teasing and making funny faces and dancing in a way that would drive the coolest person crazy, so imagine what it had done to my hot-blooded Iranian grandmother? So cunning old Jaddah just let it go, pretending not to care. Five minutes later, she was all over me, grabbed me with her two arms, imprisoned me between her thighs, got a hold of my little arm and bit right through to the tiny bones. *Remember no teeth, just gums!* Where did she suddenly get all this energy was my weirdest mystery? *They certainly manufactured great gums then!*

"God Jaddah look at what you did: you cut right through my skin with your gums only! I'm so glad you have no teeth, *Oh Granma what sharp gums you have?* Still teasing and making faces while thinking of Red Riding Hood's grandmother.

Standing in the kitchen and looking out of the window I reminisce about Jaddah's beauty at eighty. It was hard to tell what color her naturally eye-lined eyes were: gray, green, blue, orange or a mix of all; she had an oval face that was distinguished by her long sharp nose; and a mouth, though toothless, was artistically drawn with a pinkish tint color. Her silver gray hair, which used to be black as coal, was always combed in two braids and smoothed down with loads of coconut oil. My nose can't help it and I can feel it say: *"Jaddah's scent! I can smell her hair and her Vicks-rubbed tummy!"*

Oh how I loved combing that silvery soft long hair, *I was twelve,* I think. "Jaddah let me comb your hair," I would plea.

Comb my hair? You must be kidding, those few strands of hair? Touched by those naughty hands of yours? Oh never, submit my fragile old-aged scalp to your fingers! Jaddah would think to herself and would never dare speak such thoughts out and at last spoke, in a very diplomatic tone:

"Oh no my dear I don't want to trouble you."

However, pressured under such a horrible constant nagging, squeakily and annoying voice, she gave in and shut me up, handing me the comb. How I adored that old lady, but I still had to tease her so much. I didn't know why I could get away with so much when I was with her. I always felt that I controlled and held the whole universe, when she was around me; even now that she is dead she still visits me every now and then, to recharge my batteries. She had always been the strongest persistent person on this earth and the fact that she walked out on my grandfather in those *forbidden* days, gave me the incentive to walk out too and pursue my dream, which is to speak out loud and let others hear my voice as I cry in the name of every woman in my country, who just wants to be treated as an equal human being and gain her entitled rights. Now, tears gather in my eyes again as I remember the oppression we women face on daily basis at home.

I walk back to the living room and sit next to Mama. I keep looking at her, glued to that sofa; it looks as though Jaddah has spat her out. She has the shape of her eyes, but they are honey-brown, not multi-colored; her lips are so thin and hardly seen, except when she is mad and screaming, then they would suddenly blow up. No plastic surgery needed! I guess because Jaddah never beat me up, I always felt closer to her than to Mama, who did nothing but thrash me. I remember and sneakily smile at what my one best wish and prayer as a kid was: *please God I want to get older than Mama to beat and punish her in her room*, but unfortunately I was never granted that wish: the older I get the older she got as well!

Now I certainly can't upset her, as she flew all the way from home, crossing waters and so many miles for a second time to be with me. She sacrificed so much since she had been divorced and now more sacrifices and that kills me. How could I ever pay her back? I just have to be patient, nice and loving; just look at me now: I sacrifice watching my favorite programs on TV, so that she could watch all her Arabic and Western movies; now I think that this is one way of repaying her!

"Fairooz, why aren't you answering me? Say something," Mama says.

Her voice makes me jump, apparently she had been talking to me, but I wasn't there!

"This movie reminds me of you when you were little. Remember how you were Daddy's Girl?"

"Were? Sorry, but I still am," I smile saying this.

"Well, Fatin (an Egyptian actress) here, is her daddy's girl too. Did I ever tell you that story, you were around eight?"

I just smile and I don't say that I know exactly what she's about to say; she told me that story a hundred times before and she always starts with that introduction; paying no attention to my smile, she goes on:

"You were always Baba's Girl and your sister Samar was my girl."

Were? This time I only think, as she smiles, knowing that she is teasing me!

"So one day your dad came up to me and said:

'Listen Laila, why don't we try something? You take Fairooz to be your girl today, and I'll take Samar and let's see what happens.'

I just nodded, I loved the idea!" She smiles, still teasing!

"So your dad called you and said:

'Come here girls your mom and I want to try something. Fairooz from now on you're Mama's little girl and Samar you're mine.'

'What? Mama's what? Forget it! NEVER,' was your immediate response. You could never keep quiet and always spoke your mind!

'Oh come on just try to be nice,' your dad tells you, as he pats and kisses you on the head.

'Me Mama's Girl, that's the craziest idea I ever heard of.'

After all that caressing and kissing, you were still so stubborn; but then you gave in, as he sympathetically looked at you; kids then were so obedient and no matter how violent they got, they always gave in at the end. Honestly, when I think of it now," Mama laughs, "I think we were very mean because we used you as guinea pigs under experimentation, or even wooden chess pieces and moved you according to our wishes. Anyway, you were the two most miserable unhappy sad girls on earth; and you spent the whole day, in two separate corners on the huge living room floor in our big house, overlooking The Mediterranean.

'Samar come sit by Baba,' he pleaded and you know how your sister is, not as out spoken as you so she just shrugged her shoulders. Then I told you: 'Fairooz love, come by Mama.'

'I'm happy right where I am,' you answered me; 'I would rather sit on this cold dry floor freeze to death and die of starvation than become your girl!' You muttered this last sentence but I could still hear you. Your face was full of rage! I could see how red it was. It was one of the coldest days in Alexandria.

'Couldn't they have chosen a warmer day to play that stupid game of theirs?' you kept on mumbling. I was close enough to hear you again." Mama looks at me and smiles. "Then around eight in the evening, we decided that it was enough and we had to release you from this concentration camp, you were our victims for the longest time!

'O.K. kids I guess you aren't happy at all and neither are we,' your dad at last said.

'Happy? Oh God! And you want me to be good and calm?' you said as you jumped with joy and as you ran toward him; and I could hear Samar at last say:

'Oh they came to quite an interesting conclusion,' and we both laughed out loud," Mama can't stop laughing.

I was laughing too, but wondering why they had to play this game? Hitler could have been more merciful! At least he didn't watch two small girls being tortured to death! Did they really enjoy it? How mean of me to think of the two most loving people as Hitler, but that's how I really felt at that moment. Suddenly we are both so quiet, and again, watching the Arabic movie. I don't know how Mama missed a few minutes of it? Usually when Fatin's acting, she doesn't wink or budge.

Watching women driving in that movie, reminds me that at last I have my own car! I never owned one or actually driven one back home and this thought takes me back home to the burgundy Mercedes. I remember when Ali bought it, he said that it was for me, but it never was under my name. I always had to sit in the back seat, while Romeo, the Phillippino, driver drove to where ever I wanted to go. He was such a nice and loyal driver. I could really feel how he loved me and my children! But oh how at times I wished I could push him out of the car and get behind those wheels and go, but then the poor soul had nothing to do with all this; he didn't set any restraining rules for me or the other women in my country.

Never did I own anything, nothing. I didn't own the house I spent over twenty years in, my own freedom and certainly not my own body! And now I'm free. Oh! The Beetles, *my teen's first love,* come to mind and I sing to myself, *Free as a bird*. I suddenly feel so depressed; I just need to get some fresh air, so I tell Mama that I need to go out for a while and immediately leave.

Driving along the streets, I look at the people around me; everywhere I look people are talking, laughing, running, skating, touching and kissing. Real life, I certainly don't see all this life on the streets of Jeddah, all I see there is the great contrast between black and white: men in white *Thoabs;* and women always in black *Abayas*. I don't like putting the *Abaya* on. Traditions and customs strangle me to death, more than two clutched hands squeezing my throat; and although I got used to wearing it, I still don't like it. How can I? Looking like a living Mummy, dressed up in black. I remember the cultural shock my three sisters and I had, when we came back to live in such a closed society. We were raised in the fresh open and healthy environment of Alexandria, Egypt. Oh

Alex! Where my heart really belongs, but fate again, threw us right into that stale darkened and sickly dungeon. Luckily I stop at the traffic light and remember our reactions to wearing that horrible black tent.

The battle took place on that first day in summer of 1967 in Jeddah. Sue my eldest sister and I fiercely reject putting the *Abaya* on. I just couldn't understand: how they expected us to wear it, when we were used to wearing shorts and swimming suits? Samar stood by, awaiting the result of such raging anger and thought, *we left Alexandria, because of the Arab-Israeli war, though this war right here, taking place between Mama and my sisters is certainly worse!* Sunny, my youngest sister had nothing to worry about; at nine she didn't have to wear one and didn't even bother to think about it. At the end of so many days of quarreling and fighting, we unwillingly, gave in; we couldn't swim against the tide! We knew that everyone around us was thinking: *they're a couple of revolutionary girls, who are here to change and disturb the tranquility of our society.*

However, such false appearance and clothing never affected my thoughts or actions. I was never part of the flock. Maybe it was my parents' upbringing, or my school in Alexandria, but everyone around me always thought that I was the one who would cause a revolutionary change in my country when it comes to women's rights. I remember when Mary came back on her last visit to Jeddah, in 1990 during the Gulf War; she thought I was one of those women, who drove down the streets of Riyadh and told me then:

"You know Fairooz when I heard on the news about women driving over here in Saudi, I told my mom I'm sure Fairooz was one of those women, I really did."

"Wish I were, but I was in a different city, remember that it was in Riyadh and no one planned it with us back here," I disappointedly told her.

I park the car and walk down the streets of Newcastle. I can never stop taking long breaths of freedom into my lungs. No way am I going back there, *fresh air step right through and crush those lungs and squeeze them as hard as you can, fill them with freedom and don't let go, until they squeal and snap,* I thought to myself. That strange weather of Newcastle: one minute it is sunshine and suddenly it pours wet. Ever seen sunshine and snow at the same time? That is how strange the weather is around here!

I walk down Northumberia Street, analyzing with my hazel eyes everything around me. I love that cobblestone street, beautifully lined like a mosaic. I would love to skip over those tiles, just like Jack Nicholson in *As Good As It Gets*, but can't because it certainly wouldn't be British! It's a wide street with shops along both sides; people are walking everywhere, while some are sitting on the benches watching others walk by. The weather is getting warm. I take off my gray raincoat and hold it in my hand. My sleeveless black v-necked shirt reveals my olive skin. I have a pair of light brown Diesel jeans and a pair of brown sneakers. I always have my brown and silver-beaded Bedouin necklace on, which I had from my American sister-in-law, Betty. I want to let everyone know where I'm from, I feel like crying out loud but I just yell inside of me: *hey, look at me, I'm from Arabia*. I can see heads turn twice, to take a better look at me and that makes me feel great and I remember my sister Sue, one of the saddest women back home. She is highly educated, intelligent, elegant and beautiful. I often think of how different her life would have been if we stayed in Egypt. What a pity? I always looked up to her advice and tried to dress and let heads turn, as I walk down the street, like her. I remember how at around thirteen, she called me and asked me to lift up my skirt to check my legs and finally approved of them: *nice legs!* She thought. Since that day all I ever do is stand in front of the mirror and look at those legs and talk to myself and ask: *mirror, mirror on the wall, who has the prettiest legs of them all? You my dear*, answers the smart mirror!

I then see a man on the sidewalk, alternatively playing two instruments; at times he is holding his guitar with both hands, having it leaning on his knee and at others he is playing the harmonica. His blue jeans had a hole right above the knees and the shirt he had on, did not in any way match; *I remember Karen's careful and critical eyes*. A homeless, is there a difference really between the two of us? We are both homeless. I get a bit closer and I realize that his nose is hidden in his harmonica. His blue eyes are sometimes on his guitar and sometimes at by passers. There is a sad story in those eyes of his and I can't pin point the reason for such sadness, but it hits me right in the heart. I like to encourage those musicians on the road, so I open my purse and bring out some change. With tears in my eyes and a broken heart I want to touch him, give him a hug and say, "*I'm sorry. I really feel for you,*" but I cannot and I just think, *people have to hide so much of their feelings and emotions; else they will be viewed as being insane;* and I sadly smile to myself. Then I carefully and lovingly bend down and slowly place the change in his hat and he nods at my thoughtful gesture. Did he understand those eyes of mine? Maybe he sensed that I was homeless, too?

I stop at Starbucks for a quick coffee. Sitting by the window and watching that cobblestone street, takes me back to my childhood and school days in Alexandria. I remember walking down the clean streets by the sea, beautiful beaches and fresh air. Everyone is dressed in colorful clothes, reflecting the vivid colors of life down at the bottom of the sea. Life: poor or rich everyone is having a wonderful time; there goes a couple, she might be his wife, fiancée, lover or just a friend holding each others hands; his other hand is in a bag of peanuts a minute and trying to feed her the next. Probably they don't have lots of money, but they certainly have loads of happiness. There passes a man pushing a wooden cart; *smell those delicious peanuts and pumpkinseeds?* How I love walking down that coast and smelling the scent of that sea. The wind blows me off and I feel it through every part of my body: *exhale, inhale!* Walking in zigzag lines along that coast, I would tease everyone on the street: old, young, boy or girl; I couldn't walk without bugging others. I was maybe ten then, when a carriage pulled by a horse passed by and I suddenly jumped on and said:

"Sameeha, let's get on."

"How much is it?" My best friend Sameeha asked.

"One pound, Mademoiselle," answered the coachman, in such a charming Egyptian dialect.

"What?" I asked, "forty-five piasters are more than enough."

"Sorry Mademoiselle," he disagreeably answered, constantly shaking his head.

Sorry, my foot, we both thought; this happened all the time: we talked, thought and planed together, like we were identical twins.

Oh! I wish I weren't here, thought our friend Nelly, embarrassed at what was happening.

"Fairooz, Sameeha please let's just go," whispered Jeehan, our timid friend, who always wore her long light brown hair in two braids.

In one second we were on, comfortably seated and settled. The man tried to ask us down nicely, but we didn't move. We pretended to be talking and laughing, not listening to a word he was saying; and we only smiled when he stopped talking; then Nelly and Jeehan hopped on, too. The man was mad at the beginning, but he loved our naughty behavior: *naughty smart girls, I wish my passive daughter has half that character,* he was thinking.

"O.K. forty-five piasters," he at last agreed; like he had a choice.

We went on singing, clapping and dancing. Where had all this gone? I got married so young and left my childhood behind. It is a sad story, but there is no room for that now. Oh Alexandria! That was where I spent the best days of my life. It is strange, but whenever I settle in a city and love it, it happens to be by a sea! Then I remember one of those cold winter days in 1966. I can actually see that long, dark, gloomy corridor of my English school the *E.G.C. El-Naser Girl's College,* so huge; I had been to different schools in different places, but I had never seen a school as great as this. Immense playgrounds, tennis courts, a volleyball court, a handball court, a basketball court, field hockey ground, a swimming pool, and the gym where I performed some acrobatic stunts. In that gym and *at the age of ten,* Nelly and I both received two cups for the best students in athletics, during our grade-school years.

Sipping my coffee and watching people pass by, my imagination still travels in time and I think, *how I wish I can, one day, go back there and look for Nelly, maybe she has grown a bit taller.* She was so petite with straight short brown hair that covered the sides of her slim face and her brown eyes were also half hidden by her bangs. I remember that wonderful theatre, where we sat on the balcony, listening to the most boring music. Imagine eight-year-old kids sitting and listening to concerts: Beethoven, Mozart, Tchaikovsky, Brahms, Chopin, Strauss and many more, why! And when we sometimes asked why, the answer was: it is the best way to acquire a delicate taste for elite music! Elite what? What about Elvis, the Beetles, the Rolling Stones and the Monkeys? Doesn't this type of music fit the British school standards? And now, I love listening to classical music. I also remember the plays we performed on that stage. Where was Spielberg then to see such great productions?

That theatre, reminds me of one of my major childish fights with Nelly. We were both performing in *Snow White;* then I went home in tears and told my dad: "I don't want to be in that play. I don't want to be with Nelly." The next day Baba rushed to Mrs. Khaleefah, the headmistress, *another one of those really scary British teachers,* and next thing I knew was, they created a new role for me, all of my own: a salesman; nothing to do with Nelly. I wore colorful matching pants and a shirt, a hat and a well-sewn shoe; I held a flat rectangular box, with a strap around my neck and walked around saying: "ribbons, combs, laces. Who'll buy? Who'll buy?" Oh I can see those black and white pictures right now in front of me, full of color. I was a handsome salesman with a moustache and a goatee, a little more than handsome, actually one would say: *pretty!* Well, anyhow there must have been something about my dad that made them invent a new role just for me; was it his charm?

I finished my coffee just in time to bring me back to the present and walked back on the street again and took a quick look at the homeless man: still sitting there! I remember how I always wanted to learn how to play the guitar and become a singer in a band with my friends: Sameeha, Nelly and Maha; and how Mrs. Butch, a typically chubby and harsh British teacher, scolded us every time she saw us practice in the corridors and how she sent us straight to detention. I remember how she looked, as if I'm looking at her picture right now!

Her white hair was up in a bun and her nose was as sharp as a blade; with lips that curled up whenever she was crossed, which was forever. Her blue eyes scared the bravest ghost stiff; and as students we feared nothing more, except seeing a living jinni; and when she walked, her steps seemed to crack the tiles. You could hear the poor tiles screaming: *HELP!* Shattering under her steps and the whole school trembled at her sight. She was a British male soldier in a woman's attire!

Still living in my school days', I also remember our French teacher, Mrs. Natalie, who didn't stay to finish her one-year contract, because of me! She often kneeled on her knees and had her palms clutched together pleading, tears in her clear blue eyes, asking me to be good! But of course that word didn't exist in my dictionary and before the bell rang Sameeha and I were out of the window, right into the swimming pool, as we always had our swimming suits on. It took us two minutes to get into the water and our excuse was that we needed the practice, because we were on the National Swimming Team: both of us always competed in races, diving and water ballet. How mean of me when I come to think of it now; I could never forgive myself for what I had done to Mrs. Natalie.

Memories, memories and more memories, *those were the days my friend. We thought they'd never end; and sing and dance forever and today!* Dreams! Dreams! Dreams! One can only dream. The least anyone could do. I remember how, when I was only eight, I led my younger brother and two sisters, while singing the most famous songs. I was the conductor and the belly dancer of the family and I remember all the beatings I used to get from my mother, when I used to say: *"I want to be a belly dancer."* Oh all those dreams gone down the drain and I never got to be a singer in a band, or a dancer or even learned how to play the guitar; but it is never too late: next thing on my agenda is to look for a guitar instructor!

Such nice weather, a rare thing to have here, in Newcastle, the sun is shinning and no rain or windy gusts. It is ten in the morning and Karen will meet me at twelve for a quick bite. So much time on hand, and nothing to do. I just walk, try to jump and hum the most beautiful tunes from back home. I'm already homesick? It's only been six months since I've last been there. One does miss home, family and friends, but no that is hopefully a one way ticket, I can go back for visits only. Ever heard of a run-away wife; a slave yes, but never a wife, but then what is the difference? Both are oppressed, owned and robbed of the most valuable thing they can have: freedom. At least slavery was abolished way back and people were set free; maybe someday women back home will be too!

Oh no is this Mary? I can't believe my eyes, can't be! I stare straight ahead rub my eyes off like a kid, to make sure I that I'm not dreaming, then I yell her name out as I run towards her: "Mary?"

"Fairooz, my God!"

We kiss and hug jumping up and down like two crazy people!

"What are you doing here?" I ask.

"I'm on a tour to England and was told that this is a beautiful place to visit. You know what? When I thought of taking this tour, I forgot which city you were in and guess what?"

"What?"

"Well smart me! Can you believe that I lost your address and even your email? I had a virus in my computer and lost everything including your address!"

"It's O.K., don't worry, it's my mistake too. I should have emailed you when I didn't hear from you for so long, but I had been so busy with my work, I'm really sorry."

"Oh I can't believe it: fate surely has its own games to play."

"So what are you up to now?"

"Oh tomorrow we're heading to Glasgow for a night and then we'll go to Ireland for another two days."

"Ireland? Oh I forgot your grandfather is Irish."

"Ya I always wanted to visit it."

"Oh Mary I can't believe my eyes, you're really here? Come on let's have a drink. Where's the rest of your group?"

"All over this place, we said we'll meet at twelve in front of Dixons."

"Great, we have a lot of time then. I'm meeting my friend at twelve; I hope you get the chance to meet her some time, she's a lovely English girl."

We walk down Northumbria Street, holding each other's hands; just like kids; *is it a dream?* Passing KFC, we turn left into Ridley Place and there is Elula my favorite café; right across the street is Dawson Travel Agency, where I usually get my travel bookings. We walk through the store, on our way down the stairs, to where the café is; souvenirs are on display all over the first floor. Everything is fascinating and the scented candles give an alluring exotic feeling to all the hand-made Kenyan clay statues and brass ornaments.

We go down the metal spiral stairs, where dark red carpeting, with black v-shaped patterns, covers the steps. Bells lined on a string, are hanging down from the banisters: tiny bells and on other strings some larger ones. Stuffed multi-colored birds are attached together in one line and hang from the first step down. A small zebra carpet is thrown on the top of those stairs. Small bells and candlesticks are placed on the top of the stairs. Walking down I cannot, but notice every little detail of that exotically decorated setting: absolutely breath-taking!

"It's so cozy Fairooz!"

"I thought you would like it," I say, still observing, as if it's the first time I see it all! Two florescent lights, hidden in the white ceiling, give a gentle glow to the café down there. Seven oak round tables, surrounded by three stools each are set close to the built in benches and two sugar bowls are placed on each table: brown and white. The built-in benches are a mixture of red and brown brick and small printed carpets, cover their side, all the way down to the bottom. The walls are covered with brown floorboards at a corner and white bricks at the other. African drawing canvas covers each spot on those walls and different themes are portrayed on those canvas: women in their Kenyan clothes dancing, courageous men holding spears and hunting, children standing by the men and looking at their spears. I love that place; it's so warm.

Oh Kenya! I remember my trip to the most wonderful romantic place on earth, so close to nature! As we walk towards the counter, I look at Mary's eyes and can see how excited she is. I knew she was going to like this place. I walk up to the counter, to order two cappuccinos. "Hi! Can I have two cappuccinos please," I think of what Joe always told me: "*why do you say can I and please? It's either can I or please.*" Waiting for the coffee I remember how slim Mary was; she had put on some weight around the tummy, sides and buttocks; not much, maybe just six pounds, but knowing Mary, she'll starve herself to death, to get rid of those extra pounds.

"Three eighty please," the girl says, as she hands me the two cups and I look for the exact change and hand it to her.

I walk back to Mary, who's still searching the place with her baffled eyes. "Well, Mary. Where do you want to sit?" There are three empty tables. One on the right, one in the center and the third is in the corner.

"How about this table?" Mary asks, pointing to the one in the corner.

She hadn't changed a bit, I think; I knew she was going to choose that table. We had been friends for such a long time and knew what we were thinking most of the time. Mary's red hair is cut short now and she is still as pretty as ever; she has a pair of gray Guess jeans on, a black top and a white sweater is tied around her waist.

A Taste of Freedom

"So, how's life treating you? How's St. Louis? You know I hadn't been there since '72," I say that and can't stop zooming on every little aspect in that place. I'm talking to Mary, while gazing around me. I look at the wall, where an African engraved clay vase, with different engravings, portrays such a lovely part of the world; and the floor, down there, is covered with the same dark red carpet that divided each single step.

"Oh same ol' place, nothin' changed, good ol' St. Louy!" She answers. "Tell me Fairooz, how's your PhD coming along?"

"Well it's getting there, such hard work."

"So tell me, what's your PhD on?"

"John Updike's Rabbit series."

"Updike? Last time I saw you were writing your MA on Faulkner, now Updike? Boy you sure love us Americans!"

"Well, you started my love to all you Americans," I say laughing.

"Remember the canoeing trip? How we flipped over and got everything wet, our clothes, wallets and cameras," I smile that's our favorite story and whenever we meet, we talk about it.

"Oh that was so funny. How can anyone forget that?"

"Remember the Ozarks, Six Flags? Snorkeling back in Jeddah? How that gigantic horrifying sting ray came right at me? Attacking me?" She says cracking up.

"Oh, Mary, how can I forget? So what have you been doing, since I last saw you?"

"You know I had such hard times after leaving my children, but do you know that Karam and Jana are with me now?"

"Ya remember I was there two years ago and saw them with you?" *I'm really scared now; I don't know why Mary's memory's getting so bad? I just hope she still remembers some Arabic*, I think.

"Ya *min jid* ('really' in Arabic)! I can see it in your eyes; you thought I forgot my Arabic? Remember, I lived back in Jeddah for so long? And I still remember it real well."

"Oh Mary you're so lucky I wish I had my kids along too."

"You will some day Fairooz believe me, just keep on praying. You know I always remember your advice: 'leave Mary, go home; save your life and sanity; the kids are yours no matter what happens; no one can keep you apart.' Oh I can never forget these words."

"That was the worst state I ever saw you in."

"Oh what a nightmare that had been and now I have my life put together again."

"I'm so happy to hear that. You know I tried calling you several times but couldn't reach you. I guess you always changed your telephone number, till last summer, when I got your number from Amir."

"Yeah, it took me a while to settle down. Now I have my own farm. Got a pen? Write my address down."

I get my diary out and take her address down. "O.K. you have an e-mail address?"

"Come on Fairooz, I now live on a farm and what will a computer do on a farm?'

"More than you'd think."

"I guess you're right? Just let me get some money and then I'll get me one. You know it's hard to support myself and those two kids."

"What? You mean Omar doesn't help you out?"

"Well he was at the beginning, but not any more."

"My God, those men really lose it. How could he do that to his own kids?"

"Well, he does; and there's nothing I can do about it, so now we all work to keep the ball rolling."

"Listen, Mary. Remember you have a sister over here, so whenever you need me just let me know."

"Oh Fairooz I love you and know you'll always be there if I need you. Don't worry, I will. Fairooz this is all so weird. I thought this happened to me, because I'm an American and didn't fit into your society, but look at you!"

"Oh don't you worry about me, I'm so happy now and just miss the kids a lot. You know Deema is here now in London, working on an MA."

"My, my, like mother like daughter. Fairooz you see now you have Deema, just wait and see and some day soon you'll have Dalia, Rana, and Amr too. Just don't you worry, this is a test; God is testing you and wants to see your reaction. Look at me! My kids were taken away from me, when I wanted to mother them and I was forced to leave; but look how God repaid me! Two of them already graduated from the university and holding great jobs and now I have the other two. Look at the irony, I get to attend my kids' graduation and he doesn't and now I have them all with me in the US!"

I don't mean to be rude, but I can see that her tears are watering her eyes, so I instantly change the subject: "listen Mary what are your plans for tonight?"

"Nothin' much, we're going to a pub, but I don't have to go."

A Taste of Freedom 165

"So why don't I pick you up and show you where I live and then we can go to a pub or to the movies."

"Sure? Don't you have any plans?"

"No," I then look at my watch. How time flies? It's quarter to twelve. Mary notices and looks at hers, too.

"Oh Fairooz I have to leave."

"We didn't even have a sip of coffee; we'll get some at my place later on then."

"Great Fairooz, I'm sorry I brought all those memories back to you."

"Oh please, you forgive me I spoiled your day. Don't you worry about me; I really am a lot happier this way. Please Mary don't you worry; I'm just discovering who I really am and I'm starting to love me all over again; so when shall I pick you up and where from?"

"How about five? Do you know where Copthorne Hotel is? That's where I'm staying."

"Know where? That's my Hotel! That's where I stayed, when I first came over here for two weeks, till I found my flat. So I'll see you at five then. I love you."

"Oh I love you too. See you then."

We hug on our way out of the café. Mary turns left and sees her group by Dixons and she hurriedly walks over and joins them, waving back at me.

Thank God. I know she feels better now. She would be so upset if she thought I was not happy. Best of friends we had always been. Quite a combination: an American and an Arabian and still best friends!"

Now, where am I supposed to meet Karen? Mary's meeting made me forget my own name: Fa...? I get the diary out and look at my schedule. *What can I do without you?* Now I'm really losing it: talking to the diary! O.K., in front of Marks & Spencer, then I turn left and head to M & S. There she is.

"Karen you wouldn't believe what happened to me!"

"Don't tell me, you met another gypsy and gave her ten pounds!" She says teasingly.

"Seriously Karen."

"Well what?"

"Remember my American friend I keep talking to you about."

"Who Randy?" Again she's teasing.

"Oh can't you get serious?"

"Well, who?"

"Mary remember her?"

"Your friend from St. Louis?"

"Yes, I just ran into her right here, two hours ago."

"Never?" Karen asks in her cute British accent.

"I really did, come let's sit some where and talk, or do you still want to go to Fenwick and talk on our way?" I know that Karen is dying to hear the whole story.

"Oh no, I think I would rather sit and talk; I was on my feet all day long."

Ya, on your feet all day? I know that she just wants to sit and hear what I have to say. We walk for about two minutes, then I find a bench and we sit down. Karen doesn't even think of looking for an empty seat, she is too busy watching people walking up and down the street.

"Look at her," she says, "isn't she a bit too big for those jeans? Look at the skinny guy, walking next to her. Oh how I love watching people passing by," she adds with a naughty smile, a twist in her nose and a curl in her mouth with a devilish twinkle. "You probably think I'm nosy, but I just enjoy watching the way people walk, talk, dress, and even their facial expressions amaze me. Some people certainly don't look at themselves in the mirror, before leaving their house. Or maybe they don't even have one."

I smile at her and think, *not nosy, huh?* "Oh no Karen you're not nosy at all!" I tell her, with a teasing look.

"Really just look at that woman coming down here; doesn't she look like a multi-colored parrot, dressed up in such a colorful outfit."

Of course she is so critical of others, because she is so chic and is always properly dressed. Her clothes always match no matter how simple they are. *She reminds of my sister Sue, who's always elegant even in her pajamas,* I talk to myself. She has a black cotton skirt, just above the knee and a matching green shirt, pulled right over to the middle of the skirt. Her clothes don't only match, they even suite her green eyes and blond hair. Her black comfortable shoes have a diamond-shape buckle; and her handbag has the same diamond, but a bit smaller. She has two shopping bags, so I try to help her with her handbag. "God Karen what do you keep in there? Stones?" It probably weighs a hundred pounds, extremely heavy, a muscle builder!

"Nothing, my keys, my mom's keys, a diary, a telephone book, a filo-fax, papers from w…"

"Enough let me ask you differently: what don't you keep in it?"

"Oh Fairooz, you love teasing me."

Teasing you? You call that teasing? You haven't seen much yet oh no! I'm not getting to my normal self again? I talk to myself and then ask her: "so how was work?"

"Today I had so much work to do. Jane is sick and she won't be in for a week, so I had to help my sister Marge, in dealing with the customers. All day long, I didn't lift my head from all the books and papers, a lot of sorting out. I'm so tired. I wanted to call you and cancel our appointment, but I daren't; you left your studies and came all the way down here."

"It's O.K. Karen, if you want, you can go back to work. That won't bother me at all, it really won't…" I smile teasingly knowing that Karen wouldn't. *She's dying to hear about Mary,* and without giving me a chance to finish my sentence she jumps in:

"Well?"

"Well what?"

"Oh Fairooz, stop you know what I mean. Well?"

"Oh, yes. I know, I know," I love her English accent it reminds me of my own before being invaded by the sensual, delicious, softer and simpler American tongue! I remember how back in the E.G.C. in Alexandria, we weren't allowed to pronounce a letter in either American or Arabic. If caught red-handed, executions and more detentions! Arabic was spoken in our Arabic and Religion classes only, *oh how I disliked those two subjects.* Nothing but British English was ever spoken between classes, on breaks or in the garden; and spies were all over the place; comic books were instantly confiscated and the poor innocent soul was sent to the death chamber, right then, on the spot: the detention room!

I didn't like the phrase: 'five o'clock' back then, because it was not 'the five o'clock tea' to me, as I spent most of my days in 'the five o'clock detention room' than in the 'five o'clock tea room'. I was always detained in the small gloomy library room, which was located on the right hand of the main entrance to the school. It was like a grave: it took ten steps to get down there! So to me it was a grave and the ones caught talking Arabic, weren't just prosecuted, but five piasters were deducted out of their pocket money. *So forty-five piasters was more than enough for that carriage ride, as it was a life time savings to us; worth the fighting for, huh?* I smile to myself as I remember that incident. Karen couldn't wait any longer, shattering my stream of consciousness to pieces as she yells:

"Well? How's Mary? Can't believe it, what a strange coincident?"

"Isn't it so? I tell you life is so strange! I almost fainted when I saw her, and thought she was a ghost; I'm so lucky, yet I felt so bad."

"How's that?"

"You know how much I missed her."

"Well? Yes?"

"The last time I spoke to her was two years ago, when I called her from Orange County and she sounded so happy with her new life; and to hear her laugh again, made me feel so good,."

"But you met her in Boston that same year, right?"

"Ya I...," I know how desperate Karen is to hear the story.

"So? Fairooz?" She impatiently interrupts again.

God! Can't she wait? Doesn't she know that I like to take my time relating a story? Guess she can't read my thoughts after all, but then who could? I think and annoyingly smile back at her.

"Sorry. Go on please," says Karen, in her cunning apologetic manner.

"Ya I was so happy to meet her, yet, she stirred some real bad memories and experiences, right out of a pit and it all erupted like a volcano from way deep down. I didn't mean to do so! I feel so bad, because she took my experience too personal and felt so sorry for me, but when I told her that I'm happier this way, she felt better."

"Are you Fairooz, really?"

"Am I? I certainly am; no one could feel how happy I am. I feel like a bird let out of its cage. Never will it get back in again. Ever heard of one that had?"

"So good to hear that, I would hate to see you go back and leave me alone again."

"Don't worry. I won't. What ever happens we'll be great friends."

"Good, so how long have you known Mary, you said?"

"Oh! About thirty-one years."

"Wow! That long?"

"I met her when I had just got married. She used to go out with someone my ex-husband knew from home. You know that her mom was a native Indian with French blood and her dad was originally Irish with Italian blood. Yeah, I thought that I had different blood types running through my veins, but when I met her I realized that what I have is plain peanuts! Come on, what do you have at five?" I remember that I had this bad habit of repeating myself all the time, so I suddenly stop talking.

"I'll go back to work now and I'll be home at five-thirty. Any plans?"

"Well I told Mary I'll pick her up from the Copthorne at five and drive back home to show her my place. I didn't tell her that Mama is here; I want to be surprise her. She loves my mom so much."

"Who doesn't Fairooz? Your mom is so nice."

"Thanks Karen, she loves you too."

"I know I can feel that and so, what will you do then?"

"Well we'll go to a pub or to the movies. Do you want to join us?"

"Join you? I'll be home before five. Or maybe I'll meet you at the Copthorne at five? See you."

I know she can't wait till five-thirty. We are always together, the only time I feel lonely is during the long dark cold nights. So we part and I walk down Northumbria looking for Virgin stores. I walk in and look for Rod Stewart's CD: *When we were the new boys.* I know Joe would love to have it, so I buy it and walk out on the busy street. It is a Sunday morning kids are everywhere, a lovely sight. Every time I see kids I remember my own. Oh I have to buy six Newcastle jerseys! Six, each with a name and number; and I have to get them today, because Mama is leaving soon and I'll send them with her. I walk down to Monument square and right next to Dillon's bookstore is The Newcastle United sports shop, so I walk in and pick one jersey and check the price: thirty-nine pounds and ninety-nine pence. I open my purse and check my diary: thirty-nine pounds and ninety-nine pence times six is, two hundred and thirty-nine pounds and ninety-four pence. I then pick it up and walk to the salesman.

"Hi! How much will it cost to print a name and number on this, please?"

"Nine pounds and ninety-nine pence, Miss."

I bring out my diary again: nine pounds and ninety-nine pence times six is fifty-nine pounds and ninety-four pence? I start searching for the different sizes I need.

"Do you need any help?" A young salesgirl asks.

"Yes, I would like six jerseys: two extra larges, three mediums and one small please."

"Here we are, right?" The girl comes back with the jerseys.

"Yes great."

"Any names and numbers?"

"Yes, please. Can I have a pen and paper?" I start writing each name and number, next to the appropriate size. "That's it, how much is it all?"

"Two hundred and ninety-nine pounds and eighty-eight pence, thank you."

"Do you accept American Express?"

"No, sorry we don't."

I bring out my wallet and hand her the Switch card. Then I ask her when they would be ready.

"About fifteen minutes."

So I walk out and across Blacket Street towards Grainger Street. I need to buy petroleum jelly for Aunt Hala from Boots; a new one has just opened there a few weeks ago. I hurriedly go in, get two jars and come out. That was swift! I still have ten minutes. I remember that I promised Aunt Noura some Digestive Biscuits. I rush quickly into Marks & Spencer and buy them. I also need a bottle of cologne for Baba, so I literally run to Fenwick and straight to the men's cologne section and buy Opuim for men.

Now I'm on my way back to pick up the jerseys. I walk up to the salesgirl and find them all folded, so I unfold each one of them and examine them one at a time: touching each name separately. Oh lovely names! The young lady places them in a bag and I dash out of the store holding the bag close to my heart. I feel I can smell and touch each and every one of my six children. I'm so thrilled for having bought those jerseys. For a minute all six are right there with me; kissing, touching and hugging me. Now I can send all the gifts back home with Mama. However, I feel so bad I wish I had enough money to buy each of my twenty-nine nephews and nieces the same jersey, but I couldn't afford it.

Cloudy skies, it might rain; I swiftly walk to the parking lot. Oh I'm so lucky I should have taken a ticket, half an hour ago! I get to my turquoise car: a 1998 Vauxhall Corsa Breeze; I wanted it in silver, but all Benfield Motors had had was a metallic blue and I loved it! I always park it on the street in front of my flat. It is my seventh baby, all dressed up in turquoise and all four feet are coated with the loveliest rubber shoes, with a round metallic buckle in the middle. The head has a bold spot, where the sun and wind can penetrate and blow that top off. The inside is lined with checkered blue material and belts on its sides, so she can buckle up and show her slim figure. I totally fell in love with that car!

Now I get in it, buckle up, lock the door, start it and put my favorite song: Nizar Gabany's words. Nizar was a Syrian poet who bewitched all Arab women. Was it his blue eyes? Or was it his light-brown hair that turned grayish throughout the years? Or maybe it was his full lips? Or, let's face it: were his words the real spell on women? He was the Arab woman's strongest defender, spoke and felt for her as he expressed her feelings, emotions and life better than she ever could. His death, a few years ago, was the saddest event in the Arab woman's world. Who would stand up for her now? Open her secretive closet and speak her thoughts? Express her needs and emotions? What a loss! *Mais c'est le Dieu. Il fait comme Il veut*, I think, as I drive on what to me is: the wrong side of the road. My English friends insist that it is the right side of the road! I still believe that yes, it is the right side of the road, but the wrong side of driving.

I drive out of the City Center through the highway and take the Gosforth exit through the free land. Green grass all the way through on both sides of the road. Cows feeding, laying down or cuddling; cows cuddling, that is strange; am I that lonely to see the cows cuddling? I then turn on Edgefield, still singing and dancing while driving. Now I change tapes, oh those words! So true: *Some people stay far away from the dark, if there's a chance of it opening up. They hear a voice in the hall outside and hope that is just passes by. Some people live with fear of a touch and the anger of having been a fool. They will not listen to any one, so nobody tells them a lie.* Then with a high pitch I go on: *I know you're only protecting yourself. I know you're thinking of somebody else, someone who hurt you. But I'm not above making up the love you've been denying you could ever feel. I'm not above doing anything, to restore your faith if I can. Some people see through the eyes of the young before they even get a look at the young. I'm only willing to hear you cry because I'm an innocent man.* I sing along with Billy Joel: *An Innocent Man*. I love this singer and it was my brother Joe, who taught me how to love him. It is amazing how my older brothers and sister influenced my life, without maybe even meaning to! From Joe, an artist in his own rights, *how I miss reading his poetry*, I learned how to love so many singers, different type of tunes and sounds of different instruments. Sue my beautiful elegant sister gave me hints on how to look like a woman; and from Zahid, my eldest brother and the kindest of all my brothers and sisters, I discovered the love of studying. He is eight years older than me; and as a little girl I always saw him at his desk, studying and thought that he led such a boring life, but look at me now!

I'm so glad my seventh baby is automatic and I can now sing and dance, instead of concentrating on the gear. I then turn into my street Willowfield Avenue; and the good obedient car stops right in front of my house: number 29. Singing and dancing I ring the doorbell. "Hello Lena. How are you?" I tell Lena, who opens the door with a smile.

"Hello Madame." Lena is Mama's Philippino help, a beautiful young girl. Her long black curly hair, which is half way down her back, is always pulled back with a rubber band; and her black eyes are so loving and innocent. I love that girl; she's so nice, always smiling and most of all, she loves Mama and cares for her. I walk straight to the living room and find Mama nodding off on the green sofa bed:

"Hello Mama. I miss you. Mama you won't believe whom I met today."

Mama stayed in, so tired because yesterday we were shopping all day long, so today she is dead tired. She usually goes out with me and walks for about two to three hours; then for the following two days, she would sit on the sofa, with her feet up high on a stool. And she always sleeps, sitting down and when I wake her up, knowing that she has a soar neck, she would insist that she was not sleeping!

"Well Mama, guess who I met?"

"Oh I don't know who?" She is too tired to even guess.

Oh God! What did I do to her? She will go back home and sleep for two continuous days! "Well! Mary!"

"Mary! The Mary I know? Mary?" She is so excited she cannot believe it.

"Yes Mama, imagine Mary."

"What is she doing here? When did she come? How is she? Oh, I love this girl so much and feel that she's my fifth daughter."

"I know Mama, she loves you like her own mom, too; and always says that whenever she has a problem she comes to you, because you make her feel so much better; and she feels safe, when you're with her."

"So how is she? Where is she?"

My God Mama sure asks twenty questions a minute! However, she feels better when she knows that Mary is fine and that I'm going to pick her up from her hotel at five.

"Good thing, I'm glad you didn't tell her that I'm here. I want to see her surprised face. Oh I can't wait to see her. You know I didn't see her for years?"

"Ya Mama I know. She'll be so happy to see you too," I say and walk to the kitchen:

"Lena what's for dinner?"

Lena is the best cook on earth; when she started working at Mama's she couldn't cook and look at her now: a professional chef. She is good at any thing she makes.

"I asked her to make *pish madry pish*," Mama says with a smile, while twisting her palms to describe that exotic dish: *pish madry pish* which is Chinese Noodles!

She can hear me asking Lena, as the flat is so tiny that you can hear and see whatever is happening around you. "You see Mama; you could have taken some English in these past weeks. Next time you come I won't let you sit at home. You'll have to go to school and study English and maybe French," I smile teasingly. "Can we wait for Mary and then eat?"

"Of course we will, how about Karen?"

"She's coming too." Oh how she loves Mary; she is a person one can't but love. *Oh Mama if you know how much I love you. Oh I'll miss you so much, but I can't ask you to sacrifice any more. I wish I could tell you that I love you more than Baba. How can I not? Divorced at forty and buried your youth, life and beauty, to raise all seven of us. But I can't tell you that. If I do then you won't try so hard to have me on your side instead of Baba's. Oh I can see it in your eyes, always staring at me waiting for me to say it, but I can't. I'm too scared. Maybe some day, before it's too late, I will. I could see the looks on your face, when I call Baba every week asking how he is; don't ever believe that I love him more. Don't, please don't. Someday, I'll admit it all to you. I'll pour my loving to you,* I think as I open the fridge and pour myself a glass of fresh milk and look at the top of the kitchen cabinet and think more, *oh Mama you bought some green bananas, my favorite!*

"Mama would you like some thing to snack on, till the *pish madry pish* is ready?" I ask her, with a teasing smile.

"Thank you I just had some toast, butter and honey."

I know that if she isn't too tired she'll get up and hit me, so I go to her and ask if she wants to beat me and she asks me to come closer and when I do, she hugs me and gives me a kiss. I feel so good: that hug and kiss completed my happy day. I then rush to my room, take off my boots and tight jeans, put one of my lose pants on and go back out to the living room, to my dear laptop. I start it and get on line to check my email. Thank God Dalia and Rana sent me email, telling me that they and Amr passed their finals. Some day soon I'll celebrate their graduation too, now that Kareem graduated from Jordan University. I'm almost there: three down and three to go; and I have more pay back into my strenuous work account. Sam, Kareem and Deema each hold a great job and are all married. Now, I have a great son-in-law and two lovely daughter-in-laws; so my interest accumulates to nine kids now! And some day hopefully I'll have grandchildren: lots of them; and hopefully I'll willingly return home and live with my kids and family, that is when my dream comes true. I then start emailing Randy, my true love:

Subj: Special thoughts
Date: 12/11/2000 6:01:43 AM Eastern Standard Time
From: FairHoura@hotmail.com
To: RSmith@hotmail.com

houbby…I miss you…I want you to read my thoughts…
now listen…

There's so much I wanna tell you…
when I see you…
touch and feel you…

Then I'll look into those eyes of yours…
and my passionate lips will caress yours…

Your craving lips clutch to mine…
we both moan…our thighs entwine…

Wow…amazing how our souls meet…
yes…hearts with the same beat…

You read my thoughts…
I read yours…

Miles and miles apart…
yet…so close…

Suddenly tears come to my eyes…
thrilled with pleasure and ecstasy…not real tears…

Then I pass out…yes. I faint…
up…up so high…right off of this plane…

Being with you is my only yearning…
every inch of me is utterly burning…

I want you so bad…
it's driving me mad…

You know why??
yes…you've guessed it right…

I hope you like it…that's just how I feel…
love

At four I leave to pick Mary up. She was impatiently waiting for me since three-thirty. The roads were empty so we get back home around four-twenty; and as soon as I ring the doorbell, Mama's there to open it. Mary couldn't believe her eyes:

"Too many surprises for one day!" She almost screams as she hugs and kisses Mama.

"Mary, my dearest Mary I'm so glad to see you. I never thought I'll ever see you again. I always prayed God that I would see you again in good health and here you are; my prayers have come true!" Mama says with tears in her eyes.

Around five o'clock Karen comes down from her flat and we all sit and eat Mama's favorite dish: *pish madry pish,* with chicken, a salad, some humus and stir fried vegetables. After the meal Mama and Mary sit on the sofa and they cannot stop talking; catching up on all that has happened since they last met. Karen feels bored, because she doesn't understand what is going on, as we are all speaking Arabic. I know it is rude, but we couldn't help it! So she gets up and says, with a smile:

"Sorry, but I'm so tired and need to sleep. Nice meeting you Mary," and heads to her flat.

Mama then asks Mary to stay over and without second thoughts, she does. Then, the next day I drive her back to her hotel because she's leaving the next morning to Glasgow. I kiss her and tell her that we'll meet soon. I still can't believe how we met on the street, across waters: she came all the way from St. Louis and I from Jeddah; and where do we meet? In Newcastle! What a coincident? If we would have planned it, we wouldn't have met like that!

Today is another cold gray November day in Newcastle. The weather mirrors the way Mama feels: gloomy and freezing. She isn't happy and knows that I have the intentions of remaining away for good. On my breaks from summing up the third chapter of my dissertation, I go to the living room and try to comfort her and make her feel better, by touching her hands and kissing it every now and then; but that doesn't help. The fact that she's leaving me here alone, depresses her even more. She is certain that I'll never return and have asked me on several occasions:

"Fairooz, when are you ever going to finish and come back?"

"Mama, I'm almost done, but I'm not coming back. I just can't take it any more; and now my children are grown-ups; and three of them hold good jobs and have their own families, so half of my responsibility is over." Her face changes and she starts to say something, when I add: "I know what you want to say Mama. I know that they would never stop needing me and they would soon have their own kids; and that I would always miss on that, but I think it is better this way. I can always go back for visits, with a more fulfilled spirit that would get them out of their static boring lives. I know that none of them is happy living there either; and that they all hope they can get out and find their lives somewhere else. You see Mama, if I stay there, I would be miserable and that again would reflect on them and make them unhappy." You would think that would make her understand and forgive me for fleeing, but her Iranian stubbornness and pride won't let her even think of it.

Then the day comes when I drive Mama to London: she is leaving. It's a chilly Wednesday in December; she is not so happy and neither am I; and for three hours of driving down to Heathrow, she hardly says a word.

We get to Heathrow and I drive to the parking lot and ask Mama to hold on for a second and I immediately get out of the car and go to get a trolley; I place the three suitcases in it and go around her door to help her out. I know that she loves me spoiling her and that really breaks my heart, because when I was home I always accompanied her when she went shopping, to her doctor or even visited her old friends. She is certain that I'm not coming back and tears fill her eyes. I hug her when she gets out of the car; and once again kiss her hand, head and cheeks. However, being an optimist, I do have this strong feeling deep inside of me that some day I will return to my homeland!

A month later as I am sitting once again on my favorite sofa bed, now that Mama is gone, the phone suddenly rings: it's Sam; and as soon as I say hi he excitedly yells:

"Mama, Mona is pregnant!"

"Sam you're not kidding, are you? You mean I'm going to be a grandma?" I almost cry with joy, *my first grandchild,* I think delightfully smiling.

"Ya Mama we didn't tell you earlier, because we weren't sure; but we just came back from the doctor and it's confirmed: you're going to be a granny!" Sam is overjoyed and as usual, talks so fast.

"Oh my God I can't believe it!" Now tears of joy run down my cheeks.

"Mama the doctor said it's a girl; and she is due in July."

"I'll see you then. I'll make sure I'll be one of the first to meet her," I say laughing and tears are still rushing down. We then hang up and I close my eyes and pray, *thank you God. I love you.* I'm so excited and can't believe it, *at last I'm going to be a grandma,* I tell myself. I do hope, though, that I'll be a lovely grandma like my own Jaddah. Today I am the happiest human being on this earth and I'll certainly be home to welcome my granddaughter into this world; I just pray that her luck and times are better than mine.

A Prayer

I pray God, that every person or creature I have ever come across in my life would forgive me.

I pray God, to forgive and bless my parents, their parents, my children and their descendants.

I pray God, to forgive and bless Jaddah and all the deceased.

I pray God, to reunite me with Jaddah and my loved ones some day.

About the Author

Sayidet Al Hijaz is a mother of six, born and raised in Saudi Arabia. She now lives in Europe. Further details are reserved for her own personal safety.

0-595-30120-7

Printed in the United Kingdom
by Lightning Source UK Ltd.
100277UKS00001B/121-168